# HAZARDS IN THE HIDDEN CITY

# HAZARDS IN THE HIDDEN CITY
## CASE FILES OF AN URBAN DRUID™ BOOK 4

AUBURN TEMPEST
MICHAEL ANDERLE

This book is a work of fiction. All of the characters, organizations, and events portrayed in this novel are either products of the author's imagination or are used fictitiously. Sometimes both.

Copyright © 2022 LMBPN Publishing
Cover by Fantasy Book Design
Cover copyright © LMBPN Publishing
A Michael Anderle Production

LMBPN Publishing supports the right to free expression and the value of copyright. The purpose of copyright is to encourage writers and artists to produce the creative works that enrich our culture.

The distribution of this book without permission is a theft of the author's intellectual property. If you would like permission to use material from the book (other than for review purposes), please contact support@lmbpn.com. Thank you for your support of the author's rights.

LMBPN Publishing
PMB 196, 2540 South Maryland Pkwy
Las Vegas, NV 89109

Version 1.00, October 2022
eBook ISBN: 979-8-88541-177-6
Print ISBN: 979-8-88541-948-2

# THE HAZARDS IN THE HIDDEN CITY TEAM

**Thanks to our JIT Team:**

Deb Mader
Dorothy Lloyd
Christopher Gilliard
Dave Hicks
Diane L. Smith
James Caplan
Jan Hunnicutt
Kelly O'Donnell
Paul Westman

**Editor**
SkyFyre Editing Team

# THE USUAL SUSPECTS

**Clan Cumhaill**

    **Aiden** – the oldest of Fi's brothers, druid tank, Toronto police officer, married to Kinu, and father of Jackson, Meg, Ireland, and Carragh.

    **Brendan** – Fi's brother, second in the birth order, formerly deceased, given back to the family after the Culling and restricted to living on the mythical Celtic island, Emhain Abhlach with Emmet.

    **Bodhmall** – Fionn's paternal aunt who raised him and taught him how to be a druid.

    **Calum** – Fi's brother, third in the birth order, druid archer, Toronto police officer, and married to Kevin. Together they are foster parents to Bizzy, an otterkie shifter.

    **Dillan** – Fi's brother, fourth in the birth order, druid rogue, Toronto police officer, and in love with Evangeline, Angel of the Choir, formerly a reaper, and now a guardian angel.

    **Dionysus** – God of Wine and Fertility, Light Weaver, Hunter-god, guardian of the mythical Celtic island Emhain Abhlach, and honorary Cumhaill.

    **Emmet** – Fi's brother, fifth in the birth order, druid buffer, guardian and committed caretaker of the mythical Celtic island Emhain Abhlach.

**Fiona** – youngest of the six Cumhaill kids, chosen by Fionn to represent the Fianna Warriors in a new generation of urban druids, Hunter-god, Celtic shaman, guardian of the mythical Celtic island Emhain Abhlach, bonded companion to Bruin and Dart.

**Fionn, a.k.a. Finn MacCool** – Hunter-god, mythical warrior in Irish mythology, guardian of the mythical Celtic island Emhain Abhlach, ancestor of and mentor to Fi and her family.

**Kevin** – artist, high school sweetheart, and husband to Calum

**Lara** – Fi's grandmother, nature druid, and the Snow White of the Druid Order.

**Liam** – one of Fi's best friends, now her stepbrother, operator/bartender for Shenanigans

**Lugh** – Fi's grandfather, druid historian, Keeper of the Shrine, and Elder of the Druid Order

**Niall** – Fi's father, retired Toronto police officer, married to Shannon and living in Ireland with his parents

**Nikon Tsambikos** – ancient Greek immortal, Light Weaver, guardian of the mythical Celtic island Emhain Abhlach, and honorary Cumhaill.

**Shannon** – mother of Liam, became the pseudo mother to the Cumhaill kids after her husband and their mother died when the kids were young. Her husband Mark was Niall's partner and died in the line of duty.

**Sloan Mackenzie** – Fi's soulmate, druid healer, Keeper of the Toronto Shrine, and guardian of the mythical Celtic island, Emhain Abhlach.

**Wallace Mackenzie** – Sloan's father, master druid healer, Elder of the Druid Order, recently separated from Sloan's mother Janet Mackenzie.

## Animal Companions

**Aurora** – Tad's red-tailed kite.

**Bruinior the Brave (Bruin) a.k.a. Killer Clawbearer** – Fiona's mythical battle bear and Bear of native myth and legend.

**Daisy** – Calum's epileptic skunk companion.

**Dartamont (Dart)** – Fiona's Western dragon, involved with Saxa, and oldest brother to twenty-two other dragons.

**Dax** – Lara's badger.

**Doc Martin (Doc)** – Emmet's pine marten followed him home from the Santa Claus Parade.

**Nyrora (Rory)** – Dillan's Koinonos Dragon. Dark purple with gold webbing for her wings, she bonds with him at rest, creating a living tattoo on his skin.

## More Greeks

**Andromeda Tsambikos** – Nikon's younger sister, ancient Greek immortal, Light Weaver, guardian of the mythical Celtic island Emhain Abhlach, and legal counsel for SITFO.

**Nikon Tsambikos Senior** – Nikon's grandfather, ancient Greek immortal, Light Weaver, and guardian of the mythical Celtic island Emhain Abhlach.

**Politimi Tsambikos** – Nikon's younger sister and ancient Greek immortal.

## The Moon Called

**Anyx** – lion shifter, Garnet's beta, and mate to Zuzanna

**Garnet Grant** – lion shifter, Alpha of the Toronto Moon Called, Grand Governor of the Lakeshore Guild of Empowered Ones, Fi's friend, mentor, and boss at SITFO, mated to Myra and father of adopted bear shifter Imari.

**Myra** – ash nymph, Fae Historian, mated to Garnet, owner/operator of Myra's Mystical Emporium, mother of adopted bear shifter Imari.

**Thaos** – lion shifter, one of Garnet's valued pack enforcers, third in the pack hierarchy.

**Zuzanna** – lion shifter, mate to Anyx, works with SITFO as a member of the Toronto Special Investigations Unit.

## The Vampires
   **Benjamin** – vampire, companion to Laurel.
   **Xavier** – vampire, King of the Toronto Seethes.

## The Nine Families of the Druid Order
   **Lugh and Lara Cumhaill** – parents of Niall, grandparents of Aiden, Brendan, Calum, Dillan, Emmet, and Fiona.
   **James and Caitrona Dempsey** – parents of Brian and Reagan.
   **Evan and Iris Doyle** – parents of Ciara.
   **Connor and Kate Flannigan** – parents of Erik.
   **Wallace Mackenzie** – father of Sloan, ex-husband to Janet.
   **Tad McNiff** – recently took his place as a Head of the Nine Families after his father, Riordan, gave himself over to Mingin in a quest for ultimate power.
   **Finley and Elaine O'Malley** – parents of Lia.
   **Brian and Gwyneth Perry** – parents of Jarrod, Darcy, and Davin.
   **Sean and Maude Scott** – parents of Seamus.

## Friends
   **Danika** – witch from San Francisco, Nikon's ex-lover.
   **Laurel** – ghost, companion to Benjamin, Fi's high school friend
   **Merlin/Pan Dora/Emrys** – druid and wizard of legend, owner of Queens on Queen drag club and the attached soup kitchen, union bonded to the champagne-colored Western dragon, Empress Cazzienth.
   **Patty** – Man o' Green, union bonded to Cyteira the Queen of Wyrms, a.k.a. the Wyrm Dragon Queen.

**Suede Silverbirch** – elven representative on Toronto's Lakeshore Guild of Empowered Ones.

**Zxata** – ash nymph, Myra's brother, nymph representative on Toronto's Lakeshore Guild of Empowered Ones.

## More Hunter-gods

**Ahren** – Hunter-god, shaman, navigates the astral plane as a golden eagle.

**Samuel** – Hunter-god, shaman, navigates the astral plane as an ebony wolf.

**Quon Shen** – Hunter-god, shaman, navigates the astral plane as a water dragon.

## Team Trouble

**Brody** – wolf shifter/vampire hybrid, new member-in-training for Team Trouble.

**Dantanion Jann (Dan the djinn)** – djinn, member of Team Trouble.

**Diesel Demarco** – goliath, new member-in-training for Team Trouble.

**Jenna** – siren, new member-in-training for Team Trouble.

**John Maxwell** – Deputy Commissioner of the Royal Canadian Mounted Police, founder of SITFO the Special Investigations Task Force for Ontario.

## Iceland Dragons – Free Dragons of Tintagel

**Bryvanay** – black, majestic, and slightly smaller than Utiss.

**Cazzienth Empress of the West (Cazzie)** – glistening champagne-colored dragon with gold and burnt orange wings, and a strong tail that ends in a treacherous-looking ball-spike.

**Saxa** – a sunshine yellow dragon with dark, gold wings and a blunt snout of the same color.

**Utiss** – a massive purple dragon and the dominant male of the Free Dragons of Tintagel.

## Ireland Dragons

**Drakes** – Chua.

**Westerns** – Abeloth, Cadmus, Chezzo, Dart, Esym, Kaida, Scarlett, Torrim.

**Wyrms** – Scarlett, +6 we haven't met.

**Wyverns** – 7 we haven't met.

# PRONUNCIATIONS

### Pronunciations
**Adelphos** – *adelfos* – Greek for "brother" or "my brother."
**agapi mou** – *ah-gah-pea moo* – Greek for "my love."
**Cumhaill** – *Cool* – Fiona and the family's last name (modern).
**gliko mou** – Greek for "my sweet."
**mac Cumhaill** – *MacCool* – Fiona and the family's last name (traditional).
**Mo chroi** – *muh chree* – Irish for my heart/my love.
**a ghra** – *uh grawh* – Irish for my love (intimate).
**a stór** – *uh stohr* – Irish for a treasure.
**paidi mou** – *peth-ee moo* – Greek for "my child."
**Slan!** – *slawn* – health be with you.
**Slainte mhath** – *slawn cha va* – cheers, good health.

### Irish Terms
**Arragh** – a guttural sound for when something bad happened.
**Banjaxed** – broken, ruined, completely obliterated.
**Bogger** – those who live in the boggy countryside.
**Bollocks** – a man's testicles.

**Bollix** – thrown into disorder, bungled, messed up.
**Boyo** – boy, lad.
**Cock-crow** – close enough that you can hear a cock crow.
**Craic** – gossip, fun, entertainment.
**Culchie** – those who live in the agricultural countryside.
**Donkey's years** – a long time.
**Dosser** – a layabout, lazy person.
**Eejit** – slightly less severe than idiot.
**Fair whack away** – far away.
**Feck** – an exclamation less severe than fuck.
**Flute** – a man's penis.
**Gammie** – injured, not working properly.
**Hape** – a heap.
**Howeyah/Howaya/Howya** – a greeting not necessarily requiring an answer.
**Irish** – traditional Irish language (commonly referred to as Irish Gaelic unless you're Irish).
**Knackers** – a man's testicles.
**Mocker** – a hex.
**Och** – used to express agreement or disagreement to something said.
**Shite** – less offensive than shit
**Gobshite** – fool, acting in unwanted behavior.
**Wee** – small.

# CHAPTER ONE

"We call this game Flip Cup Slip-and-Slide." Emmet gestures at the sharp downward slope beneath us and the table in the clearing in the distance. "Divided into two teams, you will first dip in either the Moana or the Olaf kiddie pool."

Brendan gives us a Vanna White arm sweep to direct our attention. "Generously donated for the day's event by Meggie and Jackson."

"You're welcome." Aiden takes a bow.

"Once appropriately doused, you will climb the Little Tikes slide and wait for your cue to hurtle yourself down the slope of doom. Once you get to the bottom, it'll be a scramble to stop, get up, and chug one of the bevvies pre-poured in the line of red Solo cups. Then, you'll take your empty cup, perch it on the table's edge, and flip it to land solidly on its rim. Once the judge deems your task complete, the next person on your team slides."

I wave at the judges down at the table. Gran and Granda are abstaining from the physical part of the hilarity and will keep everyone honest.

Brenny raises a hand. "Oh, and once you're down there, you might want to choose a spotter to help slow your teammates down because a couple of times when we were practicing, Em and I shot right past the play area and into the mud bog."

Emmet snorts. "Which was also funny as hell, but we're considering it a blooper for today."

I study the land behind the table set up and make a note not to overshoot the play area. I don't want to mud-bog myself on my wedding weekend.

"Preventing yourself from becoming a bog beast is the only time anyone can use powers. This is a magic-free event."

Everyone seems clear on that.

"Is everybody ready?" Brenny asks.

That's a resounding yes.

Emmet starts pointing into the crowd. "Couples taking the plunge are plunging first. Fi and Sloan, you're up. Dillan and Eva, you're on deck."

"Moana or Olaf, lady's choice." Sloan gestures down at the blue plastic pools behind the start line.

"Moana all the way." I step into the pool, crouch, and wriggle around a bit to get wet. "Where did you guys come up with this game?"

"Facebook," Brenny says. "It's amazing how much free time we have alone on this island. It looked hilarious, and the moment we saw it, we knew it was Cumhaill-worthy."

Properly doused, I haul my wetness out of the pool and climb onto the pink and yellow plastic children's slide. It only stands three feet off the ground, but it'll do well as our launching point.

When I'm sitting on the platform with my legs dangling down the slide and my hips squeezed tight, I give Emmet a thumbs-up. "Ready player one."

Sloan has even more trouble fitting into the children's chute and opts to slide down on his right hip.

"Oh, good idea, hotness. I was worried I might wedge and get a slow start."

Sarah laughs and waves a hand at the slides. They expand and widen to accommodate our adult sizes. "Better?"

"Yes. Much better, thanks." I readjust and sit flat. "There's less chance of shooting wildly off-course if I'm straight."

"And more chance that I can fit on the slide." Eva giggles. "I've got cherub curves to contend with."

"I love your cherub curves, beautiful." Dillan wraps an arm around her and pulls her in for a kiss.

"Fraternizing with the enemy!" Kevin declares, breaking up the PDA. "We'll have none of that."

Dillan and Eva step apart and select their pools. As the "already eloped" wedding couple, this is partly their celebration too.

Which I love.

Dillan splashes around in one foot of water like a fish on a hook and gets out to offer Eva a hand. Once they're ready and on deck, Da and Shannon move in to take their turns splashing and getting wet.

"On your marks, people!" Emmet holds up his hand and points at the illuminated red light at the bottom. It's an official race car starter light although I have no idea how they got it here. "Get set..." the center light glows brightly. "*Goooo!*"

When the green light at the top goes off, I push off the platform and realize too late that I should have shimmied my butt cheeks a little before pushing forward. Oh well, slide burn on my ass is a small price to pay for eternal glory.

As fireworks explode above us, Sloan and I plummet down the wide, water-slicked alleyway of plastic, screaming and laughing and trying to stay on course.

I understand how overshooting into the mud bog is a real concern. Wobbling as water sprays up in my face, I try to use my feet as rudders to keep me on course.

I'm coming in too fast and press my feet flat. Putting my hands down slows things, but my attempts spin me sideways. I end up flopping onto my elbows and going over the line headfirst.

Getting up is an exercise in reacquainting myself with balance. I slip and shuffle over to the table. Sloan is ahead of me. He's already got his drink in hand and is tossing it back. I grab my cup and do the same.

Gran's blackberry pear wine goes down way too smoothly. It's like a burst of berry bliss.

I swallow it in three quick gulps and set my cup on the table. Poor hotness has lost his lead. He's still fussing with the mechanics of flip cup.

I, on the other hand, am a seasoned professional.

I perch my cup on the table's edge and send it up and over in a beautiful arc to land upside-down on its rim.

"Yer good, Fi," Granda says.

I wave back at Eva on the hill, and she starts her descent. Once she launches, I check on Sloan. "That's it, Mackenzie. You've got this."

Sloan's cup flips in a graceful arc and lands on its rim.

"Yer good, luv," Gran says.

Sloan waves for Dillan to launch and down he comes like an arrow shot from a bow. He's got his ankles and arms crossed to make up the extra time and is gaining on Eva.

"He's going to mud bog for sure." I laugh.

"Not on yer life, *a ghra*. Yer brothers said we could spot and catch."

*Right.* "Poop, I really wanted to see my brother fly into the mud."

With spotting in mind, I hurry out to the finish line and get ready to grab Eva's hand.

She doesn't need my help. She's sitting up in a controlled and rapid descent, water whipping past, her corkscrew curls flowing out behind her. Without effort, she launches onto her feet with the grace and coordination of an angel and runs to the table to drink her wine.

Dillan arrives a moment later, and they flip their cups in a synchronized effort.

"Yer both good."

They wave for the next two to come down and Da and Shannon launch off the slides.

"I fucking love this game!" Dillan picks up Eva in a burst of adrenaline and swings her around. "Happy not our wedding, babe."

Eva laughs. "Happy not our wedding to you too."

Gran is grinning so much she's practically glowing. "The festivities have just begun."

---

After the Slip-and-Slide, the family dries off sitting around the firepit in the clearing while Manx, Bruin, Daisy, Doc, Jackson, Meg, and Bizzy have fun sliding down the course. It's virtually the same game, just minus the chugging of wine.

Dart, Saxa, and Rory are happily playing with the Ireland Westerns and looking forward to the arrival of the Iceland dragons tomorrow morning when the guests will start to arrive.

Today is family fun fest day.

Aiden and Kinu have the twins safely tucked off to the side and in the shade. They are fourteen months old now and crazy little troublemakers. Penning them up in a play area with a ceiling was the only way not to lose control of them.

Thankfully, for the moment, they're napping.

"Matrimony looks good on ye, Fi." Wallace moves a camp chair close to mine and sits to join me. He's brought a small gift bag which he sets on the ground between his feet. "I'm so thankful Sloan found ye and that the two of ye are makin' a go of it."

I sip my wine and find Sloan fooling around with the boys and a soccer ball. He's got the upper hand in that arena. It seems endless years of having no one to play "football" with gave him time to hone his skills in footwork and perfect his touch.

It still makes me sad to think of young Sloan's life as he was growing up, but everything we experience is part of what makes us who we are.

I wouldn't change who he is for anything.

Wallace is looking upon the roughhousing with a bittersweet smile. "He's finally got the brothers he always wanted. All ends as it's meant, aye?"

"Yeah, I think it's destiny on some level. He fills the gaps in my life I never realized were there, and I think I do that for him too."

"You definitely do." Wallace sets his drink in the cupholder of his chair and wipes his hands dry on his pants. "Since I have ye to myself fer a moment, I want to give ye somethin'. I was honored to attend the handfast celebration of yer da and Shannon last year, but wondered if ye've been to a traditional druid wedding before?"

"No, this is a first for me."

"Och, grand, I was hopin' to bring somethin' to the table to contribute to the festivities."

I place my hand on his wrist and meet his gaze. "You brought the most important thing. Without you there would be no him. The two of you are in a great place, and because of that, he's reclaimed a sense of foundation and family. We're both pleased and proud to have you here representing the Mackenzies."

"The Mackenzies. Aye, well, we're a wee clan of two fer now, but tomorrow we'll be three, and hopefully in time, we'll grow." He winks at me, and I'm washed with warmth, knowing he'll do better with his grandchildren than he did with his son.

Before the moment gets awkward, he returns his attention to the gift bag. "Open it."

"Oh, it's heavy." I set the bag on my lap and rifle to the bottom to come out with a hand-painted rock.

The brown oval stone fills the palm of my hand and has four triquetra meeting in the center. Purple and blue flowers, green leaves, and little white dots that look like baby's breath decorate the outside edge.

"Do you know what it is?"

"A very pretty rock."

"Aye, it is at that, but do ye know what it is in the sense of marriage?"

"Nope. No idea."

"In a traditional druid celebration, the officiant will ask the bridal couple to present their oathing stone. It's a stone the two of ye will place yer hands upon while sayin' yer wedding vows. The belief is that by holdin' the stone during the vows in turn, yer love will be set in stone."

"Oh, that's lovely."

"Grand. I hoped ye'd think so." He smiles, looking relieved. "Turn it over."

I flip the stone and read the faded words painted on the other side. "In the middle of an ordinary life, love gives us a fairy tale."

Wallace nods. "It was a sayin' my mam used to whisper to me when life was especially hard. She painted it on her oathing stone so she would always remember the gift of their love."

I wriggle my nose as my emotions tingle and bring me close to tears. "You're giving it to us?"

"Yer goin' to do things right, I feel it. My parents had that kind of love. I never did. Maybe it skips a generation, or maybe I haven't found my other half yet, but either way, I want the two of ye to have it."

"I love it...truly. Thank you."

He nods. "Now, don't feel ye have to use it as yer stone. This is yer time to do things yer way, but I thought it was a gift that bore givin'."

I stand and set the rock in my chair to hug him properly. "We are absolutely going to use it as our stone. I want as much Mackenzie tradition as I can get this weekend. I don't know if you noticed, but we Cumhaills tend to overpower."

Mackenzie laughs. "It's a truly wonderful thing. Blessings and happiness, Fi. Forever and always."

"Forever and always."

## CHAPTER TWO

Wallace wanders off to explore the mysterious streets of Emhain Abhlach's hidden city, and I watch him go. He's finding himself after thirty years of a difficult marriage and doing well.

I wish he could find his perfect other half.

He has so much going for him.

"Greek! You're alive!"

I spin to where my brothers have stopped play in their game and are hugging Nikon. Rushing over, I wrap my arms around him and hold on tight. He returns the hug, his hold strong. "You really are all right."

"I am."

"I hate it when you die."

"You and me both, Red."

There's no stopping the tears that leak free. When Nikon sacrificed himself to Jerome St. James to give us time to escape death, he broke my heart in both the best and the worst way.

He died so we could live.

Easing back, I blink through my tears. "I love you, Nikon

Tsambikos. I hate that you sacrificed yourself for us, but I love you for doing it."

He kisses my forehead and gives me another long hug. "I love you too, Fi. You, and Irish, and Calum, and yeah, Dani too. There was no question about who had to take one for the team in that situation."

Sloan is first in line after me to start the bro hugs. "Yer a brave and selfless man, Greek. I'm proud to call ye family."

"Hells yeah." Calum is next in line. My brother pulls him in chest-to-chest and slaps his back. "Thank you for your sacrifice."

It goes on like that until Nikon has been properly hugged and thanked by the whole family. When Da steps back, he's smiling a Cheshire cat smile. "In the vein of celebratin' Greek family, can I get everyone over to the pergola fer a surprise?"

"I lurve surprises." Dionysus ushers us forward with his hands to get us moving. "Is it wedding kittens? Tell me we're getting wedding kittens!"

Dillan frowns. "What the fuck are wedding kittens?"

"Like in the wedding movie we watched when all the people got puppies. I want a kitten."

I chuckle and slide my arm around Dionysus' hips as we head over to the orchard. "We watched *Bridesmaids* last weekend on our Romcom binge to get ready for the wedding. Melissa McCarthy hogging all the puppies was our favorite part."

"Are we having guest gifts?" Dionysus asks.

"Nothing alive, no…at least, I don't think so." I haven't been all that involved in the wedding planning. Gran and Shannon took on most of the heavy lifting, leaving Sloan to work out the honeymoon details and me to enjoy the ride.

I check with Sloan. "Are we?"

"Givin' kittens to the guests, ye mean? No, I don't suppose we are."

"That's very disappointing." Dionysus' tone matches his words.

I hug his arm. "I promise, once things settle, we'll go to the Humane Society and find you a kitten that needs a good home. For right now, though, I'm not sure what we have planned."

Sloan shrugs. "I'm in the same boat. I was supposed to help more than I was able to, but New Orleans happened."

Yeah, nothing about that case was Big Easy.

It was a tough week from Monday through Wednesday night. Yesterday, we woke up and decided that instead of waiting until Saturday, we'd enjoy a Friday family fun day, and we all came a day early.

It's exactly what I needed to reset my world after Dionysus almost died and watching Nikon die.

I side-hug Dionysus and reach over to squeeze Nikon's wrist. "I'm not okay."

Nikon shakes his head. "We're not going there, Red. Not this weekend. This weekend is a celebration of love and a look at the future."

"And Gran making cake and me singing at the wedding," Dionysus adds.

"Och, there will be cake," Da says, shaking his head as he looks at me. "Mam and Shannon spent the entire week in the kitchen while Da and I were out back wranglin' the monkeys in the yard."

I laugh. "You raised six kids, and if you add in Liam and Kevin, that's eight. Of them, seven were boys. You can wrangle kids as well or better than anyone else I know."

Da winks at me. "Nice of ye to say, *mo chroí.*"

The pergola we built is at the front of the orchard Gran made, above the meadow and below the wall to the hidden city. To the left of the city gates, an area with a few citrus trees has become a beautiful and productive fruit grove.

Here Gran wove several benches for people to sit under the shade of the canopies to reflect.

When we round the bend from the meadow area, I see the

four women reaching up to smell the fruit hanging on the branches above, and my heart races. "Tarzan, look who it is."

Dionysus' steps falter, but I've still got my arm around his hips, and I pull him along, hoping this is what I think it is.

Like many stories of lore, the tales about the Moirai being blind, one-eye-sharing hags are way off base. The Fates are graceful, resplendent women who share an incredible likeness with their mother.

It still blows my mind that because goddesses live immortal lives, the visual cues of age and lineage are lost.

The daughters look the same age as their mother.

"Dionysus, I am pleased to see you looking better than a few days ago," Themis says as we approach.

Her daughters, the three goddesses of fate, Clotho, Lachesis, and Atropos, turn to greet us. They are stiff and seem quite uncomfortable.

It's Clotho who approaches, holding out her hands. "We too are glad to see you are well, *gliko mou*. It seems in our effort to impress a lesson upon you, the powers have seen to impress one upon us in return."

Dionysus stiffens at my side and lifts his chin. When he doesn't say anything, I realize he's having a tantrum moment.

I intervene to fill the awkward silence. "Everyone, this is Clotho, the Fate who creates the thread of our birth and begins to spin and record our lives."

Brenny nods. "I've seen the tapestry you wove for me. It's as stunning as the woman who labored over it."

Clotho seems surprised by his words but inclines her head and accepts the compliment.

Lachesis is the second sister to come forward. "There was an oversight in our plan, cousin. Since you are not of the mortal world, your life in progress wasn't visible to me as I tended to my charges."

I gesture at the second sister. "This is Lachesis. She allocates the fate of lives in progress."

Atropos is next. "The idea that the actions of a mortal could cut your thread never occurred to us, my friend. The fault is ours you suffered. For that, we offer you our heartfelt apologies."

*Hubba-wha?* They owe him a shit ton more than that. "He almost died. It was only because we destroyed the lich and his soul jar while Evangeline kept him alive that he's even here to enjoy my wedding."

"And pouring that much power into him nearly killed her," Dillan adds.

Themis points at an empty spot on the grass, and Lady Justice's scales appear. "I believe a measure of justice should be assessed. If you would, *paidi mou*."

She signals Dionysus to stand beside the weigh scales and hands him a basket of stones. When he's in place, she raises her hand toward the low platform of the scales, and they tip dramatically to one side.

"The weight of staying the life of a mortal is heavy. Dionysus, you were aware of this when you asked this of the girls, correct?"

"Yes. I was."

"And so, you offered them payment in return for the sparing of Sloan Mackenzie's mortal existence."

Dionysus nods. "I did."

"What was your offer?"

"That I lose the privilege of my powers and the life I love with my mortal family until such a time when it was deemed I had rebalanced the debt owed to Atropos."

"It was a life for a life in a sense."

He shrugs. "In a sense. I forfeited spending time with Nikky, the Cumhaills, and Contessa McSparkles and gave up the life I knew as a god of the pantheon."

"The nature of your repayment was never meant to end your

existence or endanger the lives of those around you in their efforts to save your life. Your repayment was not a life for a life."

Atropos shakes her head. "No, Mother. It was not."

"Yet, through no fault on their part, he and those who love him suffered grievous and bodily harm, have they not?"

The girls all nod.

"Yes, Mother," Lachesis says.

As Themis makes her points, she pulls stones from the basket and places them on the higher scale. "Dionysus' powers were bound. He spent time away from his life and friends. He was unable to contribute to the quests of his group. He was injured in both human trials he's faced since. He became an anchor for a lich and all but perished. An angel nearly perished trying to sustain his life. Fiona and the others were put in grave danger to find the lich's phylactery and destroy it."

With each stone she places, the scales shift toward becoming more level. When she's finished, they are close but still tipped toward him owing a debt.

Themis takes a final stone and looks at her daughters. "Dionysus also suffered, once again, from the neglect of his immortal family. He trusted you to govern his penance and intercede if things went beyond the scope of the agreed absolution. You did not."

She sets the final stone in place and the scales balance. When she extends her hand to him, he accepts. "Dionysus, your actions have been weighed and measured. Officially, I find your debt to the balance repaid. Personally, I find your compassion and growth inspiring. I am proud to witness the man you've become."

She places a palm against his cheek, and he jolts and staggers back a step. "Congratulations, *paidi mou*. Enjoy your new life. You deserve nothing less than a family who loves you."

Then she looks at me. "Take good care of him, Fiona Cumhaill. He is a unique treasure in our world. He deserves to be treated as such."

"I couldn't agree more."

Themis hugs Dionysus and kisses his cheek. Holding both his arms in her hands, she smiles. "Be fabulous my friend."

"Aren't I always?"

"Without question."

When she steps to the side, she looks at her girls and gives them a head tilt in urging. It's funny, but it's the most motherly thing I've seen pass between them.

Atropos leads the charge and opens her arms. "Your string remains uncut. Mother's right, it was our responsibility to watch over your well-being, but in the end, you are fine. Let us speak no more about it."

Clotho nods behind her. "Well said, sister. It is done."

Lachesis nods as well. "Best to forgive and forget."

I cast them a look. Seriously? That wasn't even close to the heartfelt apology he deserves.

Dionysus shrugs and hugs each of them. "Saving Sloan's life far outweighs everything I went through over the past months. I don't regret it. Still, I neither forgive nor forget the careless disregard with which you treated my life."

The three of them look alarmed.

"Perhaps in time," Lachesis says.

Atropos nods. "Yes. Time is something we all have plenty of. In time you shall forgive us."

Clotho releases him and moves to stand with her mother and sisters. "We look forward to making amends, dear cousin."

When the four goddesses dissolve into the air in a sprinkling of golden mist, the crowd whoops and we all move in to congratulate Dionysus.

"The best wedding gift I could've gotten." I hug him. "Congrats, Tarzan. You got your mojo back."

He hugs me, and I'm thrilled to feel the energy of his power tingling over my skin. "Thanks, Jane."

We go through the ranks, everyone wishing him the best. Then everyone breaks off to return to what they were doing.

When it's only the two of us, I grip Dionysus' wrist and hold him back. "Come here, sweetie. Sit with me."

Settling on one of the benches, I pat the seat beside me. "Why aren't you happy?"

The smiling façade he's wearing falls, and he sighs. "I am happy."

I pull his hand to mine and link our pinky fingers. "Try again. This time with the truth."

He squeezes his hand and shoulder bumps me beside him. "I *am* happy about having my powers back. I feel whole and strong and indestructible again instead of vulnerable."

"But?"

"I truly thought the Fates would care enough to watch over me. Of all the pantheon members, we've shared the best times. I thought we were more than pantheon family. I thought I mattered to them."

"Well, their apology was shit. They futzed around with saying it was unfortunate and that it's in the past, but none of them said how horrified or sorry they are."

"Because they're more worried about Zeus finding out than about my well-being."

"Is that what all the 'let's forget this happened' stuff was about?"

"Yeah. It's tough having the king of the gods as a father. People pretend to care about me, but they're more concerned about what Zeus will think or do if they treat me wrong." A sharp edge cuts the air as he speaks, and I wish I could wash it all away for him.

"I'm sorry, dude. If it makes you feel any better, I don't give a flying fig what Zeus thinks of our friendship. In fact, I don't think he deserves you as a son."

Dionysus leans sideways and rests his head against mine. "I

know. That's one of the reasons I love being a Cumhaill. Zero fucks given."

I chuckle and take his hand. "How about you exercise your powers and the two of us pop over to Italy to get a couple of tubs of cherry gelato."

"Just us?"

"Yep."

"But this is your wedding weekend."

There are times when it's important to include Dionysus in the group chaos of our family, and there are other times when he needs one-on-one. I suppose it stems from his lacking one-on-one positive reinforcement while growing up and getting to know himself.

He didn't get that then.

I ensure he gets it now.

"It'll still be my wedding weekend when we get back. We won't be long." I squeeze his hand and pull him to his feet. "Come on. It'll be fun."

## CHAPTER THREE

With our trip to Italy over and three large tubs of gelato in the freezer, the distraction has worked its magic. Dionysus' disappointment with the Fates has faded, and he's ready to get back to the family shenanigans of the wedding weekend bonanza.

"What are we doing next?" he asks.

"That is exactly the right question at the right time, Greek," Emmet joins us in the Great Room. My brothers lead the troops and Sloan, Kev, Liam, Nikon, Eva, and Da follow. "For tonight's fun, we're pulling out one of our childhood favorites and giving it a Team Trouble twist."

Brenny joins us carrying a large pirate's chest with iron bands and a lock plate. "The name of the game is Assassin Double Trouble."

Liam waggles his brow. "Assassin, finally, a game where we're all on equal footing for a bit of murder and mayhem."

I laugh. "Trust me, the murder and mayhem part of our lives isn't much fun."

Emmet points at the two of us and pegs us with a look. "Stifle the chit-chat, you two."

Liam laughs, and we straighten.

"What's Assassin?" Eva's expression lights up with excitement.

Dillan lifts their joined hands to his lips and kisses her knuckles. "Oh, babe. With your reaper skills, you're going to rock at this."

Emmet continues. "For those who haven't played before, each of you is an assassin and will be given one target. You must hunt your target and shoot them with these."

He gestures at Brenny opening the chest and pulling out one of many black pistols.

"Welcome to the new age of paintball guns," Emmet announces. "The new .68 caliber paintball pistol boasts an innovative, compact design, specially engineered to be lightweight, easy to maintain, and best of all, dependable. These pistols now include two, Tru-feed, seven-ball magazines to take Assassin to a new level."

"There's a catch." Brenny holds up a finger. "Only you can know who your target is, there can be no sharing of sensitive information, and no one can see you make your hit."

"You are an assassin, after all," Emmet concurs. "Anonymity is your bread and butter."

Brendan sets the chest down and starts setting up three stacks of equipment: pistols, magazines, and hip holsters. "It should go without saying, but no powers, no fae sight, no super sneaky cloaks, no flashing, snapping, *poofing* out…this is a test of stealth, skill, and strategy. Everyone is on even footing."

Dillan chuckles. "If you say so. Some of us are just naturally superior even without cloaks."

"And humble," Calum adds.

I laugh. "Look at the cute holsters."

Brenny scoffs. "Holsters aren't cute, baby girl. These are adaptable, ambidextrous holders for a finely tuned weapon."

"I stand corrected. Does that mean I can't bedazzle mine?" I make the comment just to poke the bear and the expression of horror he flashes me is too funny.

Man, it's good to have Brenny back.

There's a general buzz of excitement as everyone steps up to collect their weapon, holster, and magazines.

"Each pistol has one pink paintball magazine inserted for Assassin."

"Only seven bullets?" Dionysus asks.

"For the moment, yes," Emmet answers. "There's more to it. We'll circle back to that in a moment. Patience, Grasshopper."

"You likely won't need more than that anyway, Greek," Calum informs him. "You're only targeting the person on your target list. You'll need to line up your shots like an assassin. A concise attack uses less ammo."

I strap the holster around my waist, insert my first magazine into the handle of the pistol, and check the feel of the paintball gun in my hand. "They're a lot heavier than the plastic water guns we used to use as kids."

Brendan grins. "They are, but these won't empty in our pocket and make us look like we pissed ourselves. Will they, Em?"

Liam snorts. "Grade ten was hard on you after that, wasn't it, Em?"

Emmet rolls his eyes. "You two, fuck off. Everyone else, write your name on one of these wooden disks, and we'll start picking targets."

My brothers and I practically stampede to grab a Sharpie and write our names on one of the smooth, wooden coins. Sloan, Liam, Kevin, Nikon, Dionysus, and Eva are much more civilized.

When I've got mine written, I step back and blow on it to ensure it doesn't smear. Then, when Da lifts a velvet bag, I drop it inside and make room for the others to do the same.

"I'm the sheriff in these here parts, kids. I'll be patrollin' the streets on a Segway. If I catch ye firin' off yer guns or targetin' someone, I'll arrest ye and ye'll be out of the game."

*Rude.* Da has eyes in the back of his head and is crazy stealthy. That makes things more difficult.

When everyone had dropped their token into the bag, Da pats the bottom and invites Sloan and me up to pick first. "The bag is spelled so ye can't pick yerself, so off we go. Pick yer target and step away to look at it in private. The game won't begin fer a bit yet."

I reach into the bag, swish my fingers among the wooden discs and close my fist around one, clenching it in my palm. Stepping back, I retreat to the rear of the crowd and read the name I chose.

*Aiden.*

I make a concerted effort not to look at my oldest brother and start to plan my strategy.

"How long does a game usually last?" Sloan asks. "Ye'll not be shootin' people at our weddin', will ye?"

"Great question, Irish." Emmet raises a finger. "If this rolls over to tomorrow, there will be a truce on all fronts from the time the guests arrive until after the cake. We're not going to affect the wedding."

Sloan looks relieved about that.

Honestly, I am too. I don't want a giant paintball splotch on my— "Oh, and be very careful to only hit below the shoulders. I don't want a black eye for my wedding."

Everyone agrees on that point too.

"What's our battle zone?" Dillan checks out his gun's features. "Are we playing this like a Hide-and-Seek sorta thing or are we continuing with the festivities in the meadow?"

Emmet grins. "That brings me to the Team Trouble twist. As kids we played this around the neighborhood over a weekend and had fun, but we're adults now, so we needed to up the points for difficulty."

Brenny and Emmet are practically busting with excitement, and I'm both intrigued and afraid to hear what more they've planned. "Yes, you are all assassins and will have your targets, but for the next family event, we are playing Capture the Flag."

I blink at them. "Seriously? We're playing both at the same time?"

Brenny offers me a wide grin. "I know, right? Your mind is blown. You need to trust your Capture the Flag team while at the same time wondering if anyone and everyone around you might assassinate you."

"I fucking love this game!" Dillan exclaims.

"Mind-bendy, right?" Emmet agrees.

"What's the course for Capture the Flag?" Kevin asks.

Emmet points at the balcony off the Great Room, and we all step outside. The sky is darkening as dusk sets in. We'll have another hour of daylight at most.

Watching the dragons swoop and play in the sky above squeezes my heart. Dart and Saxa are much happier here where they can stretch their wings. Merlin told me once I wouldn't be able to stay in Toronto indefinitely.

I have a union bond with a dragon, and my dragon is stuck hiding in a den in a forest in my back yard.

I need to do better for him.

That's a worry for another day.

Emmet points at the hot pink glow outlining a section of the hidden city. It divides a bunch of the buildings from the prana river, goes down to the gates, then across toward the Boundary Gate, and back again. That leaves us with a massive rectangle.

"Around the game quadrant of the city, you'll find the glowing magical ward to keep you in play. Sarah set up the flags, so she will oversee the games but not be participating. She's also got a spell working to track any magic. Use it and lose it, boys and girls. This is mortal abilities only."

When everyone is clear about the battlefield, Da leads us back inside and points at a second set of wooden discs. "Divide for yer Capture the Flag teams."

We go through the same process as we did for our Assassin targets, and I write my name down on a wooden disc and drop it into the bag.

"The first six names I pick are Team Marvel. The remaining six will be Team DC." Da gestures at the stack of colorful character bandanas on the table.

He sticks his hand into the bag, jumbles things up, and starts pulling names. "Eva, Aiden, Liam, Calum, Kevin, and Fiona, grab yer Marvel gear. Sloan, Brendan, Dillan, Emmet, Dionysus, and Nikon, yer DC, boys."

The Avenger's bandanas are bright blue, and I pick Black Widow. Natasha Romanoff and I are soul sisters, and yeah, she was also a badass assassin.

I fold my bandana into a two-inch band, wrap it over again and again, and tie it around my forehead, Rambo-style.

I poke a finger into Sloan's chest and bite my bottom lip. "You're going down, Mackenzie."

He tightens his Aquaman bandana around his lovely, sculptured bicep and laughs. "Is this the love and affection I get on the night before my wedding?"

I shrug and throw up my hands. "You knew what you're in for long ago and haven't run for the hills yet."

Emmet laughs. "I think that's her telling you that time is running out, Irish. If you have plans to hightail it, you better get gone."

Sloan shakes his head. "I'm not goin' anywhere. I'm exactly where I want to be."

I tilt my head up and kiss him. "Good answer, Mr. Cumhaill."

Calum snorts. "Are you taking Fi's name, Irish? Good choice. It rocks."

He arches a brow at me and shakes his head. "It does, but I'm a Mackenzie. I can't abandon our line and leave Da as the last of us. No. I intend to create an entirely new generation of Mackenzies."

"Yeah, you do." Aiden grins. "Be aware that twins run in the family. Don't go there until you've prepared."

I laugh. "Can you ever be prepared for twins?"

"Good point."

Emmet claps once. "Enough talk about procreation. This is war, people. Get your game faces on. Now, your holsters hold two backup magazines and your pistols hold one. Your first strategic decision is whether you want two green paint magazines for Capture the Flag and one for Assassin or the other way around."

"There's no going back. Your choice may decide your fate," Brenny warns.

I laugh and consider that. Deciding that Capture the Flag is more of a firing-on-the-run game, I go with one pink set and two green.

When I've chosen and my holster is full, I step away from the table to join Team Marvel. "All righty, then. Let's get the Assassin Double Trouble underway."

"Marvel rules, DC drools," Calum says.

The room erupts into schoolyard banter and we ready for the fun ahead.

Geez, if I knew getting married was this much fun, I might've considered it sooner.

## CHAPTER FOUR

The night goes on, and the hilarity continues. It's an exercise in self-preservation trying to do a "trust your team" event at the same time as an "everyone's your enemy" event. Points to Emmet and Brenny for putting this together.

The only person I trust is Calum...because Kevin assassinated him off the games' starting blocks. We didn't see it happen, but it was hard to miss the hot pink splat on Calum's stomach.

He has sworn revenge and demands a post-wedding mulligan as soon as this weekend's excitement dies.

Forty-five minutes after that, I now trust Liam. He's had ample opportunity to shoot me without anyone seeing, and he hasn't made a move. He also had no opportunity to shoot anyone else to acquire me as his target, so I'm giving him the benefit of the doubt.

He must've come to the same conclusion because we're working together with the easy rhythm and good humor we always have. I press my finger to the comm in my ear and wait for the *beep*. "The Barkeeps are deep inside enemy territory." I give a progress report to our team.

The line crackles to life, and Eva speaks next. "Guardian Angels have our flag secured."

"Left perimeter covered," Kevin advises.

"Right perimeter covered," Aiden adds.

"S'all quiet," Calum finishes. "Go team."

While Calum and Eva guard our flag against being taken, Liam and I make our way straight through the center of the grid. Aiden and Kevin are flanking us a couple of streets on either side, and we're making good time as we hop rooftops and race through buildings.

"I know where we are." I glance around as we seal ourselves into a building along the main corridor. It's a welcoming space with a long bar along the back wall and stairs off to the side. "I came into this pub when we got pulled back in time. I had a drink up those stairs on the balcony with Patty's sister."

Liam chuckles while shuffling through the moonlit space. "Figures. Even sucked back in time, you end up at a pub. You're a lush, Cumhaill."

He's not wrong. "Although, I think this is technically a tavern inn."

"My mistake."

The wooden tables and chairs, which should have disintegrated over time, still stand strong and intact like the building itself. I figure the Light Weaver spell that kept the city hidden and preserved protected everything from wear and age.

"If you ever feel like making Shenanigans a franchise, I bet you could get a deal on this place."

Liam laughs. "Who's coming to drink?"

"I guess only us."

"Well, I'll consider it if you retire from crime-fighting and come tend bar with me."

I laugh, but part of me truly loves that idea. "It would be great to get the band back together."

He pauses outside the door to the kitchen in back. "I admit, when the empowered world isn't trying to kill me, it's cool. The past six months of having Brendan back and now with Kady and me back on track, it's been an incredible time."

"Agreed. Now if we could only get the world back in order." I ease open the back door of the large tavern inn and check out the dark back alley.

"It's not up to you to save the entire world, Fi," Liam whispers. "You can only do what you can do."

"I get that." After checking the sightlines and listening for any sign of an ambush, I deem the alley safe.

Stepping out into the narrow, cobble-stoned corridor, we keep to the shadows, searching for any sign of the flag we're supposed to capture.

Starting in the middle of our zone, the four of us moved forward while Eva and Calum went back to get into position to defend.

I forgot to ask what we're defending.

The two of us move along in the darkness, and I pause to ensure I've got my bearings and am not twisted around.

*Which way should we go?*

I've barely thought the words when a glowing gold arrow appears on the wall across from me. It's beside a ladder up the back of the adjacent building, and I tilt my gaze to follow it toward the velvety darkness of the night sky.

"Where did that come from?" Liam whispers.

"No idea. I was just wondering which way would be best and it appeared there."

"Did you use magic? I don't want to get chucked from the game for cheating."

"Of course not. I wouldn't cheat. What fun is it to win if it's not on our merit."

The two of us fall quiet and stare at the arrow.

"So, do we follow it?"

I shrug. "I've always been a fan of Wonderland."

"Then follow the white rabbit, Alice."

I check both ways before darting across the street to start up the ladder's rungs. Hand over hand and foot after foot, we hustle to get where we're going.

We're close to the DC endzone.

There's no telling where the DC guards have set up to keep us from finding their flag.

In a crouched jog, Liam and I make our way across the flat roof of the inn and end up peering over a half-wall to the streets below.

"There," Liam whispers, pointing at the glowing glass dome covering an Oh, Henry! bar. It's propped high in a lush, bushy tree and will be a bugger to retrieve with their guards waiting to take us out. "Found it."

"It's damn lucky we're up here because I'm not so sure we would've found it on foot."

"I'm not so sure it's luck." Liam frowns as he glances around. "Do you think Sarah tipped us off?"

"No way. She's a white witch. The ethics of fair play and harm none are her tenets in life."

"A trap then?"

I glance around at our position. We've got good cover, can see the target, and there are no sightlines to us. "I don't think so."

"Well, however we got up here, let's guide Aiden and Kevin into position, so we can get back to our territory and win."

"Good plan. You call it in, and I'll go down and help with the extraction."

Liam chuckles. "You realize it's a chocolate bar in a glass dome and not a kidnapped head of state, right?"

I grin. "Perfect practice makes perfect. Give every drill one hundred percent."

Liam laughs. "You're a nutbar."

"No, *that's* a nutbar." I point at the illuminated prize across the courtyard.

Liam chuckles. "I teed you up on that one, didn't I?"

"Maybe a little."

He waves away my laughter. "It's fine. You go. The three of you are better shots than me. You help with the extraction, and I'll be the voice in your ears."

I nod and get moving. "Don't get dead."

"Good advice. Try following it yourself."

---

"Is there any sign of them?"

Aiden, Kevin, and I are in high-alert recon mode, assessing our surroundings and searching for the DC guards. There's no way they're not here, but the question is who, where, and how many of their team stayed back on defense?

"Does everyone have their green paintballs in?" Aiden asks.

*I do.*

As much as I want to peg him with a pink paint pellet, now is not the time. We're deep behind enemy lines, and Kevin is right here looking at us.

Chocolate bar retrieval ranks higher.

"Let's think this through," I mutter. "We're dealing with Brenny, Dillan, Emmet, Sloan, Nikon, and Dionysus."

"I'm with you so far," Aiden confirms.

"Guaranteed, Dillan and Brenny are offense. There's no way they'd be content sitting back and letting the others take on the danger and glory."

Kevin nods. "Agreed."

"Dionysus and Emmet lean more toward defense and foiling people."

Aiden nods. "I can see that."

"Nikon and Sloan are the wildcards."

"Well, they wouldn't have four defenders and two offensive

players, so at least one if not both of them are probably in our zone searching."

*Agreed.* "Okay, so let's go with what we know about Emmet and Dionysus. Where would they be?" I scan the scene below and see nothing.

Then it hits me.

"They're in the tree perched in the elbow of a branch somewhere, waiting for us to climb up."

Aiden nods. "Yep. I'm with you on that."

"Not Irish," Kevin says. "If he stayed back, he's much too logical and strategic to sit around in the tree. He'll be somewhere with high ground and a good view of the park area around."

"Yeah, he would." I scan the area, searching for the place Sloan would choose as his crow's nest lookout point. "There. Do you see that temple-looking stone building with the tall spires facing the play area? It has those tall, skinny archer windows that make it impossible to see inside. If he's guarding, he's there."

Aiden follows my pointed finger and nods. "Okay, Fi, what if Nikon hung back? Where would he be?"

I consider that. "They know what direction we'll be coming from, so he'll be dug in somewhere over there so he can see us approach."

Kevin sighs. "I'm not sure Nikky would hang back. He loves the thrill of the quest."

"That's true. He does." I tap the comm in my ear. "Barkeeps to Guardian Angels. Have you seen anything? Any idea who's coming your way? How many are you dealing with?"

"They haven't shown their faces, but we've got at least three creeping closer. They're still several hundred feet out and haven't seen us, so they're taking it as slow as molasses in February."

"Roger that. We have eyes on the flag and are readying our approach. Advise if anything changes on your end and we'll do the same."

"Roger that."

The three of us regroup, assessing the situation. "The only way we're getting up that tree is from the bottom, isn't it?"

"As opposed to what?" Aiden asks.

"Not sure. I'm trying to think outside the box."

The three of us sit there a moment and ponder. After a few minutes, Kevin grins and points at a building with a strange, almost futuristic canopy sticking out of the storefront. "If one of us takes a flying leap off that, we could surprise them by launching ourselves into the branches."

Aiden worries his bottom lip and tilts his head from side to side. "Well, if one of us flings ourselves across the gap in a Spiderman leap, the other two would have a better chance of getting a shot up from beneath to take them out."

"You're our best shot with a pistol." I consider the strongest positioning for our attack. "I think you should take a ground position with a good sightline. Kevin is our best climber. I'll do the kamikaze jump."

The two of them consider that for a moment, and we all agree.

"If we coordinate the surprise to our advantage, it might work," Aiden admits.

"Take that one step further," Kevin suggests. "Let's assume all goes as planned. I'm climbing, Fi's jumping, and you're shooting. Do we have a plan for who's going for the retrieval and who's making the run back to our territory?"

I point at Kev. "You're our fastest runner. If this cockamamie plan works, I say you grab the chocolate bar and run. Then you dart and weave back to our territory as fast as you can."

Aiden checks our surroundings. "Agreed. I'll still be on the ground, and Liam's our eyes in the sky. He can fire at your pursuers and slow them down. I'll run with you and try to give you cover for as long as I can keep up. If you outrun me..."

"Which he likely will," I add.

"Which you probably will, then beat feet and we'll pray you have the luck of the Irish with you."

Kevin laughs. "I'm the only one of us who isn't Irish. Do you think that rubs off by prolonged exposure?"

I nod. "Oh, for sure it does."

We mull that over for a moment, letting the plan sink in. When everyone's gazes meet and we nod, we know it's a go and update Liam on the details.

"Okay, we all know what we have to do," I say.

"Please don't break your arm the night before your wedding," Kevin warns. "Or your dad will kick our asses."

I laugh. "True story. I'll do my best. Worst case scenario, we've got Wallace here to back us up."

Aiden laughs. "Yeah, well, in that case, there's nothing to worry about, amirite?"

---

It takes a moment for Aiden, Kevin, and I to get into position. Kevin managed to get around the park square, so he's coming in at nine o'clock while I've climbed to the top of this weird canopy directly opposite him at three o'clock.

Aiden won't make his approach until the two of us are a go. Hopefully, we'll distract Emmet and Tarzan long enough that he can get a couple of solid shots off.

I tap the comm and wait for the little *beep*. "Barkeep, get ready. Big Daddy and Brush Boy are moving in. Five, four, three, two, one...go!"

I rear back and run up the steep slope toward the awning's edge. Thankfully, the building materials are rigid and have enough grip that I'm not worried about slipping.

If it was glass or metal, I'd seriously risk breaking my face before I launch into the air.

I've got good traction, so I give it.

The wind picks up around me, and I gain air. Branches come at me like craggy spears and only then do I think maybe this wasn't such a great idea.

I do have to look presentable tomorrow.

*Meh, this is me.* No one coming tomorrow would be surprised if I'm banged up. Or that I did something recklessly stupid in the name of a good time with my brothers.

My aerial arc doesn't last long before I crest my jump and descend into the leafy foliage. From the moment I climbed onto the canopy, I've been projecting where I would land.

Unfortunately, Fiona unplugged doesn't have the same oomph and finesse as Fiona with druid powers.

It's a humbling realization that comes too late.

I grapple with the incoming branches, and it's not a pretty sight. My hands sting as sharp sticks poke my skin and gravity takes hold. I'm a hot mess of flailing arms and legs, but eventually I grab hold of a decent-sized branch and stop my crashing descent.

Well, if that didn't work as a distraction, nothing will.

There's no time to worry about where the guards of the Oh, Henry! are. The longer I stay in one place, the easier I'll be to pick off.

So, I climb.

The air rings with the snapping branches and cursing of men. The arboreal attack is upon me.

Pulling myself up branch to branch, I find fast footholds and push higher as quickly as possible.

I landed higher in the tree than I thought I would and I'm not far from the glass bell cover.

"She's making her move, Greek," Emmet shouts. "Get over there and stop her."

*Perfect.*

I might not have been able to outclimb and outmaneuver

Emmet in a tree, but I'm sure Dionysus doesn't have the experience points I do in this childhood event.

Booking it as fast as my grip will allow, I get over to the glowing dome of chocolaty delight. The moment I lift the cover off the platform, I worry about what I'll do with it.

No need for concern.

Sarah must've spelled the glass container to dissolve into nothing once it's released and the chocolate bar is in hand.

The *splat* of paint follows the *whiz-thwap* of a projectile firing past me. My head turns on a pivot as I assess my situation.

*Am I hit?*

*Nope.* The center mass of the paint explosion is on the branch to the left of my shoulder. I got shrapnel spattered, but that's it.

Still, that was close.

With new urgency, I scan the tree's interior and find Dionysus and Emmet coming at me full-bore.

Without magic, I'm as good as dead.

"Kevin, fire in the hole." Before the boys get another couple of rounds of paint fired, I torpedo the Oh, Henry! through the biggest canopy opening I can find.

The hits come hard and fast after that.

One to my side, one to my ass.

"Fi is out," Emmet shouts below me. "Irish, close in for ground support."

"Rude. Which one of you targeted my butt?"

Dionysus snorts. "You know I love your bootay, Jane. You can't blame a guy for noticing perfection."

*Har-har.*

"Flirt later, Greek. We have family to shoot right now." Emmet has changed course and focuses on climbing down to catch Kevin.

"Liam, get ready. The DC Guardians are coming."

"I doubt I'll hit them from here," he says in my ear.

"Doesn't matter. Getting close will slow them down."

"I'm almost at the base," Kevin shouts, navigating the bottom branches. "Aiden, get them off me."

My brother is positioned at the tree's base, aiming and firing up at Em and Tarzan.

Once Kevin gets to the ground, he tears off with Aiden at his side.

"Run like the wind, Bullseye!" I shout, cheering Kevin on from my position high in the tree.

Damn, we've got a good chance.

Dionysus squeals and I stop climbing down to see what I missed. Liam is firing and almost got the Greek. He and Emmet change course to take a different path and avoid Liam's cover fire.

"They have the flag," Emmett shouts. "Kevin is coming your way. Do not let him get to home territory."

"Go, Kevin!" I shout.

"Irish, where the hell are you?" Emmet's words hang in the air, and I pause to listen and watch.

*Yeah, where is he?*

It's not like Sloan to flake out on his team, especially when it's something like this. Left alone beneath the branches of the DC home tree, I glance around for any sign of him.

Something's not right.

## CHAPTER FIVE

I'm known for having keen instincts even without the telltale sign of my shield igniting on my back. Sloan wouldn't flake on his team. They have comms too, and if he'd heard Emmet call him out for backup, he would've been there.

Unless he couldn't be.

Deciding to go with my instincts, I abandon the Capture the Flag game for now and head toward the interesting old building at the back of the square where I figured he'd take up position.

The first thing I notice as I approach the fifteen-foot bronze doors is one has been left open.

That's good enough for me.

I call Birga to my hand, push the door open a couple more inches, and peek inside. This city has been abandoned for centuries but is coming back to life. There's no telling what might be lurking in the shadows.

Maybe something surprised Sloan.

Maybe the city has taken possession of him as it did with Emmet last week.

"Sloan? Are you in here, hotness?"

Everything in me tells me he's close, but why isn't he responding?

My shield isn't firing to life, but maybe that's because the danger isn't directed at me. It's possible he's in trouble, and that's why he didn't join the chase to guard the chocolate bar.

"Mackenzie? Olly olly oxen free."

I'm not sure that Sloan knows the significance of the phrase, but in the Cumhaill world, it's the step before panicking and calling Da to help find the one of us who has gone missing.

The *click* of a shot sounds a split second before a paintball cracks me square in the thigh and the sting of the hit takes hold. I glance down and curse.

Now, to match the green splotches on my ribs and ass, I have a pink one. "Dammit!"

Sloan steps out of the shadows and blows on the barrel of his gun as if he's a Wild West outlaw. I see how pleased he is with himself, but that was bad form. "I can't believe you made me worry about your safety to lure me to my death. Not cool, hotness."

Sloan chuckles, holsters his pistol, and holds his hand in front of me. "Yer target chip, if ye will."

"Rude."

"Och, luv, all is fair in love and war. Ye've heard that one, have ye not?"

"Yes, I've heard it." I give him the wooden coin with Aiden's name on it and sigh. "Emmet's going to be sooo pissed that you didn't come when he called for backup."

Sloan's expression blanks out. "I didn't get any calls for backup." He taps his comm but no *beep* sounds. "Maybe my battery is dead."

"I'm glad you're not actually in trouble. I was genuinely worried when you didn't join the chase."

He squares off in front of me and rests his arms across my shoulders, linking his fingers behind my neck. "I knew ye'd be part of the offensive force of the Marvels. That's why I picked this wonderful old building as my kill zone."

"Because you knew I'd know you felt drawn to take shelter here for your surveillance."

"Exactly right. See, this is why we'll make a great married couple. We already know each other's hearts and minds and anticipate each other's moves."

*True story.* "Yeah, it's a lock." I land a light punch in his gut and make a face. "But you sacrificed your soon-to-be-wife to advance your standing in a game of murder."

He laughs. "And if the roles were reversed? Would ye not do the same?"

"Oh, no. I totally would kill you. I'm just sad you killed me first."

Sloan laughs. He kisses me before stepping back and pulling me along with him. "Come, I want to show ye what I found."

Sloan drags me deeper into the building, calls faery fire to his palms, and reaches toward a small trough high on the wall.

The moment the fiery blue gets close, the trough ignites, and blue flame races along the ceiling line. As the flames spread, they illuminate the inside wall by the doors in both directions, turn the corners and burn along the sidewalls, then across the back.

The fiery *whoosh* of illumination is sudden and jarring and at the same time stunningly beautiful. "Nice special effect. Did you know that would happen?"

"I suspected. Seeing it firsthand was a wee bit sexier than I imagined in my mind's eye. How do ye think the fuel in the troughs remained flammable after all this time?"

I wander around the space, studying the runes and depictions carved into the stone walls. "I have a theory about that. I think whatever the Light Weavers did to secure the city also preserved it. Liam and I were in the tavern where I met Betrys for a drink that time, and everything looks the same as when I was there a thousand years ago."

"So, the important question is, did the whiskey age a thousand years, or was it held in stasis too?"

I chuckle. "That's the important question, is it?"

"Och, I suppose there could be more than one."

We meander through the open space, and I turn in circles, studying the carvings and trying to piece together what this place is. "Are those spells?"

Sloan steps closer to the firewall and nods after a few moments of examination. "Aye, I think this is the Light Weaver temple. If I'm reading the symbology correctly, these spells record their accomplishments."

"Does it say what happened to them?"

"Not here, no, but perhaps back there." He points at a section of carved stone on the back wall. "Unless I miss my guess, that looks like the perfect place for a spelled panel for a hidden door."

I assess the section of the wall he's indicating and yeah, I can get behind that. "Cool. Then let's see if you're right."

The two of us move to the back of the vast, open temple and examine the seams and carved relief of the stone wall. "I'm thinkin' perhaps this is the community forum, and they kept the private information and records in a private sanctum."

"Ooo, then by all means, let's have an adventure the night before our wedding. Seems oddly appropriate, doesn't it?"

"Aye, it does."

---

If I had to describe my life since getting my druid abilities, I'd say I'm a mash-up between Lara Croft in *Tomb Raider* and Batman trying to straighten out conflicts in Gotham. To be fair, no city I've worked in so far has yet been so bad as that.

Usually, there's a rotten apple to be rooted out or an event that needs addressing.

Tonight is much more on the Lara Croft, Tomb Raider side of things, and if I'm honest, I prefer that side of my life.

There's nothing like the mystery and adventure of discovering forgotten worlds to get the blood pumping.

That is…if you can figure out the mystery.

Sloan and I spend the next five minutes trying five different spells to gain access to what may or may not be a panel to a hidden inner sanctum.

"We're getting nowhere. What if we—"

Heavy footprints *thump* up the steps, and the two doors burst open. Da barrels through the entrance followed by my brothers, the Greeks, and everyone else.

"Fi? What happened to ye, *mo chroí?*"

I take in the panicked looks and shrug. "Nothing happened? What's wrong?"

"Why the hell didn't ye respond to our calls to check in?" Da rushes forward to pull me against his chest. "Ye robbed years from my life."

"Sorry. I didn't hear any comms calls." I touch the earpiece, and like Sloan's before, it doesn't beep. "Maybe the signal doesn't work in here."

"How did you get in here, anyway?" Brenny asks, looking around. "The three of us tried dozens of times, but nothing we've done could open those front doors."

I check with my guy for that one.

"It was odd. I was wonderin' where to take up my position, and an arrow appeared on a building's wall. I knew the city has a mind of its own, so I decided to follow and see where it took me."

"That happened to Liam and me earlier too," I say.

Dillan nods and raises his hand. "Yep. Same."

"It seems the city is feelin' energetic tonight," Da notes. "It wanted to play in our games too."

I'm not sure how I feel about that.

"I guess the city decided tonight was a good night to let us into this temple," Emmet offers.

Seems so. "Emmet was shouting for Sloan when he took off, and I got worried. I came here because it's exactly the kind of place he would seek out. I figured he'd be watching the tree from one of the little windows to take us out when we come for the Oh, Henry! *Hey*, did we win?"

Liam grins and comes forward with a tangle of yellow wrapper. "Team Marvel is a marvel."

Aiden chuckles. "To the victor went the spoils. That's your share of the winning chocolate bar."

I accept the last bite of the chocolate bar and eat it with pride. "Victory never tasted so good. That takes a bit of the sting outta getting killed in both games within five minutes." I gesture at the two green paint blobs and the pink splat on my thigh.

"Sucks to be you, baby girl." Dillan laughs. "So, Sloan took you out?"

"Yep. So much for marital devotion. He shot me. Can you believe that?"

Emmet snorts. "You would've pegged him and laughed about it if you pulled his name."

"Who, *me?*" I feign innocence but no one buys it.

"This place is wondrous." Eva stares up at the rune-covered walls. "The magic in here is nothing I've ever felt before. It's similar to Emmet's but different…and it's building."

That last statement has us all falling quiet.

"Building? Building toward what?" Da asks.

I reach out with my connection to the Source and see that Emmet and Sloan are doing the same thing.

Eva's right. There is a building energy signature, but while she may not have felt it before, we have.

"It's the city," I say.

"It's waking up this building," Emmet adds.

Magic tingles over my skin and I shiver at the goosebumps. I access the communication channel I share with Bruin and send a message to my bear. *Bruin? Not sure if there's an issue, but would you mind joining us in the city center?*

*On my way, Red.*

I'm not sure if there's any cause for alarm, but after the city taking Emmet over the last time, I don't trust our family is safe. Not that I know what Bruin could do against a sentient city, but still.

"Check it." Dillan points at the back wall.

The stone wall shimmers with magic and shifts as the image of five oddly tall women pushes forward out of the flat surface. A moment later, the carvings and spells on the side walls sparkle with silver light as if the stone is backlit somehow.

The same silver energy washes over the surfaces of the walls, highlighting things not visible to us before.

"Wow, that's impressive." Liam blinks up as the ceiling of the building seems to stretch and distort to accommodate for the height of the thirty-foot likenesses of Kyna and her Light Weaver sisters protruding from the wall.

"Who are they?" Eva asks.

"That's Kyna." Dillan points out the woman who hosted our stay in the city when we visited. "Those are her sisters, Syma and Lyri."

"They were the original protectors of the city?" Eva runs her hand over the massive depictions.

Emmet steps back to tilt his head and take in the grandeur of the space. "They trained me to use spatial magic. Honestly, 'trained' is generous. I had a crash course on how to do one spell and its reversal. I can hide and unhide physical things from this world."

"Do you think that's maybe what happened to them?" Kevin asks.

Calum's brow pinches. "What? Do you think they're here somewhere, phased by spatial magic?"

Kevin shrugs. "I was wondering out loud."

"I don't think they're here." I walk the perimeter of a mosaic circle appearing beneath our feet. "If Kyna and her sisters were here—even if they had been frozen in some kind of a state—they would've thawed themselves out over the past six months."

"Maybe this *is* them." Emmet looks horrified. "Maybe they're frozen in carbonite like Han Solo. This could be their true form, and they're awaiting rescue."

"I don't think so, Em." Sloan is studying the glowing runes and swirls on the side walls. "If I'm reading the symbology of their language correctly, I believe this is the telling of the arrival of the Light Weavers to the island. They came through the Boundary Gate."

I shuffle over to check out the symbols and signs he's studying, and yeah no, I've got nothing. "Well, if they came through the portal door carrying their belongings, they weren't supersized."

Emmet exhales a long breath. "That's a relief. Those women were intimidating enough with their naked netting and their power. I don't know if I could take it if they were also thirty feet tall."

"Naked netting?" Sarah asks.

I wave away that tangent for the moment. "Sloan and I figured this room is their community worship forum and there might be a hidden sanctum on the other side of the back wall. We were trying to find the opening when you arrived. Dillan? Can you have a go?"

Dillan holds out his hand. "Babe, can I get a ride up to our room to grab my cloak?"

"Oh, let me take you." Dionysus rushes over. "It still feels like I'm dreaming. I want to use my powers and make sure I am me."

"You are you, Tarzan," I assure him.

"There can be only one," Aiden says in his best Christopher Lambert impression.

My brothers and I laugh, but Dionysus misses the *Highlander* reference altogether. He clasps Dillan's hand, and they're gone and back in a few seconds.

Dillan holds his cloak, swings it over his shoulders, and clasps the collar. Once the hood is up, he heads back to examine the wall with Sloan.

Bruin breezes in and takes form among the group. "This place is rife with magic."

"Yeah. It makes me wonder how powerful the city is." I return to the mosaic pattern on the floor and continue to study it. "Something about this has me mesmerized. My instincts are pulling at me."

Da, Nikon, and Dionysus come over to see what I'm talking about. Having walked around the circle's perimeter clockwise a few times, I try withershins this time and reach out with my connection to earth magic.

The island is a supercharged battery of prana energy, but I don't get anything specific coming back at me.

Before I can figure out what piqued my attention, Dillan shouts in triumph, and a section of the stone wall swings out of the way. "Never fear, my peon friends. The master of discovery is here."

I roll my eyes and am about to toss an insult back at Dillan when I make it to the door of the hidden sanctum and my jaw drops. "Holy crapamoly. Look at this place."

## CHAPTER SIX

The group fills the opening to the private room behind the back wall of the Light Weaver temple. The procession stops inside the opening, and we stand there with our mouths agape.

"Holy shit." Dillan's words echo my thoughts.

The space reaches high above and is as breathtaking as the forum temple. The spires I saw rising to the night sky outside stretch above us.

During the day, sunlight would stream through the windows high above and fracture through the myriad of crystals strung above our heads.

The effect must be one of a total prism explosion.

My heart stalls in my chest and starts back up at triple time. "It's incredible. I bet it's even more spectacular in daylight."

"And slightly creepy," Emmet says.

Sloan glances at my brother and scowls. "What part of this do ye find creepy?"

"The part where the women we met a thousand years ago considered this their private space and now we're invading it…

and we have no idea what happened to them…and no idea if they rigged this room to blow when infiltrated by strangers."

"I would say that's imposin', not creepy."

"Semantics, Irish. It's something anyway."

"Aye, it's somethin'."

Our group enters, but we take things slowly.

I watch my footing, reaching out with my power, ready for anything. "Emmet's not wrong. It feels like a booby trap kind of place. If it's all the same to you guys, I'd rather not get poison darts shot into me or have the floor drop out from underneath me the night before my wedding."

"There's your sweet spot, Irish." Calum points at a floor-to-ceiling, wall-to-wall bookshelf filled with wide leather spines.

I grin. "True story. This is a Sloan Mackenzie trifecta of intrigue. We've got the ancient stone building with spires and magical alcove lighting. We've got the mystical library of the ancients filled with hundreds of books. And we've got a mystery to solve."

"Which mystery do you mean, Jane?" Dionysus asks.

"Take your pick. What happened to the Light Weavers between the time we met them with Bodhmall and Fionn until now? Where did they go? Why did they hide the city? Why did the city go dormant?"

Sloan has his hands up and is scanning the bookshelves for magical energy.

"Do you think Patty knows?" Calum asks.

"I think he would've told us by now if he did."

"Have you ever asked him?" Dillan asks.

"I have, but he doesn't like to talk about that time in his life. Things were rough for him while he lived here."

"Aye, we remember." Sloan gravitates toward the bookshelf.

I draw a deep breath and sigh. "You'd think the air in here would be musty and stale after being sealed up for centuries."

"Magic is a funny thing, luv," Da reminds me.

"Maybe there's a magical equivalent of Febreze," Emmet says. "You know, so wizards and faeries can keep things fresh."

I laugh. "Or maybe this island hasn't been hidden and spelled shut for as long as we think. Maybe people still live here, and we haven't seen them."

"That's unlikely, *a ghra*," Sloan points out.

Brendan nods. "Yeah, the three of us have been all over this place and other than last weekend when the island possessed Em, we haven't seen or heard anything that wasn't us."

Sloan finishes with his search of the books and eases a couple off the shelves. "Do ye mind if I spend a few minutes havin' a look at some of these books?"

I point at the ornately carved marble table. "Take a seat. This is your wedding weekend. Have at it."

While he looks at his chosen books, the rest of us explore.

"I'm coming back here tomorrow to see what it looks like in the daylight," I declare.

"Ye might be a wee bit busy tomorrow, *mo chroi*. Ye know, with yer weddin' and all."

My brothers chuckle, and I wave away their amusement. "I *know*. I didn't forget."

"I can help you see the effect now, if you like." All attention turns to our guardian angel. Eva is grinning wide, her joy dimpled in her cheeks. "What do you think? Anyone interested?"

"Yeah, babe. Do your thing." Dillan gives her a gentle nudge into the center of the room.

Eva focuses on the ceiling for a moment and bursts into the air. Her white dove flaps feathered wings, gently lifting her toward the ceiling.

Her dove always glows with the light of Heaven's rays, but when she gets high above our heads and centers herself over the prisms, she holds out her wings and bursts into a supernova of golden light.

"Holy shit," Dillan repeats. "She never ceases to amaze me. You're incredible, Angel!"

*Seriously...wow.* Eva is so lovely and unassuming it's easy to forget what an exceptional being she is and the magical power she possesses.

It takes a moment for my eyes to adjust to the sudden brilliance, but when I stop blinking and my vision clears, I'm taken away by the beauty around us. The prisms above aren't strung willy-nilly as I thought at first glance. They're placed to ensure rainbows of light cover every part of the room.

It's like standing in the center of a diamond as the world around us sparkles.

"That was worth the effort of getting in here," I say.

"Aye, and then some," Sloan agrees.

Brenny raises his hands and waves them around like a magician. "For my next trick, folks, Heaven's light will shine down on you."

The awe in Brendan's voice rings clear.

Dillan smiles proudly up at his mate. "She's fucking incredible, isn't she?"

"She is at that, brother. The question is...why the fuck is she with a loser like you?" Brenny is ready for the flying fist and laughs, blocking the assault.

"Speakin' of newlyweds, it's gettin' late, kids." Da taps the face of his watch. "Do ye think maybe we should pack it in fer tonight and get everyone settled? We've got a big day tomorrow."

It's a testament to Sloan's love for me that he lifts his nose from the book he's devouring and closes the cover. "Aye, yer probably right, Niall. Let's head back to the palace. Nothin' here is goin' anywhere. It'll keep."

I hear the self-restraint he's forcing into his words and laugh. "Why don't you take a couple of them back with you. Since I'm staying with Sarah tonight, you can flip through the ancient texts as some relaxing, light reading."

He grins and starts to stack a few books.

Liam brushes my shoulder with his as he leans in to whisper, "He missed the sarcasm in that completely, didn't he?"

"Uh-huh. To him, tackling four ancient texts *is* light reading. He'll be in his glory. Still, someone will have to take the books away from him and force him to go to bed at some point, or he'll lose track, and it'll be morning before he realizes it."

"We'll take care of it," Calum says.

"Niall, do you need a lift back to Lugh's and Lara's?" Nikon asks.

"Not tonight, son. I'll be stayin' at Sarah's with Fi."

This is news to me. "Why? What's up? I figured you'd go back to the shire after game night and return in the morning with Gran, Granda, and Shannon."

Da shakes his head. "Och, no. I know how ye tend to go missin' and tomorrow's an important day. I'm stayin' in the bedroom next to yers fer tonight to keep watch."

I burst out laughing. "Come on. I'm not that bad."

The raised eyebrows around the room tell me they disagree.

I hold up my palms. "Fine. I won't argue, but I'm sure I can get through one night without having a guard."

Sloan winks. "Aye, yer probably right, *a ghra*, but humor us. It'll make *us* feel better if nothin' else."

---

Less than an hour later, Da and I are hunkering down in the home Sarah claimed as hers. It's not far from the palace, and she's made it quite homey over the past six months. I recognize some of the furniture and textiles from the times I visited her little cottage home in Blarney.

"It's lovely, Sarah. Thank you for inviting us to stay."

Sarah pulls the elastic out of her ponytail and shakes out her blonde hair for the night. "Yer always welcome in my home, Fi.

It's been too long since I've had company. I miss having people rattling around the house with me."

"Have you thought of bringing some of your coven to spend time with you?"

"I've thought about it, but my friends don't have the same access to portal magic as yer lot. As well, they wouldn't necessarily get past the island's wards."

"Then we'll arrange with Dionysus or Nikon to bring them over. Schedule yourself a girls' week, and we'll make it happen. I'm sure they wonder what you're doing here and would love to stay with you."

"Aye, they do and would."

"Then it's settled. After the wedding, we'll make a plan. The Greeks won't mind, I promise."

"The Greeks won't mind what?" Dionysus, our God of Festive Fun, materializes in front of me wearing cotton pajama pants with wedding bells and confetti on them and a toothbrush in his hand.

"Are you staying here too, Tarzan?"

"It's a sleepover, isn't it?"

Da frowns. "Aye, son, in a fashion but Fi needs her rest tonight. There won't be any movie marathons or staying up late. It's straight to bed to rest up fer a big day tomorrow."

Dionysus acknowledges him with an exaggerated nod. "I understand. We're getting married tomorrow. I've gotta rest up too because I'm singing."

Sarah gestures at the stairs and starts moving. "Shall I make up another bed then?"

I follow her up to the bedrooms. "Not necessary. If I know my Tarzan, he'll be bunking with me tonight."

Dionysus frowns as if he's confused. "That's what you do at a sleepover. What fun would it be to sleep in my bed?"

Da glances sideways at me and frowns. "Do ye think yer

husband-to-be will appreciate ye spending the night before yer wedding sleepin' with another man?"

I laugh. "Sloan will be fine. He's used to it. The fact that he trusts me and has never questioned me, or the guys I'm close to, is a huge reason I love him so much. He knows my heart and never doubts me."

"Or me," Dionysus says. "Irish is a rare man. I hope I find a partner who loves me that way one day."

"You will, sweetie." I point at the bathroom, then at the room we'll be staying in. "Why don't you take first shift in the bathroom and settle in? I'll be there in a second. I want a minute with Da before I turn in."

"Okeedokee." Dionysus bounces off toward the bathroom with his toothbrush, and I glimpse the butt of his pajama pants.

"I love your 'Just Married' sign."

"Jane, eyes off my very fine ass. I know you can't help yourself, but you're getting married in the morning."

"My bad." I laugh and draw a deep breath. "Man, it's good to have him wisecracking again. Losing his powers really rocked his foundation."

Da leans his shoulder against the wall of the upstairs hall and crosses his arms. "As it would."

When the bathroom door *clicks* shut, I focus on my father and point at his room. "Can we sit and talk for a minute?"

He pushes off the wall and gestures for me to go in ahead of him.

Sarah might have brought some of the furniture from her cottage home, but this building is still older than any castle or home in the real world.

The architecture is similar, but where we're accustomed to square rooms and ninety-degree angles, this house is all curved lines and a domed ceiling.

I sit on the bed and tip toward my father when he sits and the mattress dips. He lifts one leg to lay it on the mattress in front of him and shifts to face me. "So, what would ye like to talk to me about, *mo chroi*?"

"Nothing specific. I just thought…you know, that you'd give me one of your Da pep talks to start me off on the right foot."

Throughout all the days and nights of my life, Da has been my guiding force. He's praised me when I've gotten things right, suggested a new course if he's seen me heading in the wrong direction, and pulled me up short on the occasions I've gone off the rails.

He's exactly the kind of parent every kid needs.

He wasn't only raising six kids.

He molded six adults.

"Do ye *need* a pep talk, luv? Is all well?"

"Oh, yeah, I'm good—great even—I've just missed our daddy-daughter talks and figured you'd have something inspired you'd like to say."

He chuckles. "Weel, I don't know about inspired, but I have a few heartfelt thoughts that have been bumpin' around in my mind the past few months."

"I'll take what I can get."

He holds out his hand, and I make the connection, squeezing tight. I'm not sure why I feel so emotional, but at this moment, I'm not a twenty-five-year-old independent adult with her own home and life. I'm the little girl who sat in his lap so many days and nights and cried because I missed my mom.

Even thinking about that has me blinking fast and my eyes glassing up.

"Och, now, don't be doin' that, or ye'll get me started. Then where will we be?"

I chuckle and try to blink back the tears. "I'm being stupid. Nothing's really changing. Sloan and I are already married in our hearts, and no one is leaving or moving on. It's just…"

"Ye miss yer mam and wish she could've seen the life ye've built."

*Is that what this is? Yeah, I guess it is.*

Huh…once again, Da knows me better than I do. "I hadn't even figured that out. How did you know?"

Da winks. "I've made it my business to know yer heart since ye first opened yer eyes and wrapped yer wee fist around my baby finger. Grown or not. Druid or not. In the same house or not. It'll never matter. Yer my wee girl…the touchstone of our family."

"Our family sure looks different now than it did a few years ago."

"Aye, that's true, but no matter how it looks, it always feels the same. We Cumhaills are a funny bunch that way. We love bone deep. We're in each other's minds and hearts but also in the bones and blood."

"Tomorrow I'll be a Mackenzie."

"To some extent that's true, but bein' added to the Mackenzie clan doesn't remove ye from ours. The way I see it, Wallace and Sloan are lucky to have ye. They missed out on the joy of family and couldn't have a better liaison to teach them in the future."

"Wallace said as much to me this morning. He regrets what he missed with Sloan and is looking forward to getting it right with his grandchildren."

"I have no doubt he is."

The two of us sit quietly for a little while. Then I squeeze his hand. "Thanks, Da. For being everything I've ever needed and more. Yeah, I'm sad Mam can't be here with us, and maybe I'm a little spoiled by getting Brendan back that I kinda hoped Eva or the Fates might surprise me with her, but I've never lost sight of how fortunate I am."

"How fortunate we *all* are, luv."

I draw a deep breath and let that sink in. "I've been blessed in so many ways, and they all stem from you. You and the boys say I'm the touchstone. If that's true, you're the mortar that cements us all in place."

"I'm touched ye feel that way, but in truth, ye made it easy. Ye were a joy to raise and a pleasure to watch grow. Now that yer off to start yer own family, I hope ye take the lessons and fond memories we've shared and put them to good use."

I lean forward and wrap my arms around him. "I'll try my best, Da, but if I screw up, you'll still be here to dust me off and give me a kick in the pants, won't you?"

"Och, baby girl. I'm not goin' anywhere."

# CHAPTER SEVEN

"Fi, wake up. It's our wedding day, and they're here." In my hazy daze of slumber, I hear Dionysus and try to focus on his words. "Who's here, Tarzan?"

"The guests. They're arriving. Myra and Shannon are downstairs with Sarah, waiting for you to start your wedding day preparations. Come on. You're sleeping our day away."

It never fails to make me smile when he calls it *our* wedding day. "All right. I'm up." I force my eyes awake and smile at the elaborate chiton he's wearing. "You're already dressed?"

"Of course. I was first in the bathroom to make sure I didn't get in your way."

"That's very thoughtful. Okay, let me get showered. Tell everyone I'll be down in ten when I'm ready for them to start futzing with me."

Dionysus pushes off the bed with such force that I bounce off the pillow. "Okay, I'll tell them. Ten minutes, Jane. No snooze buzzer."

I laugh at the admonishment and sit up. "Understood. No snooze buzzer."

Breathing to the depth of my lungs and holding it for a few

beats helps with the sudden rush of excitement that hits.

*OMG, I'm getting married today.*

Wedding day or not, it doesn't take me long to shower and dry off. I towel my hair and run a brush through it to keep it from tangling. I pull on my undies, bra, and robe and tie the silk belt ready to greet my ladies-in-waiting.

When I return to my room Dionysus is back. He's sitting cross-legged in the middle of the bed, smiling at me. "They're waiting to glitz your glam, ma'am."

"Are they now?" I chuckle, grab my makeup bag from my duffle, and turn toward the door. "Then I guess we shouldn't keep them waiting."

Dionysus flashes to my side and flashes us downstairs. "Ladies, I bring you the bride." Dionysus sweeps his hands to the side with a flourish and back to his body, one across his front and the other behind his back as he bows.

I accept the theatrics and hold the sides of my robe out as I curtsy. Taking them in ratchets my excitement up another ten notches.

Sarah's in a pretty cornflower blue sundress with spaghetti straps. Her blonde hair has been left long, and two small braids at the side of her face have been pulled to the back like an elven laurel.

Shannon's wearing a lovely sage green dress with Celtic embroidery at the cleavage. It sets off her strawberry hair and her pale complexion beautifully.

"Look at all of you. I hope someone is taking pictures."

Sarah nods. "A few of us have raised our hands to make sure yer covered there."

"Excellent."

Myra comes over and hugs me. She's wearing a champagne-colored dress that contrasts the electric blue of her hair and the gold of her vertically slit eyes. "Big day in the life of Fiona Cumhaill, eh?"

"Yep."

"Then we better get you fed so you don't faint in front of all your family and friends."

"It wouldn't be the first time I did something mortifying in front of them, but yeah, let's try to avoid that."

"Got you covered there, duck." Myra guides me over to the dining room table. "Come, feast your eyes and fill your belly."

She lifts a serving dome off a plate, and I smile at the chocolate chip pancakes with raspberries and icing sugar. The chocolate chips form a heart, and I sigh. "I'm a lucky girl."

"Yes, you are. Nikon brought these and said to tell you Sloan is showered and cooking wildly to remain calm. No one up there is complaining."

I laugh and take my seat, reaching over to grab the syrup. "I suppose not. Hotness likes to cook when he's anxious or excited about something."

Myra laughs. "Garnet likes to snap people's bones, so I think you're already ahead of the game."

While Sarah and Shannon bustle around in the living room getting ready to get me dressed, I take a moment with Myra. "Thanks for being here."

"Oh, duck, where else would I be? You're my girl, and today you're getting married to the man of your heart. All is right in the world."

"I think so too. How's Imari?"

"Oh, she's fine. She's excited about the wedding and spending the day with Jackson, Meg, Bizzy, and Bruin. She's excited to see dragons... She's as happy as any eight-year-old could be."

"How are Mommy and Daddy?"

"I'm relaxing into her being marked. Sloan saying she's physically fine helped. I'm anxious for her to spend time with Wallace though to be sure."

"We mentioned it to him last night. He's happy to help whenever there's a break in the festivities."

"Thanks, duck."

I dig into my bridal breakfast and moan. "So good."

The sweet treat derails my train of thought but the out-of-body moment soon ends, and I'm back in the present. "How is the king of beasts? Is he still all growls and claws?"

"Yep. I invited Anyx and Zuzanna to escort us. I hope you don't mind."

"Of course not. My wedding is your wedding."

She chuckles. "Not really, but I get your meaning. Yeah, so they're here under the guise that they might babysit Imari while we have adult time."

"Does Garnet realize he's the one being babysat?"

"If he does, he's not protesting, so I'll take it."

"Excellent."

Dionysus is eyeing my plate, and I chuckle. "Snap up there and get yourself something, Tarzan. I promise I won't start anything exciting before you get back."

He grins and is gone.

Myra laughs. "Does Sloan realize he's marrying you and inheriting an ancient demi-god in the package?"

"He does. Dionysus is mine. We're a package deal."

"Well, he seems to be finding his footing in our world. I haven't seen him this happy in weeks."

"He got his powers back." I spend the next few minutes finishing my breakfast and catching Myra up on the visit from Themis and her daughters.

"Well, good. He deserves to get them back. In my opinion, there was nothing to make up for in the first place. He had friends who could save the life of someone we love. That's something to be celebrated, not punished."

"Thank you, Myra," Dionysus says, materializing at the end of the table. He has a plate in hand and sits. "Here, Sloan sent you bacon. Mine's crispy. Yours is chewy."

I grin and reach across to accept it. "He gets me."

Dionysus chuckles. "Oh, Jane. This is just the beginning. Irish is working his magic behind the scenes like you wouldn't believe. This is going to be a great day."

"Behind the scenes? What do you know, Tarzan? What does he have planned?"

Dionysus grins and fills his mouth with pancake, then points to show me his mouth is full.

"Not talking, eh? Well, that's fine. I guess I can wait to see." I finish my juice and wipe my mouth. "Okay, you can finish that in the next room. It's time to decide what I'll be wearing."

"You haven't *decided*?" Dionysus stops chewing and stares at me as if I've just blown his mind. "Jane, the wedding is in less than two hours."

The panic in his voice is too funny. "Dude, don't you think I know that? Come on. I'll show you the problem."

The three of us head into Sarah's living room, and I take it all in. Last night, I didn't explore the house so much as go straight upstairs to get cleaned up and ready for bed. I was worried I might not be able to get all the paint off me, but Dionysus took care of that with a flick of his finger.

He really is *soooo* happy to have his powers back.

"Good morning, *mo chroi*." Da is sitting on the window seat, looking out at the hidden city below and sipping coffee. He's got a white dress shirt, his black leather kilt that the men of the Order wear at formal occasions, and his dagger strapped to his hip. "Did ye sleep well?"

"I did. Like the dead."

"No nerves or worries keepin' ye up?" Shannon blinks at me expectantly, but I've got nothing.

"Nope. I sawed logs all night until Dionysus woke me up this morning."

She laughs. "Och, weel, that's good. I was a bundle of nerves last year when we wed."

"Nope. The only thing I'm worried about is what to wear.

Once we finally figure that out, I'll be fine."

Dionysus moans. "I still can't believe you don't know. Isn't that the first thing brides choose?"

"That and how they want their hair and makeup," Myra says. "Fi and I have been playing with her red curls for weeks, trying to figure out how she wants to wear them."

I shrug. "I can never decide."

"The problem is ye don't know what yer wearin'," Shannon says. "Once ye have that, it'll fall into place."

"Then let's get this party started," Dionysus urges. "What's the issue? Tell me, and I'll fix it."

I laugh at his confidence. Most men would throw up their hands and stay miles away from a woman picking out her wedding outfit.

Dionysus isn't most men.

Three dress bags hang on a dressing screen around the room. I move to the first one and look to see which it is.

"It's not that I haven't thought about what I'll wear since I was a little girl—I have—but my choice changes with my mood. At first, I wanted to wear a sleek, silky dress that clings to all the right curves and makes me look sophisticated and glamorous." I unzip the first bag and pull it out.

"Sloan's jaw would drop if he saw ye in that, *mo chroi*. He'd love it."

"I think so too. Only, I'm not really a sleek and sophisticated girl. I want him to see what he's signing up for when he sees me. I want to be authentic."

"Got it." Dionysus flicks his hand. "It's stunning, but it's not the one. Let's see the next one."

"The next one is sentimental." I unzip the front of the garment bag. "This was Gran's dress. She saved it hoping that I might want to wear it someday. It's beautiful too…but Gran practically raised Sloan, and I don't want him to look at me on my wedding day and think I look like my grandmother."

Dionysus makes a face. "Yikes, definitely not. It's lovely, but we want to fan the flames of passion for the honeymoon and the years ahead."

"Perhaps ye can wear it for part of the reception so yer Gran can take some pictures," Shannon suggests.

Myra nods. "That's a good idea. Then you can show her you love it and still shine as yourself on your day."

"What's in the third one?" Da asks.

"Since this is a simple celebration of our nearest and dearest, I also brought a pretty, champagne-colored knee-length dress that's much more my style. It's cute but understated and practical."

"Fail!" Dionysus shakes his head. "Sorry, Fi, but none of these speaks to me."

Da looks at him and his brows arch. "Ye realize this isn't yer weddin', don't ye, son?"

Dionysus nods. "Yes, but it's my best friend's wedding. What kind of a Man of Honor would I be if I failed in my duty to get the bride to the altar in anything less than an outfit that makes all the men throw wood and twist in jealousy."

I blink and shake my head. "Yeah no, that's *not* the goal. The men are my family and friends. No wood is to be thrown. That is…well, icky."

Dionysus is ignoring me.

He's propped his hand under his chin and is studying me as if he's Michelangelo's Thinker.

*I'm scared.* What's going on in that head of his?

"I've got it." Dionysus snaps his fingers.

Magic washes over me, and a moment later, I'm clothed, and Shannon, Myra, Sarah, and Da are all staring. Looking down at myself, I take a beat. It's nothing like what I imagined, but it feels good.

Stepping over to the full-length mirror, I look at myself. "Wow, this is…"

"Perfection, I know. You're welcome."

"I think we should let the lady decide fer herself." Da stands and comes to get a better look.

Dionysus chuffs. "What is there to decide? Fi knew the dresses weren't right. This is perfect. It's wedding sleek, authentic, and practical. *Annnd*, when Irish sees you in this, he knows exactly what he's signing up for. This is you, Jane. The real you."

I stare at myself in the mirror. Dionysus dressed me in white leathers that are more soft and supple than anything I've ever worn. The bodice is strapless, and the boning makes the girls look good. Over the pants, there's a leather overskirt around my back and a gossamer front piece that flows freely and matches my veil.

It's nothing like anything I pictured, but he's right…nothing I pictured felt right. "I love it, Tarzan. You're right. It's perfect."

"What can I say, except you're welcome," he sings, swaying his hips and dancing around the living room. "I'm just an ordinary demi-guy."

I laugh and step back while he breaks into a full rendition of Maui's solo from *Moana*.

Da looks at me, but I shake my head.

Dionysus being himself is as good as it gets. Besides, it's a rocking song, and he's killing it.

Myra, Shannon, and Sarah have never had the pleasure of experiencing Dionysus unplugged. I'm happy they got to have this moment. When he finishes, I clap and give him a standing ovation.

"You'll have to do that again for the kids," Myra says. "That was amazing, and they'll love it."

I nod. "*Moana* is Meg's favorite Disney movie. I bet she never realized you're a demi-god like Maui."

Nikon snaps in and stops dead when he sees me. He presses a hand to his chest and shakes his head. "The radiance of the sun pales in comparison, Red. You are breathtaking."

"Nailed it." Dionysus does another twirl, and the skirt of his chiton flares up to reveal the commonality between the men of kilts and chitons.

I close my eyes and make a mental note not to let him go wild on the dance floor.

Nikon laughs. "I feel like I've missed something, but that's okay. Sloan is in the meadow welcoming the guests. He asked if you have his grandparent's oath stone and said you'd know where it is."

"I do. It's..." I think about how to explain where I put it and figure it's likely easier for me to get it. "You're sure he's at the meadow?"

"That's where I left him."

"Okay, then I'll show you, and you can snap me right back to finish getting ready. Tarzan, will you go to the meadow and make sure Sloan doesn't come back to our room at the palace?"

"Will do."

I smile at the others. "I'll be right back."

Myra waves that away. "If you weren't running off to do something yourself, you wouldn't be Fi. Take your time, duck. Hair and makeup can wait. You don't get married for another hour at least."

I squeal and link my arm through Nikon's. "Got it. We'll hurry."

---

Nikon snaps me to the bedroom that Sloan and I use when we're here on the island, and I hurry over to the suitcases and boxes of wedding supplies we brought with us for the weekend.

I didn't want Nikon going through our bags on the off chance he chose the wrong one and opened the honeymoon bag.

I've got a few X-rated honeymoon surprises in that one for Sloan's eyes only.

When I find the little gift bag Wallace gave me yesterday morning, I lift it out of the pile and give Nikon the painted stone. "Here. It's pretty, isn't it?"

"Gorgeous." But he's not looking at the stone.

"You're not so bad yourself, Greek. You and Dionysus are rocking the chitons. Who knew you boys had such nice knees."

He chuckles but says nothing as he studies me.

I draw a deep breath and address the elephant in the room. "Are you okay? I don't want my happiness to hurt you. I know your feelings or at least what your feelings used to be, and I need to make sure you're okay."

Nikon takes my hand and presses it to his chest. "I love you, Fi. There's no getting around it, you're amazing, and you bring me joy."

"You bring me joy too. I do love you back."

He presses his fingers over my lips. "Don't worry about me. I've lived long enough to learn how to be happy for the people around me, even if I wish my life were different. The fact is, you and Sloan are amazing individually and together. I'm truly happy for both of you and look forward to sharing your lives."

I hug him and give him an extra tight squeeze. "Thank you. I needed to hear that."

Nikon eases back and winks. "I don't want you to think I'm standing in the corner pining away and trying not to implode. I'm good. I'm thinking about rebuilding with Dani. Maybe it works, maybe it doesn't, but we had something special once, and I never stopped loving her."

"Well, she'd be a fool not to realize what a catch you are. I'm sure you'll woo her back."

"We'll see, but for today, you need to finish getting ready, and I need to deliver this rock to your guy."

I hug him once more before giving him the go-ahead. "All right. Let's do this."

## CHAPTER EIGHT

When my hair is swept off my neck, and my veil is pinned to the crown of my head, I clutch a bouquet of exotic-shaped flowers blooming in ivory and the softest blushes of pink. I'm as ready as I'll ever be. I check the time, and my heart flutters with a rush of adrenaline. "This is it."

Da smiles and folds my hand over his elbow. "Yer a vision, *mo chroi*, an absolute beauty."

Dionysus snaps back from portaling Myra, Shannon, and Sarah to the meadow to take their seats. "Everything's set. They're ready when you are, Jane."

"How are things set up? Is there an aisle? I don't want to look confused when I get there."

Da shakes his head. "Yer Gran and Sloan agreed to a traditional druid ceremony. The chairs will be in a circle, and the two of ye will stand in the middle to say yer vows, surrounded by family."

Dionysus nods. "Gran told me to bring you to the opening of the circle. You and Niall will walk inside together. Then, it's pretty much the same as most wedding ceremonies…except for ancient Roman. There will be no sacrificing of a white bull."

"Oh, excellent. I'm good with that." I extend a hand and pull him close. "Thank you, Tarzan. You're the best Man of Honor I could've hoped for. I heart you hard."

Dionysus bends down so I can kiss his forehead and grins. "You're going to rock this, Jane."

"Yeah, I am."

A surge of Dionysus' magic tingles over my skin, and we flash out, arriving outside a circle of chairs. It's exactly as Da and Dionysus described it and I'm glad I asked. I don't want to look lost.

"We meet again, fair Fiona," a man says, turning from facing the circle to greet us.

I meet the twinkling gaze of my great-great-great who knows how many greats-grandfather. Fionn's usually messy flaxen blond hair has been groomed and braided to fall beside his face. Probably for the first time, his tunic is clean. "Hello, oul man. I'm thrilled to see you, but how are you here?"

He tilts his head to where Samuel, Ahren, and Quon Shen are sitting in the circle. "Yer Hunter-god friends have quite a bit of pull in the Nether. They sprung me for a few hours."

I clasp wrists with him and squeeze. "I'm so glad they did. Thank you for coming."

Fionn harumphs. "Fiona mac Cumhaill, blood of my blood, my heart sings to know I played a small part in the journey that led ye to yer man. There's nowhere else I'd rather be."

Merlin joins us. "Then we should get started, yes?" He tilts his head toward the circle of people standing and waiting. "How about we catch up after?"

"Oh, right." I blink and get back to the now. "My bad."

Merlin takes the lead and starts the procession into the center of the circle, followed by Fionn, then Da and me. The men ahead of me screen me from getting a good look at Sloan and vice-versa.

When we arrive at the center, the wait is over. They all step into their positions, and I'm left standing face-to-face with the man of my heart.

My breath freezes in my chest.

My pulse races in my veins.

*This man is mine.*

He looks me over, and I guess I pass muster because he presses his palm to his heart and blinks fast against the moisture rising in his eyes.

Merlin clears his throat and stands at our shoulders. "We gather today as friends and family on this most sacred of occasions, the bonding of marriage between Fiona and Sloan."

I draw a deep breath and lock my knees. Faceplanting during my wedding isn't going to be part of my blooper reel of life.

"Our circle is woven and consecrated, blessed by each soul and spirit gathered and blended in one sacred space. We share the weight of one purpose—to witness two unite as one."

I swallow and waggle my brows.

"Who brings this fair maid to be wed this day?"

Da steps forward and inclines his head. "I do."

Merlin nods. "So mote it be."

Fionn is standing behind Da, and I don't miss the significance. Yes, Da is giving me away, but Fionn brought me here today. He chose me, empowered me, and set me on this path from the beginning.

"We gather beneath the watchful eye of the sun and moon, upon this hallowed earth, to witness this sacred bond of marriage between Fiona Kacee mac Cumhaill and Sloan Lincoln Wallace Mackenzie. We honor the life they have built over the past two years and the life they plan to build in the years to come."

*The years to come—I love that.*

"Fiona and Sloan, do you come to this place of your own free will?"

Sloan and I speak as one. "I do."

"Then may you be blessed by the powers of the earth. May

your love root in sweet fertile soil, so your union may continue to grow strong. May your lives together be rich with fertility and its perfect fruitfulness."

"Hello, God of Fertility, right here," Dionysus points at himself. "I got you covered on that front."

I laugh. "Thanks, sweetie."

Fionn steps around us, takes my bouquet, and hands it to my father. While Merlin continues, Fionn wraps our joined hands in a beautiful emerald green silk handfasting cord.

"Vows bind a couple together, soul to soul, heart to heart. They join the bloodlines of your ancestors and those of your descendants, in spirit and in body. Fiona and Sloan, are you ready to declare your vows?"

"I am," Sloan and I say together.

Fionn finishes with the handfasting cord, and Merlin holds the Mackenzie oath stone under our joined hands.

"Fiona and Sloan have prepared their own vows and will exchange them now. Fi, go ahead."

I suck in a breath and squeeze Sloan's hand. "I thought love was only true in fairy tales, meant for someone else but not for me."

My brothers all bust up at the same time.

Dillan snorts. "Seriously? You're quoting a Monkees song for your vows?"

I scratch my cheek with my middle finger. "You lost your say, D. You eloped. My vows, my choice."

He laughs and holds up his hands. "Fair enough. You do you, baby girl. Carry on. I believe love was out to get you. Or that's the way it seemed."

I chuckle and meet Sloan's arched brow. "This is us."

Sloan chuckles and shakes his head. "May the goddess help us. Aye, this is us."

"Congratulations to you both." Laurel hands me a glass of champagne, and I pull my attention away from Gran and Granda gliding over the dancefloor. "That was a lovely ceremony. I especially like the part at the end when Merlin sealed your bond with a kiss. The way the two of you glowed was cool."

"Yeah, weird, eh? At the time, I wasn't sure if it was my imagination or the excitement of the day playing tricks on me, but the moment our lips touched, the magic of our bond washed over me."

"Why is that weird?" my high school friend asks.

"Because we didn't plan it. Merlin says he didn't do it, and neither Sloan nor I did. We haven't figured it out yet, but with my track record, there's no telling what it might mean."

"You sound worried."

"Not so much worried, but cautiously unsettled. Maybe it's totally fine and it's nothing, but my instincts are usually solid."

The two of us watch the guests mingling under the faery lights strung across the meadow.

It's really beautiful.

Eva brought back the dance floor from last weekend, and Dionysus set up a line of gossamer-draped tents along the back. With the drapes tied back and decorated with bunches of flowers, it's like something out of a magazine.

While I know it was a joint effort, I see thoughtful touches of Sloan and Gran everywhere I look.

"So, how do you feel?"

"Honestly, I didn't think the ceremony, a paper, or a ring would change anything between us..."

"But it does?"

I meet her gaze and smile. "It's like it makes what we share... more. Does that make sense?"

"Perfect sense. It was like that after I pledged my oath to Benjamin as his companion. It didn't change anything we were doing or intended to be to one another, but it solidified things in a way I hadn't expected."

"Yeah, that's it exactly."

The two of us stare at my guests as the dance floor undulates with the elegant ebb and flow of crisp suits and colorful, flowing gowns. The sea of bodies shifts in a coordinated rhythm. It's mesmerizing.

Brenny's wedding soundtrack is working its magic.

It's funny. The longer the day ticks on, the more I realize how many people pulled together to make this happen.

It takes a village…or in this case, a clan.

Sloan joins us with a tray full of finger food in one hand and a drink in the other. "Hello, Mrs. Mackenzie."

"Hello, Mr. Cumhaill."

He kisses me and when he eases back, his beautiful mint green eyes sparkle with emotion. "Are ye enjoyin' yer day, luv?"

"Very much, thank you."

He winks and offers us our pick of the food on his tray. "Och, ye don't have to thank me, *a ghra*. It's my deepest pleasure to put a smile on yer face."

"The way she put a smile on yours when you saw her in that outfit?" Dionysus asks.

Sloan looks me over and smiles the same way he has all afternoon. "I can't even begin to tell ye…it's perfect."

Dionysus gives me a sly grin behind Sloan's back and uncurls his finger until it's sticking straight up. *Mission accomplished, Jane. Your boy's been throwing wood every time he looks at you. You're welcome.*

I swallow and try not to laugh. "Don't you have a song to sing to the monkeys, Maui?"

He grins. "Yeah? You were serious about that?"

"Oh, yeah. The kids will love it."

"Cool. I'll be back."

Dionysus snaps away, and Sloan sets the tray down. After

tipping his drink back, he sets the tumbler down too and holds out his hand. "May I have this dance?"

I lay my hand in his. "You may have all the dances."

"I like the sound of that."

Sloan leads me out and spins me to face him, securing me in his frame as he leads us into the flow of traffic. He's an incredible dancer. The years of grooming a perfect son might not have been ideal for Sloan, but it worked out for me.

As we glide across the dancefloor, him leading us all the way, I smile at the circle of family around us. "So, this happened."

"Aye, it did, and it's a good thing. A very good thing."

I'm not sure how long we dance. It could be a few songs or a few hours. Lost in the music and magic of the night, the only thing I notice when we finally leave the dance floor is that the sky is darkening and the winnots are coming out to dot our sky.

"Oh, can we say hello to Samuel and the guys?"

Sloan changes course toward where my fellow Hunter-gods are standing with Fionn. "Of course, luv. We should spend time with everyone."

---

Our light lunch and appetizers are replaced by an incredible buffet table several hours later and the night marches on.

I'm enjoying a drink with Xavier and Garnet when the music stops and Dionysus taps on a microphone. "Can we get the bride to the center of the dance floor, please? It's time to really get this party started."

"I hope he means that in a normal way and not in a Greek god orgy kind of way. There are children in the crowd."

Garnet's scowl is too funny.

I laugh and pat the lapel of Garnet's suit jacket. "It's fine. He's been looking forward to singing for me all week. S'all good."

Dionysus points and a sleek black grand piano appears on the corner of the dance floor. "Irish? Are we doing this?"

Xavier leans in and frowns. "He is an excitable man."

I chuckle. "That's a gross understatement, but I wouldn't change him in any way."

Dionysus looks over from across the meadow and smiles. "Thanks, Jane. I lurve you too."

Sloan *poofs* beside me and wraps an arm around my hip. "Gentlemen, if ye don't mind, I'd like to steal my wife." Then he *poofs* us again, and we reappear over by the piano.

"Enjoy the show, *a ghra*. Happy weddin' day." He strides off to the piano bench, sits, presses his fingers on the keys, and begins to play.

As the first notes of the song coalesce, I smile. Sloan's playing *Slow Hands* by Niall Horan. The first time he played this for me, we were at the funeral home run by the West Village Wizards, tracking down my trickster stalker, Discord.

I didn't know he played until he sat, and his fingers started dancing over the keys. He started playing something else but then mentioned he was an acquaintance of Niall Horan.

As silly as it sounds, he won big points with that.

As the two of them finish the song I raise my hands to clap but the final refrain blends into another Niall Horan song and the dulcet voice of Niall himself fills the air. *Are you freaking kidding me?*

I spin and just about die when I see him walking toward me. OMG, he did it…Sloan really did it.

Callum, Dillan, and Emmet each have their phones up recording my expression and laughing.

Emmet lets out a long whistle. "I told Irish this will come back to bless him on his wedding night. He's going to get soooo lucky."

Nervous excitement bubbles up from my chest, and I feel like a fifteen-year-old girl again. Niall Horan is singing at my wedding.

I rush forward, stopping directly in front of my teenage heartthrob. When he extends his hand, I respond so quickly that it's a little embarrassing. He squeezes my hand while he sings *Nice to Meet Ya* directly to me.

The world spins around me, and I think I might faint.

Sure, I've met famous and important people over the last couple of years, but this is Niall Horan, and he's serenading me at my wedding.

If the end came right now, I'd die a happy woman.

Of course, I don't want the end to come yet.

I'm just getting started.

I'm frozen in place for more songs: *Put a Little Love on Me*, *No Judgment*, then *Black and White*.

When he finishes singing, Sloan stands and comes around to introduce us. He has to pry Niall's hand free from mine.

*Awkward.*

"Thanks fer comin', sham. I think ye can see how much it meant to Fi to have ye here."

"Och, no trouble. I was happy to do it. How's a guy to say no with the promise of a magical portal to an enchanted island of fae wonder?"

"Oh." The static finally clears in my mind, and I come back to my senses. "Bruin! Come meet Niall." I wave over my bear. "He's a big fan too. We stream your songs when we're working out, don't we, Bear?"

Bruin lumbers over and lifts his chin in greeting. "Howeyah."

Of course, Niall can't understand him, so I relay the greeting.

"Shall we cut the cake?" Gran calls.

"Yeah, Gran. Two minutes." I check with Niall. "Come eat cake. Have you ever wanted to ride a dragon? After dessert, I'd be happy to take you up for a spin."

Niall looks at Sloan and my guy chuckles. "There's a fair bit about our world we haven't made public yet. Dragons are real, and Fi is the one we can thank fer bringin' them back from the brink of extinction. If ye've got the stones, she'll take ye up on her mount."

Now it's Niall Horan who looks like he might faint.

---

The night progresses, and I'm so glad my family gets me. There is laughter and drinking, and the children are going wild in the bouncy castle Dionysus brought here. He told everyone it was for the kids, but the moment Kinu and Kevin round them up and Nikon flashes them back to the palace to go to sleep, the adults invade.

Thankfully, Wallace is here because I have no doubt that with my family, tons of alcohol, and an adult bouncy castle, there will be injuries.

Garnet and Myra take more than a few spins around the dance floor, and my heart swells to see their happiness shared with mine.

Gran is in her glory.

The celebration has brought her many stomachs to fill and her week's worth of efforts are well received. She and Shannon have become quite a team.

I'm not surprised.

Both women are strong and skilled in their own arenas, and both have loved this family for decades.

Nikon and Andromeda are having a blast, and I'm happy to see that Maxwell was able to come after all.

They seem to be enjoying themselves.

I hope Nikon finds someone to share his love. He's an incredible man, and after a millennium of being stalked by Hecate, he deserves to have the family he's always wanted.

"How's yer night goin', Mrs. Mackenzie?"

Sloan wraps his arms around me from behind and kisses my temple. "I couldn't imagine it any better. We made it through the entire day and not one disaster in sight. Could it be my luck is changing?"

Sloan laughs but before he can reply Garnet steps up to us and interrupts. "It seems we have a problem, Lady Druid."

I wince. "Dammit! I jinxed us."

Garnet gives me a long look and waits for me to shake it off.

"Okay, I'm calm. What kind of problem?"

# CHAPTER NINE

It looks like the honeymoon is over before it even begins. The tension in Garnet's muscular frame tells me he's worked up. Even more worked up than he's been all day. "Is Imari all right?"

He nods. "Yes. This isn't about her mark."

That's a relief. "Then what are we talking about?"

"Now that the children are turning in, Zuzanna and Anyx were taking Imari home to allow Myra and me some grown-up time. They tried to leave but don't seem able to get off the island."

Weird but not as bad as I worried.

"Maybe it's the protective wardings. Dionysus or Nikon should be able to take care of that for you."

"They tried. They can't snap out either."

"Okay, that's weird." I raise my hand and catch Nikon's attention across the crowded dance floor. *Can you join us, please?*

I'm still not totally sure how our mental connection works, but if I have his attention or am close to him, there has never been a problem communicating.

Sloan gestures for us to step off the dance floor and we claim one of the gossamer tents. When Nikon arrives, I don't mince words. "What's happening? Is it the island's warding?"

He shakes his head. "I don't think so, but Dionysus and Bruin are checking that out now. They're trying to get through the access point into the shifting forest. We could always do that even before we could portal in and out of the island."

"Good idea. I don't want my wedding to be remembered as a Hotel California celebration."

Dionysus snaps back looking befuddled. "How do you feel about your wedding becoming a Hotel California celebration?"

Sloan rolls his eyes. "It's no wonder the two of ye get on so well. Yer both cracked along the same fault line."

I ignore his chastisement and stay on point. "You guys couldn't get out through the forest either?"

Dionysus shakes his head. "No. It looks like we're stuck here until we figure out what's going on."

I glance at my guests, and while most of them won't object too strongly about a glitch like this, people like Garnet, Xavier, and Merlin have duties of their own they need to stay on top of back home.

And... "OMG, we've kidnapped Niall Horan!"

"Maybe the dragons can portal us out." I pinch my thumb and forefinger together and press them under my tongue. Letting out a shrill whistle, I call for Dart across our mental union bond channel. *Dart, we need to do a bit of intel gathering, buddy. Bring Saxa to the bottom of the meadow.*

*On our way.*

"Sloan and I will go up on the dragons and see what we can find out. If it means a dragon shuttle out to the beach to flash, that's what we'll do."

Garnet nods, but he's clenched his jaw, and the muscle at the side of his temple is pulsing.

"Easy, lion. I'm sure it's nothing."

He arches an ebony brow and scowls. "Nothing is ever nothing around you, Lady Druid."

The fear I see in his amethyst eyes isn't about him getting

trapped on the island. It's about Myra and Imari being caught in a potentially unknown situation.

He doesn't respond well to his girls being in danger. I'm sure that protective impulse is already exacerbated by Imari's crescent mark appearing.

"Nothing will happen to them, bossman. We all love them, and we protect our own. There are enough warriors and powerhouses here to fend off Morgana and ten armies. Let's figure out what's going on without assuming the worst."

I leave Garnet to brood and growl while Sloan and I strike off toward the meadow's edge. Dart and Saxa are there waiting, and I call *Feline Finesse* to give me the oomph I need to vault onto Dart's back.

Sloan arches a brow. "Showin' off, are ye?"

"I gotta make it look good. Niall Horan is watching. Maybe if he sees how much I rock the dragon transport, he'll trust me enough to come for a ride."

Sloan laughs. "Ye realize ye married *me* only a few hours ago, aye? Should I be worried?"

"No way, no how. Being married to you has been the best hours of my life."

He shakes his head at me. "Then here's to many more hours of marital bliss."

"Works for me." Jogging up the uneven scales of Dart's back, I rush to his first spike and grip the handle of my saddle. "Take us up, buddy."

With the sheer power unleashed, he launches us straight into the night sky. Saxa is right behind us, and I glance over my shoulder to ensure Sloan is good.

I don't doubt his coordination or Saxa's skills. Still, dragon-riding is new to him, and I worry. When he was unconscious back during those horrible hours during the Culling, Saxa offered to bond with him.

The gesture came from a good place. She wanted to help

bring him back to me. When Sloan eventually woke, he wanted to wait and give her time to think about it without the pressure of saving his life.

I still hope the two of them will form a union bond. That would grant him the longevity of a dragon rider and give us a better chance of living a long life shared.

The wind feels good in my hair, and I realize too late I should've pulled my veil free before takeoff. The sheer fabric catches in the wafting air and tugs it free.

I glance back to watch it float on the night breeze like a ghostly film fluttering gracefully back to the ground.

*What's the concern?* Dart asks me.

*There's a problem portaling off the island. We need to gain some speed and test the warnings to see if you dragons can get through.*

*And if we can't? How much speed do you want behind us if we find out the portal won't open?*

*How about enough to trigger the portal but not so much that we crash and die on my wedding night?*

I feel Dart's amusement over our bond. *I suppose being robbed of the consummation part of being married would put a damper on the entire celebration.*

*Yes, it would.*

*Congratulations, by the way. Sloan's a good man and a good match for you.*

*Yes, he is. Thank you.*

Dart pumps his mighty wings once, twice, then a third time. I tuck in behind the spike and widen my stance.

Saxa picks up speed, and a moment later we're racing through the skies side-by-side.

*Here we go*, Dart says.

The two of them make no attempt to slow down. They commit to engaging the portal and give it everything.

This is how we arrived in the early days of coming to the island. We'd approach from the beach, fly into the area of the hidden city, and fight the urge to turn back. The warding magically imposes a sense of foreboding sending people back.

The island's security keeps outsiders from entering, but tonight we're merely soaring through the clear blue sky.

"I don't feel anything," I shout over the rush of air in my ears. "Is the portal even here?"

*If it is, it's not activating for us,* Dart says. *What do you want to do next?*

*I guess we go back and tell the others. It seems a mystery is afoot.*

Just like that, the magic and mayhem of my life impose themselves on my wedding.

---

Dart and Saxa drop us off at the meadow, and a crowd welcomes us. I don't think many of them know what's happening, but many have never seen a dragon before.

"Hello again, Dart." Myra strides forward to join us.

Samuel looks wary about getting anywhere near the dragons, and I struggle not to laugh. The day Scarlett grabbed him and dragged him through the tunnels will be forever etched in our joint memories.

For completely different reasons.

In hindsight, I think it was hilarious.

I don't think he's gotten to that point yet.

"So, no portal then," Garnet growls.

"No. It seems there is an issue." I read the questioning looks from my family and friends and elaborate. "For right now, it seems we're in a lockdown."

"What kind of a lockdown?" Xavier asks.

"It's the wardings or some kind of island glitch, we don't know yet, but it seems none of the access points to the island will release to allow anyone to leave."

"So, this is Hotel California," Dillan says.

Sloan shakes his head and rolls his eyes at me. "It's like ye have a language of yer own and everyone else is forever trying to make sense of it."

"Has this happened before?" Quon Shen asks.

"Not that I know of." I search the group for the only person here who might be able to answer that. "Patty? Do you remember anything like this happening before?"

I find my leprechaun friend among the crowd. "Not that I recall, Red."

I hear the unspoken words that echo as subtext.

He doesn't recall much about that period of his life.

"All right, well, let's assume it's a new problem. We have enough combined wisdom here from gods, angels, kings, immortals, and alphas that we should be able to figure this out."

"Unless we can't," Xavier snaps. "Then what do we do? Some of us are needed back home and have certain dietary needs that require us to get back to Toronto."

*Craptastic.* I didn't think of that. He and Benjamin will need to feed off a female if we can't get them home. I don't relish the idea of being his juice box.

Been there, done that.

Got the nightmares to prove it.

"I understand. Let's focus on the fact that this has only been an issue for half an hour. Let's not get ahead of ourselves. For now, let's consider this license to keep the party rocking without the worry of going home."

Sloan steps in beside me and wraps his arm across my lower back. "In the meantime, we'll do our best to figure out what happened and why."

Emmet joins us in addressing the group and points at the golden obelisk glowing up the hill at the top of the hidden city. "If anyone has had enough partying for one night and wants to stay over and see where we are in the morning, there are thirty bedrooms in the palace to be claimed."

"We've got more than enough food," Gran says.

"It's turned into a destination wedding," Myra adds. "Fun. The adventure never stops around you Cumhaills. Emmet, if it's all right with you, I'd like to claim two of those bedrooms. I'll put Imari to bed in ours and Anyx and Zuzanna will stay close until we know what's happening."

Emmet nods. "The rooms across the hall from Kinu and the kids are vacant and have an adjoining door. Nikon, can I get you to give them a lift to the third floor?"

Nikon steps in and nods. "Of course. Anyone else?"

It seems it's too early in the process for anyone else to be packing it in for the night.

Brendan takes that as his cue to restart the music. "Enjoy, everyone. There is still plenty of night to be had and love to celebrate. Fi and Sloan will update us as soon as they know more."

---

Gran and Brendan take control of entertaining the guests. Although there is tension in the air that wasn't apparent previously, everyone is taking things in stride. Then again, it's only been half an hour.

Emmet snaps back with Nikon, and they join us in the gossamer tent. My brother goes straight to Garnet. "Myra wants you to know Imari is super excited to sleep over in the palace with Jackson and the kids and that she is turning in so you can focus on the problem without worrying about either of them."

"Anyx and Zuzanna are there with them?"

"Yes. Anyx asked her to leave the adjoining door open until you get there to join your family."

That goes a long way to taming the king of beasts. "All right. Now let's figure out what the fuck is going on."

"There's a security control center in the city's heart." Patty gestures the way. "We might start the investigation there."

"Sounds like a great idea." I glance around at the group. "Who's staying and who's going?"

When the group weighs in, it ends up being me, Sloan, Patty, Nikon, Emmet, Merlin, Garnet, and Xavier tackling the warding issues and everyone else staying back to keep the party going.

"I've got your back, Jane," Dionysus says. "Consider me your good-time ambassador."

There's no doubt about that, but... "Just to be clear, everyone's clothes stay on, and no guests get roofied. I don't want any Mad Max moments."

He frowns. "One time. A guy makes one mistake and never lives it down."

I chuckle. "I thought it bore mentioning."

"No worries, *mo chroi*." Da winks. "We'll take good care of the party-goers. Yer only task is to figure out what's gone wrong and why."

"Thanks, Da. Call us if you need us. Otherwise, we'll be back...hopefully with good news."

---

We navigate the city streets by the light of faery fire, Patty guiding us along the way. "It's been a great many centuries since I walked these streets, Fi. I hope I don't get turned around."

"Don't worry about it. The fact that you knew there was a security building is more than we knew. If it takes us a couple tries to find it, that's fine."

"What does it look like?" Emmet asks. "Brendan, Sarah, and I have explored most of this section of the city. Maybe I can help you find it if you tell me what we're looking for."

"If I remember correctly, it was a shiny bronze building with engraving across the roof line like the Grecian Marbles."

"Huzzah! I *do* know where that is. Sarah and I tried to get in there a couple of weeks ago, but like most of the buildings, it was locked down and wouldn't let us in."

"Do ye think it's possible that the city is decidin' what ye can and can't gain access to?"

Xavier casts Sloan a dirty look. "What do you mean 'the city deciding?'"

I take that one on. "We discovered last week that when Mother Nature asked Emmet and Sarah to help wake the city, she meant it literally. Last weekend when we were here, we found out the city is sentient and able to communicate."

"How did you discover this?" Garnet asks.

"It spoke through Emmet. There was an issue with a portal gate on the other side of the city. Through a kind of possession takeover of my brother, the city instructed Nikon how to secure the gate."

Xavier curses. "Possession? The city is alive and can possess the people within its boundaries. Did you not think that something to mention to people coming here?"

"The city can't possess just anyone," Emmet says. "I was its vessel because I reside here as its champion and protector. It's not going to possess you or any of the other guests."

"Can you guarantee that?"

Emmet hasn't had as much experience dealing with the stern, angry vampire king and seems a little rattled by the hostility.

I step in to rescue him. "Obviously, with a situation like this, there are no guarantees. Emmet got a sense of the city's intentions when it used him as a communication vessel. To the best of our knowledge, it merely wanted to communicate a pending danger."

We continue to wind through the streets, and Emmet moves forward in the group to walk with Patty and put some distance between him and Xavier.

Sloan's stride matches mine, and he takes my hand raising my fingers. "Weel, at least no one will go away thinkin' our weddin' was borin'."

I chuckle. "Look at you, finding the silver lining. Well done, hotness. It seems like only yesterday we were cursing and brooding."

Nikon laughs. "That *was* yesterday."

"Oh, right. I thought so."

The two of us chuckle at Sloan's expense, but it's nice to see that even with the current craziness unfolding, nothing seems to be touching Sloan's good mood. Maybe he finally realizes that chaos doesn't always mean calamity. Sometimes it's just adventure.

"Here we are." Emmet gestures at a sleek, four-story building with a flat brass front. There are no windows, but I suppose if it is a security building, that makes sense.

"Aye, this is it." Patty squares off in front of the building and cranes his neck back to look up at it. "Now to see if we can get inside."

Garnet growls. "Oh, we'll get inside. Even if I have to rip the fucking walls apart to make an opening."

*All righty then.* "It's good to be motivated."

"If the city spoke through Emmet, is it possible that Emmet can speak to the city?" Merlin asks.

"Great question." I meet Emmet's gaze to gauge what he thinks about that. "Have you ever tried?"

"Nope. I think in the week since I was possessed, I was trying to avoid a repeat performance of having a sentient city inside my head."

"I get that, but maybe if you're speaking to the city, it wouldn't have to be so invasive. When I speak to Nikon, Dionysus, Dart, or Bruin, it's nothing more than a conversation in my mind."

Emmet considers that and shrugs. "I'll give it a go. What do you think I should say?"

"Ask the city to let us into the building," I suggest.

"Ask the city what the fuck is going on," Garnet says. "If it's sentient, it might know."

"Or be behind it," Xavier says.

*That's a thought.* "Why would the city want to keep my wedding guests hostage?"

"Maybe it's lonely," Emmet says. "It's been abandoned and dormant for who knows how long. Maybe it's happy to have people within its streets. Maybe it doesn't want the party to end."

I have no idea if that's even possible. "Okay, try to get us inside first."

Emmet closes his eyes.

A moment later, there's a soft *click*, and the door to the city security building swings open.

"Good job, Em."

## CHAPTER TEN

The eight of us step over the threshold and into the security building, none knowing what to expect. Even though Patty knew about the building, he's never been inside. However, several security officers visited him when he lived here.

I let that one drop. That Patty isn't this Patty, and we all have the right to leave our past in the past.

Without windows, the interior is pitch black.

There must be motion sensors or something because when we step deeper into the darkness, the lights fire up around the room.

"That's better." I take in the surroundings.

Seating stations line the outside walls of the twenty-by-twenty space, and a control console is in the center of the room.

"Welcome, strangers, to Isilon. A city forgotten but not gone."

Everyone's heads pivot as we look for the source of the welcome.

"Who's there?" Garnet snaps.

"Is it an AI welcome?" Nikon asks.

"Does a hidden city from a thousand years ago have AI?" I ask.

Patty rolls his eyes. "No, Red, but it did have magic."

"Right. Sometimes I still forget to think like a druid."

I'm not sure what Patty thinks about that because he steps forward and raises his hands in welcome. "Hello, Astrid, this is Padraig of the Northern Hills."

A four-foot female with purple and turquoise spotted wings appears in front of Patty. "Welcome, Padraig. A long time it's been. Your hair is white, but your mind is clean."

"Aye, a lot has changed over the years."

The little fairy doesn't set off any of my warning systems, but that doesn't seem to hold true for Xavier and Garnet. The two are as tense as a strung bow and have murderous expressions as they glare at the little turquoise-haired greeter.

"She doesn't have a scent," Garnet snaps.

*Weird.* "Is she an illusion?"

Astrid flaps her wings and flutters over to land directly in front of me. Without preamble, she punches me hard in the right boob.

I shout and take a swing. My hand passes straight through her, and she grins. "Illusion, I'm not. My presence is real. Say that again, and more pain you shall feel."

I call Birga to my palm and grip her staff, ready to ram Tinkerbell through. "Punch me again, and I'll kick your ass. I'll find your master switch and kick your ass."

Emmet's laughing. "I don't think you can rhyme kick your ass with kick your ass. And I don't think you should piss off our fairy welcome committee."

"Piss *her* off? I'm the one that got sucker-punched to the right tit."

Sloan moves forward and raises his arm as a restraint to keep me back. "How about you release Birga, and we'll try this again."

I don't see what I did that was so wrong.

I only asked if she was an illusion.

How was I to know she was sensitive about it?

Sloan bends slightly to meet Astrid's gaze. "Hello, little one. I am Sloan Mackenzie of Galway. Can you tell us what's happening with the city? The friends we've brought here for a family gathering can't leave the island. Do you know anything about that?"

"I know everything about everything," she says.

"Challenge accepted," Emmet says. "Who shot JR?"

Astrid faces him and bows her head. "In the 1980 television drama series *Dallas*, the character JR Ewing was shot by Kristen Shephard, JR's former mistress, in the final episode of season three."

Emmet's eyes widen, and he takes in the room. "Not bad."

I throw him a look. "Did you know who shot JR?"

"Oh, hell no. That was way before my time." He turns back to the little faery. "Who was the first girl I ever kissed?"

"Your mother."

Emmet looks at me. "Not what I was going for, but I suppose that could be the right answer."

Before he rhymes off his next question, I hold up a finger. "Maybe we should focus on the current problem before Garnet's head explodes."

Emmet casts a glance at the alpha lion and makes a face. "Oh yeah, good call. Astrid, I am the champion of the island and the caregiver for the hidden city. Can you please tell me why our friends can't portal back home?"

She bows to him and smiles. "Whether or not your party has ended. Permission to leave the isle is suspended."

"Suspended by whom?" I ask.

She turns to frown at me. "Identify yourself, and I'll answer your query. There are rules to addressing a custodial faery."

Are you freaking kidding me? "If you know everything, you already know who I am."

"My directives are clear, for you to inquire, identify yourself or the consequence is dire."

"Well, I guess she told you," Emmet says. "Astrid, could you please tell me why permission to leave the island has been suspended?"

"Isilon wishes for the people to roam. Those who have gathered shall not go home."

"Who is Isilon?"

Sloan raises a finger. "I think what she's sayin' is Isilon is the name of the sentient city."

"Dark skin pale eyes, this male is wise."

I arch a brow. "Huh, your charm even works on magical faery greeters. It really is a superpower, hotness. I think she's flirting with you."

Sloan rolls his eyes. "Astrid, is there a way we can speak to the city to request that permission to leave the island be reinstated?"

"No."

Nikon snorts. "No rhyme? Just, no? That's anticlimactic."

Astrid grins and fists her hands at her tiny hips. "The answer is a simple no. Your party guests aren't cleared to go."

"What about arrangin' an audience with the city?" Sloan asks.

"The city is Astrid. I am he. The answer is no from both of we."

Emmet pulls up a finger and moves in next. "If we knew why the city felt so strongly about keeping people here, perhaps we could come up with an alternative that was more agreeable to everyone."

"Isilon is all. Agreement is moot. Since the people have come, the power takes root."

*Now that makes sense.* "If the city gets power from people being here, it makes sense that while it was abandoned, Isilon fell dormant. So, he wants people here to prevent himself from falling back to sleep."

Emmet frowns. "Maybe we can get him other people. How can we repopulate the city?"

"I don't think we can, Em," I say. "Not without knowing why

the city evacuated in the first place and where everybody went. If a threat or a plague put everyone in danger, we can't simply repopulate for our benefit."

A long low growl rumbles out from Garnet's lion. "If a threat or a plague put everyone in danger, that's exactly why we need to get the fuck out of this city."

"I feel you, bossman, but we've been coming here for six months, and there hasn't been one moment where we worried about threats of any kind."

Emmet screws up his face. "That's not really true, Fi. Last weekend, the island seemed to think there was a threat coming from the other side of the Boundary Gate. That's why it had Nikon reinforce the wardings."

"Astrid, if you know everything, what was the threat to the Boundary Gate last weekend?" I ask.

"Girl with red hair not so bright. Must state her name to make things right."

*Oh, for fuck's sake.* "Hello, Astrid. My name is Fiona Cumhaill. I am a druid from Toronto, and I'm a Taurus. I prefer street hockey over long walks on the beach, I have a ticklish spot behind my knees that makes me almost pee my pants, and my right boob is aching and sore. Would you like me to go on?"

"Please don't," Xavier says.

"Yeah, I'm sure that covers things well enough for everyone here," Garnet adds.

I'm not sure that's true, but I've run out of steam. "Look, I'm tired of this runaround. This is my wedding day, and I hate that people I love are being inconvenienced, so please tell me what we can do to make this right."

"All is well, for Isilon has risen. Fret over nothing. This isn't a prison."

"This is pointless. There must be another way—one that doesn't involve talking in rhyme with a boob-punching fae poet."

No one seems to want to back me up on that.

I roll my eyes and wash my hands of the whole exchange. There has to be another answer.

As I'm storming toward the exit of the security building, an image on one of the terminals draws my attention to a group of six cat people pounding their fists and shouting up at the camera.

"Hey, what is this?" I gesture at the scene, and Emmet jogs over to see what I'm looking at.

"Yeah, Astrid, who are those people?"

"Feline folk in dire straits, requesting entry through Isilon's gates."

"Dire straits? Do you know what has them so panicked?"

"Most seeking refuge in Isilon arrive after all other hope is gone."

I scowl at the pain in the ass fae welcome wagon. "Refuge from what?"

"Have ye forgotten the folks who lived here when you visited last, Red?" Patty wanders over and glances at the scene. "I remember ye telling me when ye got back that it was the island of misfit toys."

*Right, I remember.* "People who need help or a safe place come here to live. So, why did we barricade the doors and seal all the wardings extra tight?"

Astrid doesn't want to answer me.

Emmet takes a shot. "Astrid, why did we seal off the city if this is supposed to be a safe place for people in trouble?"

"With people in need come people with greed. We cannot be certain, so why risk the burden?"

If I could only skewer her with my spear, I totally would.

Nikon comes to the front of the crowd to look at the image of the cat people knocking on the doors. "If they're in trouble, Sarah and I spelled the Boundary Gate to shut them out. If this is supposed to be a refuge, you made us complicit in turning them away."

"Part of that casting mentioned allowing worthy people to pass through." Emmet frowns. "I thought we were supposed to determine who is granted access to the city, not lock everyone out completely."

"To allow access of people in need allows access to people with greed," Astrid states.

"Not good enough," Garnet growls. "If this city is designed to be a haven for species from different realms and pantheons, you don't get to lock the doors because you might get some bad ones in with the good. That's not how it works."

"Isilon suffered years of neglect. He is all, and now will select."

"Select implies there is a chance for people in need to get in here." Nikon points at the family of feline folk on the viewscreen. "This is not a selection process. This is isolation. Fi, didn't you say this race lived here when you were here?"

I nod. "Yes, the feline folk were the royal guards to the Light Weavers."

He turns back to Astrid and scowls. "If they are inherently a duplicitous species, the Light Weavers wouldn't have made them their guards. There must be some who have moral fiber and a code of ethics."

Emmet turns once again to the faery. "Astrid, what is the general characteristic of the feline folk? Are they a dangerous species?"

"The feline folk are honest and just. Well known for heroics, goodwill, and trust."

"That's good enough for me. I'm going to get Sarah. I'll meet you guys at the gate."

When Nikon snaps out, I check in with Emmet, Sloan, and the others. "Are we doing this?"

Emmet considers that for a moment and after another look at the screen nods. "Hells yeah, we are. If I'm going to live in this city for the rest of my life, I'm making it the kind of city I want to live in. Fantasy Island doesn't turn away people in need. Irish, take us to the Boundary Gate."

---

We arrive at the ornate bronze doors a moment before Sarah and Nikon. Brendan and Dionysus have tagged along and are joining the fun.

Nikon gestures for us to give them space to work. "Wish us luck. We had instructions on how to fortify the gate. That doesn't mean pulling down the wards will be a simple reverse engineer."

I wave away his concern. "You've got this, Greek. Between you and Sarah...piece of cake."

As we step back to give them room to work, Dionysus smiles at me. "Speaking of cake, Gran outdid herself. I've had three pieces of each kind and still can't decide which is my favorite. I would even go so far as to say it's as good as the ambrosia of my pantheon. Although, Gran's cake doesn't grant immortality or god powers."

I chuckle. "I guess now that you have your powers back, you don't have to worry about adding on extra weight. Three pieces of each kind, eh? Good for you."

Dionysus pats his flat stomach and grins. "Doesn't get any better than this. Welcome to the pleasure dome."

Emmet laughs and raises a fist. "Well said, Greek."

Those of us not actively unraveling a sentient city's warding spell chat quietly among ourselves while Nikon and Sarah do their thing.

"This still doesn't get us any closer to getting us home," Xavier says. "Not unless this gate also holds a portal destination that can lead us back to Toronto."

"Yes and no," I say. "If Isilon doesn't want to be abandoned again because the energy and power of the inhabitants fuel his sentience, adding more people does get us closer to getting you home."

"Maybe we can make a quid pro quo exchange," Garnet suggests. "If we let in six people, maybe the city will approve six people to leave."

I like that in theory, but I have a feeling the city isn't feeling all that logical. Still, I think it's a step in the right direction.

I've been watching Sloan's expression from the corner of my eye, and I know that look. His mental cogs are turning, and he's probably five moves ahead of us on the chessboard.

"What are you thinking, hotness? Is that a worried look, or are you on board with us breaking the seal of the ward and letting in a few refugees?"

"Och, I have no objection to lettin' the feline folk inside, but several worryin' things come to mind. First, why are these people poundin' on the door now if the city has been closed to them for millennia? We still have no idea why the city evacuated in the first place. Once we open the door, does that signal to the rest of the realms that the vacant sign is lit up with neon?"

Emmet frowns at Sloan and looks at me. "Why does he always have to do that? Why can't we be happy in the moment? We're helping people who need help. That's nice, right?"

I chuckle and pat a gentle hand against Sloan's abs. "He's a thinker, my guy."

"There's nothing wrong with that." Garnet nods at Sloan. "Honestly, with you Cumhaill kids, having someone cranial within the ranks makes the rest of us far less nervous."

"Rude," Emmet says.

Garnet arches a brow but doesn't begin to apologize. "Your father is a strategic man who sees the world as it is. It seems he raised you kids without the cynicism and skepticism we share."

"Dillan does," I counter.

"Yes, Dillan would be the exception. He has a healthy dose of contemplative judgment that will be useful in keeping your family safe."

A *crack* of sound and a pulse of light brings our attention back to the Boundary Gate.

A magical explosion detonates and knocks us staggering back a step or two to regain our balance. My skin bursts to life with the sensation of ants crawling over every inch of me and pulling at the hairs on my body.

Thankfully the sensation is momentary.

As quickly as it hits, it ends.

The air falls still, and I draw a deep breath.

"Help me with the door." Nikon grips the long brass pull at the seam of the double doors.

Garnet steps in to help, as do Dionysus and Sloan.

It doesn't escape my attention that arguably the strongest among them, Xavier, makes no move to get involved. Other than him, Benjamin, and Laurel being stuck here, none of this involves him.

I would get in there and help with the heave-ho myself, but with two on each side of the double doors, there isn't much room for any other eager helpers. Besides, the druids can call for added strength if they need a little more muscle power.

The doors stick at first but whatever resistance they've built up over centuries of disuse is no match for our determined men.

Soon enough, the doors swing free and allow the entry of the people on the other side.

"Welcome to Fantasy Island." Emmet holds his arms out in a valiant Ricardo Montalban impression. "I am Emmet Cumhaill, and this is Sarah Connor. We are two of the three full-time guardians of the city."

The man who steps forward is a black panther man wearing a leather sash slung from one hip to his opposite shoulder. He holds his arm forward with his fingers extended. "It is an honor and a blessing to meet you. I am Kidok of the Great Plains, and this is my charge, Lady HaiLe, and her young."

I scan the scared faces of the young kitten people and fight the urge to pet them and snuggle them up.

"Oh my, you're so cute." Dionysus drops to his knees to meet their gaze on their level. "Don't be afraid, little kittens. I would never hurt you. In fact, you look hungry." He twists to peg me with a question burning in his gaze.

*Fi? Can I take them to the party and feed them?*

I meet the gaze of their mother and smile. "I am Fiona. You have arrived during our wedding celebration. There is more than enough food for everyone. If you wish to join us, you and the children can eat, and you can tell us about your ordeal and how we can help."

The woman looks apprehensive, but even I see the hunger in their gazes. "Our sincere apologies for interrupting your mating celebration."

"No apology necessary. You are welcome to join us."

She studies our wedding clothes and draws a long breath. "That is kind of you, Missus. We accept with great thanks."

I glance back at the guys and the open doors. Sloan's worries have crept into my mind now, and yeah, I know Garnet is right. It's good that we have him to think ahead about the consequences of our actions. "Dionysus and I can take them to the meadow if you guys want to resecure the doors and the warding."

Sloan nods. "I think that's best. At least for now, I don't feel comfortable having easy access to the city."

Emmet checks with Sarah, and they come to the same conclusion. "Perfect. While they stay and help with the warding, I'll come with you guys and welcome the guests."

I extend my hand to the woman, and Kidok steps between us as if to protect her from me.

"Dionysus will portal us to the main meadow where my

wedding celebration is in progress. I only meant to hold HaiLe's hand to complete the connection for the portal."

"Then you won't object to taking mine instead." He extends his palm to me while reaching back to take the woman's hand with his other.

"That's fine. Everyone hold hands."

When the connections are complete, Dionysus portals us back to the meadow.

## CHAPTER ELEVEN

Dionysus, Emmet, and I escort our feline folk guests back to the meadow and they seem to relax a great deal when they see the welcoming faces of our family and friends milling around, eating, and laughing.

"Come, please. Let me show you where you can eat."

Three of the littlest kittens jump back and hiss when they see Bruin lumbering toward me.

"Oh, no, kids. Don't be afraid." I hold up my hands and hurry over to run my hand over my bear's boxy head. "Bruin is part of my family. He won't hurt you. No one here will hurt you."

HaiLe picks up the youngest of her children, and the oldest pulls his younger siblings tight to his body. With his ebony paws draped protectively over their chests, everyone settles down.

The boy couldn't be more than ten, but when he meets my gaze, it holds a challenge that speaks to his expectation of confrontation.

Then I see it...the crescent moon pattern in the sleek, black fur of his forehead.

"Will ye look at this? We have more guests." Gran rushes in

and goes straight to the children. "Hello, wee ones. I'm Lara, Fiona's grandmother. Welcome."

HaiLe and Kidok don't seem to know what to make of us. I'm not sure if that's on them or us. Either we're so far beyond what they're used to that they're befuddled, or they've been so badly mistreated they're unsure how to accept simple kindness.

"You have nothing to fear from us. Gran, will you help Lady HaiLe and Kidok navigate the food tent? I think our weary travelers are hungry."

I try to sound nonchalant and not to stare, but things just got more complicated.

When Gran gestures the way, the woman nods at her son, and they take the children to follow.

Kidok remains. He steps before me and raises his splayed hands in a show of force. "You saw the mark and reacted. What does it mean to you?"

Dionysus is at my side in a snap and steps between us, his chest lifted and his fingers twitching. "Step back, puss. Whatever hostility you've got brewing, let it go, or I'll put you down before you can release your claws."

Kidok tilts his head to recapture me in his line of sight. "Tell me what you know."

I run a gentle hand against Dionysus' arm. "It's okay, sweetie. I'm good. Can you do me an important favor? Can you snap to the palace and see if Anyx and Zuzanna are good to watch over Imari so Myra can come down and speak to our guests?"

Dionysus twists to look at me over his shoulder. "I don't like the way he's looking at you."

I give him a reassuring smile. "It's fine. He's being protective of his charges. He doesn't know us yet. He doesn't understand we would never hurt an innocent and especially not a child."

"Children are sacred to our family." Dionysus squares off against Kidok. "Fi and our guests are sacred too. If you do anything to harm them, you will face the wrath of the gods."

To punctuate that, he holds his palms up, and as they glow with silver power, he levitates off the ground.

Kidok doesn't show fear, but he grasps how incredibly outmatched he is against Dionysus. He wriggles his whiskers and drops his gaze. "There is no threat as long as my people remain unharmed."

Dionysus eases back to the ground and stops glowing. "Then there is no danger of threat."

When he snaps out, I'm left with a distraught panther man and a ring of family who have closed in during the altercation.

I hold up my hand. "It's fine, everyone. Just a misunderstanding and a little flexing of muscles."

Da and Granda don't take that as enough of an explanation and join us. "What seems to be the trouble here, *mo chroi?*"

I hold up my hand. "Kidok, this is my father and my grandfather. It seems you're getting a shot across the bow from the entire family. Don't take it personally. It's how we are. Anyway, all is well."

I take a step back and let him see that HaiLe and her children are gathering heaping plates of food and are in good hands.

Dionysus snaps back a moment later with Myra at his side.

Myra does a double-take at the warrior panther man but recovers quickly. "What's up, duck? Dionysus said you needed to see me."

I nod. "Do you see that family of feline folk in the food tent?"

Myra glances at where Emmet and Gran are playing host. "I do."

"The oldest boy there, the tall one with the ebony coat and the white patch on his chest...he has a crescent mark on his forehead like Bella and Imari."

Myra's attention focuses and Kidok shifts behind us. "What does it mean to you? What will you do to him?"

Both Myra and I swivel to peg him with a look.

"What do you mean *do* to him?" Myra asks. "We won't do anything. Why would you think that?"

"Because HaiLe has been on the run for weeks, trying to keep men cloaked in green from taking him from her. Since the moment that mark showed up on his forehead, there has been no peace for her family."

"That's awful, but that has nothing to do with us. That's not how we roll. We met a young girl a couple of months ago that had a mark show up."

"My daughter received one a few days ago," Myra adds.

Kidok glances into the night sky and nods. "From what I've been able to learn, the marks appear during the phasing of the full moon cycle. Binx's mark appeared when the full moon was at its zenith."

"I'll have to look back and see if that's when Bella's mark appeared too. It sounds about right, though."

"Who are you to them?" Myra gestures at the feline family.

"HaiLe's mate and I served in the Protection Forces together. When Binx's mark showed up and men attacked them in the street, it was all Morok could do to gather his family and get them to safety."

"What happened to him?" I ask.

Kidok shakes his head. "He held off the Hunters in Green so his mate could get away. She sought me out, and I brought them here. Now, if you assure me they are safe, I must return. If he is alive, I am duty-bound to try to save him."

I nod. "If you give us time to change, we'll pull together a rescue party and join you."

Kidok frowns. "Why would you do that?"

Dionysus shrugs. "That's what we do."

By the time Sloan, Nikon, and the others return to the meadow, Dillan, Calum, and I are already changed and making a plan with Kidok.

"What's goin' on, luv? What did we miss?"

I meet Sloan's question with a smile and a quick kiss. "The men hunting the feline family are after Binx, the oldest boy. He has a crescent mark and became a target the moment these Hunters in Green saw it."

"And now?"

"While they didn't get Binx, they took his father and older brother. Kidok believes they'll keep them alive to try to make a trade for the boy they want. We're putting together a rescue party."

Nikon nods. "Give me two minutes to change."

The furrow in Kidok's brow deepens. "Why would you leave your celebration to risk your life and fight for someone you don't know?"

"It's what we do," Sloan says, echoing Dionysus' words from earlier.

Merlin waves down the front of his suit and in a quick-change move, he's left wearing battle fatigues. "Dionysus, pack food and drink to take with us and ask the Iceland dragons to ready for a quest."

I blink. "Do you think they'll be able to get through the Boundary Gate?"

"I do. From what I felt while Sarah and Nikon were working on the portal wards, the energy of the warding spell is much the same as the magic I placed on the druid stones to activate them as a dragon portal. I believe with a bit of modification, I can tweak the doors to permit dragon transport as well."

"Well, I'd love to have the backup." I turn to ask Kidok about that. "Does your realm have dragons?"

By the blank expression, I take that as a no.

"Dragons…large, flying, fire-breathing mythical beasts of magic and might."

That shakes something loose. "From where we hail, they are called Zunass. They are long extinct."

"Extinct due to what?" Merlin asks.

"Generations ago, Zunass were hunted down and destroyed by the same men we seek."

"Oh, I dislike them more by the minute." I turn to Sloan. "Do you mind if we postpone our honeymoon until after we try to rescue HaiLe's husband and son?"

"Of course not, luv. Give me time to change and tell my father what's happened."

Garnet growls, his gaze locked on the food tent across the meadow. "You assured me Myra and Imari turned in and were under the protection of Anyx in the palace. Why is she down here mingling with strangers?"

*Oops.* "The reason these strangers are on the run is that the boy had a crescent mark emerge on his forehead. Sorry, but Myra knows the most about that."

"Still, she knows very little."

"True, but she also wouldn't appreciate being stowed on a shelf if there is something she can help us with. She's in no danger. Like I said before, we'd never allow anything to happen to her or Imari."

"If you can help it." He pegs me with a poignant look. "Things happen, and well-meaning declarations go to hell."

I'm not about to argue. He's right. There are no guarantees. "Now that the children are fed, we'll have everyone move up to the palace to lock down for the night. Myra can return to your suite, and we'll look at getting everyone proper housing after we've evaluated the dangers these Hunters in Green pose."

That soothes the alpha beast.

I check the time on my phone. It's not even midnight. Not at all how I thought my wedding night celebration would end.

"Sloan, you go change. I'll speak to Da and Brendan and see who is staying here to guard the palace in case of trouble."

"Benjamin and I will stay," Xavier says, a little too eagerly. I'm not sure what's going on with him, but I don't have time to play the mind games it takes to get anything out of the King of Vampires.

"That works. Thanks."

Sloan *poofs* out, and Nikon returns. "The Hunter-gods are staying to safeguard the home front. Quon Shen says they're much too drunk to be wielding magic."

"In hindsight, we might need you to stay too, Greek. Once we leave, you and Sarah will need to seal the Boundary Gate to keep out unwanted guests."

Nikon doesn't look happy about that.

"Your strengths cast you as the right person to lock down the fort this time around."

After another moment he sighs and concedes. "Fine. Sarah and I will seal the doors when you leave, and I'll man the station in the security building to watch for your return."

"Perfect. Thanks."

"No problem."

"From what I figure, there will be you, me, Sloan, Calum, Dillan, Dionysus, Garnet, Merlin, the Iceland Free dragons—"

"Count me in, Red." Patty steps into the mix and—

My shield flares in a fiery warning.

"Die, you foul beast." Kidok throws his fist forward, and a sword extends from his empty paw.

I call my armor and launch myself between the tip of the thrusting blade and Patty. Kidok fails in his attempt to skewer Patty but won't cease his attack. He roars and tries to come through me with claws and fangs extended.

Merlin thrusts his palms forward, and Kidok is knocked thirty feet back to skid across the dance floor on his ass.

Still, he rounds onto all fours and pounces like the fiercest of panthers.

Dionysus raises a hand before Kidok and I hit head-on and freezes the moment. We're all locked in place for a heartbeat. Then we're released, and it's only a murderous Kidok held in suspension. "Bad form, puss. We're trying to help you here. You can't go all wildcat on us."

The cat lets out a feral growl and HaiLe races back to intercede. "What happened?"

I shake my head. "No idea. We were planning a rescue for your mate. Then Kidok went nuts and tried to skewer Patty."

HaiLe follows my extended finger and shrinks back a few feet looking pale. "You said we would be safe. I trusted you."

The venom in her hissed words has me even more baffled. "What's gotten into you people? Nothing has changed on our side. You're all going ballistic for no reason."

"No reason? You have one of the Hunters in Green in your presence, and you dare assure me we'll be safe?"

My mental hamster stumbles a bit, but I get there. "Your Hunters in Green are our Men o' Green. Okay, so, yeah, I guess we could've put that together, but whatever the opposition you found in his kind in your realm doesn't apply to Patty. He's our friend and has been here for over a thousand years."

Kidok is still growling like a feral cat, and I return my attention to Dionysus' hold on him. "If we set you free, you must promise you won't try to kill Patty. He's one of us, and we protect our own. I don't want to fall on opposite sides about this, but there's no question where we'll land."

"You would truly defend him over us?"

I shrug. "HaiLe, I met you less than an hour ago. Patty has been one of my closest friends for years. Yes, I would truly defend him. The same way I'll defend you as long as you aren't trying to attack one of us."

That gets through to her.

She pegs Patty with a distrusting stink eye and swallows. "Apologies. In our homeland, his kind are the root of all greed and suffering. We have lost a great many to the wicked whims of his people."

Patty shakes his head. "They haven't been my people for almost eleven centuries, ma'am. I assure you, when I parted ways with my kin, it was a severing of all connection. It's the reason my family and I first ended up living here in the city of safety over a millennium ago."

I did not know that. All I knew was that he was very distraught and very drunk. I suppose being exiled or excommunicated from your realm and your people could do that to a guy.

Astrid appears in the mix. "He speaks the truth. Padraig came to us to seek refuge from the death sentence of his people. He was found worthy to remain and remains worthy even still."

HaiLe considers that for a moment and nods. "Very well, I suppose we can't judge all men on the same scales. Kidok, we will not endanger our welcome over deeply rooted prejudices."

I check to see if Kidok agrees. His fangs are still bare, but he seems slightly less hissy. "Okay, Tarzan, set him free."

The moment Dionysus releases Kidok onto the wooden platform of the dance floor, Garnet steps into his path, and his lion growls. "Easy. I feel the fury of your cat. You need to rein that in because we've all got family here and you're so fucking outmatched you have no idea."

Knowing alpha-dominant species as I do, I'm sure that little ray of reality doesn't sit well.

Thankfully, however, Kidok gathers his wits and gears down.

After a long, tense moment, my shield stops burning.

I exhale and try to reset the atmosphere of calm and trust. "All righty then, that happened. Are you sure you still want to join us, Patty? By the sounds of things, we're going into your old stomping grounds, and you are *persona non grata*."

"Aye, I'm sure. I may not have been around in the past

centuries, but my people are quick to judge and slow to change. I may be able to offer some inside insights only a Man o' Green would know."

*That's true.* "Still, I don't like the idea of you being in danger simply for being there."

Patty waves away my concern. "Yer sweet to worry, Red, but I was a grown man makin' my own mistakes a thousand years before ye were born. I don't need yer permission to do somethin' reckless."

"I get that…I just worry."

He winks and takes my hand to pat it. "Aye, I know ye do, and I love ye for it. Still, I might be in a unique position to help on this quest, which rarely happens."

I think Patty's helped on dozens of quests, but I won't argue or split hairs. "Fine but be careful. If you get hurt, I won't forgive myself. You matter to me, oul man."

He chuckles. "I matter to me too. Don't worry. I don't plan on gettin' hurt. Come now. We've got feline folk to rescue and a family to reunite."

## CHAPTER TWELVE

"Does anyone know how to target our entry through the Boundary Gate?" Garnet asks, frowning at the tall, bronze doors. "I expect that back in the day of this city functioning as a respite for persecuted people, there was likely a group who covered the security building who knew how the gates worked."

"Are you saying we don't?" I ask.

"Are you saying we do?"

I hold up my hands in surrender. "Not at all. I was helping you make your point."

Emmet frowns and looks around. "Astrid, can you come here, please?"

The four-foot, turquoise-haired faery appears within our group. "You call my name, and here I be. Tell me what you need of me."

The way she beams up at Emmet is nauseating.

I'd say something about her having a crush on him but that would likely incite her to do terrible things to me when I'm asleep. No thanks.

Emmet's smile is warm and endearing. "Astrid, when the city was inhabited before, whose duty was it to navigate the destinations of people traveling through the Boundary Gate?"

"Sometimes Zislah, when he free, and sometimes it was the walking trees."

Patty nods. "Zislah was a centaur warrior, and the walking trees were the Forest Lords who lived here. I couldn't tell you which of the walking trees was involved in programming the gate, but I don't suppose any of them are alive now."

Emmet takes another stab at it. "Astrid, seeing how you know all, are you able to navigate the destinations of the Boundary Gate?"

"Able yes, I suppose I might, but maybe not without a fight."

*Could she be any more difficult?*

Emmet knows me well enough to shake his head at me. "Play nice, Fi. Flies and sugar, amirite?"

*Fine.* I make the universal sign of buttoning my lip.

"So, why the fight?" Emmet asks. "What about helping us bothers you? Maybe if you tell us, we can fix it."

Garnet growls. "For the sake of my sanity and everyone else's safety, please stop rhyming. My lion is about to break past my tether."

*Right?* I'm with him.

Emmet presses his hands together. "Please, Astrid, if you will, stop the games and help us help people. You want to help people, don't you?"

"Of course. Aiding the citizens is my purpose."

"Excellent, well, Kidok came from his realm an hour ago and wishes to return with my friends and family in the hopes of rescuing two of their party who were captured and left behind."

Astrid examines the black panther warrior. "Captured by whom?"

"By my kind," Patty says. "The world hasn't changed so much after a thousand years as ye might think."

Dillan shifts and Rory bursts from beneath his shirt. His purple pseudodragon companion soars around Astrid a few times and lands on Dillan's shoulder.

"Hello, dragon." Astrid reaches up to scrub Rory's snout. "What a pleasure it is to see you again."

Are we always this unfocused and annoying?

"So, Astrid, will you help us?" I ask. "Can you program the gate to direct us to the home of Kidok and the feline folk so we can attempt to bring back two people lost in the shuffle?"

"It would be my pleasure. Emmet, if you will accompany me back to the security console, we can begin."

Emmet looks as surprised as I am that the faery simply agreed. "Okay, perfect. Nikon can snap me back to the security building, and maybe we can learn something about the process. Then, once we set the destination, he can snap back and help Sarah lower the wards."

"Sounds like a plan, Em. Go be the great island champion and we'll catch up when we get back."

I hug my brother, and he gives me an extra squeeze. "Be safe, Fi. Know that I wish I was with you."

The sadness in his voice hurts my heart.

Sure, he and Brendan have a great new adventure to navigate, but we were always a dynamic duo and destiny took us in different directions.

"I'll be back soon, and we can compare stories."

When Emmet and Nikon snap out, I check in with the others. "Let's get the dragons and be ready for when Emmet and Nikon give us the green light."

---

No matter how many times I ride upon Dart's back, part of me still *squees* in delight like a little girl. It's magical. He's magical.

When the two of us are together and doing our thing, it's like our magic merges somehow to become more than the sum of two parts.

It's synergistic.

I glance sideways at where Sloan stands on Saxa. He doesn't talk much about things like hopes and things he's excited about, so I wonder if it's the same for him. Is his magic merging with hers or will that only happen after they bond?

*If* they bond.

Hokiedoodle, I hope they bond.

Then, I glance the other way and find Merlin riding upon Empress Cazzienth's back. The two of them have a bond on another level entirely. They share a love that transcends.

More than a dragon and her rider, the two of them are mated.

It's rather beautiful.

I've seen Merlin's dragon form, and he's as formidable as a mythical beast as he is a druid spellcaster as he is a drag queen on stage.

I suppose when you've got it, you've got it in all aspects of your life.

*Okay, Red. Astrid and Emmet have the destination locked in. Sarah and I are about to take down the wards.*

*Perfect. Thanks, Greek.*

I relay that info to the others and twist back to meet the tense gaze of Kidok death-gripping the saddle handle on Dart's second spike. "Almost time. Once we're through, we'll find a place to land and—"

*Fi, we have a problem.*

*Why? What's wrong?*

*We've got people on the other side of the gate trying to get in.*

*Men o' Green?*

*No, immigrants from another realm. Our vacancy shingle is swinging.*

*Does that affect us? Can we exit and go to our realm with them there or are we going to buzz past them on the dragons?*

*I'll ask Astrid.* I wait for a moment, and he comes back. *She says you're good to go. Emmet is here, and we'll deal with the incoming.*

*Okay, thanks.*

I steer Dart away in a wide arc and ready our approach.

I've watched Nikon and Sarah work on the wardings of the doors two or three times before and create a mental image in my mind. The bronze doors are massively wide and twenty feet tall. When they're open to their full extent, the opening is about twenty by twenty.

Surely, we can maneuver five full-sized dragons through there.

*Hopefully.*

I envision the hidden city like Stargate Atlantis and all we need to do is pass through the gate.

And hey, it's magic.

That should work in our favor.

*Fi, I can sense your apprehension. What's wrong?*

*Oh, nothing. I'm just considering the logistics of getting five dragons and eight warriors through the bronze doors.*

Dart chuckles in my mind. *You're hilarious. It'll be fine.*

Sometimes I wish Dart was still my excited little hatchling cooing when I rubbed the horn on his snout. In only two years, with the influence of the Iceland Free Dragons and through accessing the wisdom of dragon ancestry hardwired into his DNA, he's grown up too fast.

Does every mother think that?

I don't have time to dwell.

Dart dips low in a smooth arc toward the gate. Nikon's hands are up, and the portal is glowing with the power of his spatial magic. Sarah is standing beside him, and the soft, white glow of her magic bolsters his in a beautiful way.

Something in my heart *clicks,* and I wonder if that's not an indication of something great to be explored.

Before I have a chance to think more about that, we drop to

street level and shoot forward like a five-car dragon train racing along the tracks.

The doors open and I close my eyes, giving over total control to Dart.

*Please don't crash. Please don't crash.*

Passing through the barrier of the Boundary Gate magic is jarring. I grimace and grip my saddle tighter. It feels like a metal barb hooked my intestines and yanked them out of my belly button.

I cry out, my body trembling under the force of the power, and...

It's over.

Straightening, I draw a few deep breaths to steady my nerves and gather my thoughts.

We did it. We jumped realms.

---

Since it became apparent we would try to rescue HaiLe's husband, part of me has wondered what the realm of leprechauns and feline folk looks like.

Is it a realm of rainbows and pots of gold?

Is it all jungle growth with cat people purring and grooming themselves on rocks lying out in the sun?

*Sad face.* It's neither of those things.

We soar across the rich, purple sky and I study the land below. For the most part, the land is a wide, flat plain with areas of vegetative growth, areas where the water glows pink, and other areas where small oasis pockets of villages and cities dot an almost desert tundra landscape with little in between.

The ground is dark, but I can get a read on things by the light of the four yellow moons and the orange stars.

It's a dry and rocky terrain. We travel for a long while before

Kidok calls to me. "There, on the right between those two plateaus. That's Laristar. That's the holding fort for the Hunters in Green. If they live, that's where they'll be."

I catch Merlin's attention and point at the distant city surrounded by a stone wall. Merlin leads our descent, taking Cazzie down toward an area heavily shadowed and out of the way.

When we land, I jog back to check on Kidok. "That distance must've taken you, HaiLe, and the kids weeks to travel across. Bringing the dragons was an amazing cut in time, don't you think?"

With the feline's coat being ebony, I don't know if his being pale is a possibility, but if it is...I'd say he's very pale.

Or at least nauseous.

"Sorry. I guess if dragons are extinct in this realm, you've never had the chance to get your sea legs."

He blinks at me like he doesn't know what I'm talking about. Not the first time someone has given me that look.

"So, are you ready to dismount and get us where we need to go?"

I resist the urge to hold out my hand to coax him. The man is brawny and dominant. Handling him the same way I do my nieces and nephew won't go over well.

Thankfully, he gathers himself enough to pry his white-knuckled fingers off the handle of the spike saddle. "Come. If they didn't see us flying in the sky overhead, we have a good chance to make it to the breaker unchallenged."

"And if we were seen?"

"I couldn't say. There's no way the Hunters in Green are prepared to take on five Zunass."

"Then let's get this done."

Our rescue party leaves the dragons tucked in the shadows and Dionysus portals us to the area Kidok indicates. The moment we're in place, I release Bruin to do our groundwork. *Be careful, buddy.*

*Ye don't need to be careful when yer incredible, Red.*

I chuckle. *I stand corrected. Okay then, be incredible.*

*I'm all over it.*

Kidok brings us in to give us the lowdown, and we all gather close. "This wall is called a breaker and acts as a way for the Hunters in Green to control who gets into the prison town within. It's manned heavily and not only by hunters but by violent, mindless creatures called Talpidae."

"What are these Talpidae like?" Garnet asks.

"They are sightless monstrosities that live in the darkness and have extra fingers and thumbs to aid in digging and burrowing underground."

"So, they're mole people," Calum says. "That doesn't sound so bad."

"They bite, and their saliva paralyzes their victim so they can eat through your stomach to your lungs. They love eating lungs."

Calum makes a face and sticks his tongue out. "My mistake. They sound repulsive."

"They're also hard to kill," Kidok continues. "In fact, they're nearly impossible to kill. They scurry on all fours and launch into the air when they're about to attack."

I blink. "Is anyone else expecting weeks of nightmares after this?"

Dillan and Dionysus raise their hands.

Calum calls his weapons forward, slides his quiver off his shoulder, and hovers his hand over the flights of his arrows. "Maybe we can spell my arrows to take them down faster. What is their weakness? Poison? Magical spells?"

Kidok frowns. "Water. The easiest way to eliminate them from a battle is to drown them but they know this and are very careful to live nowhere near large bodies of water."

I can certainly call moisture from the air, but the air here isn't all that moist to begin with.

*Disappointing.*

"What about chopping off their heads?" Dionysus asks. "That works on most living things."

"If you can manage it, sure, but it's rare that you'd ever get the chance to get close enough to decapitate a Talpidae. They're incredibly fast."

*I hate these things already.*

It makes sense why the Men o' Green recruited them as the front-line defenders.

"All right, so let's assume we get in there. We're past the mole men and going in for the rescue. What's our next obstacle?"

"Then we have to get through the watchtower guards. Those will be hunters."

"Okay, so we take on the Men o' Green." I envision that. "How many should we expect?"

"There will be two on the door and four more on rotation along the city wall."

"So, two, possibly six Men o' Green to take on. Then what?"

"The igniting fire pockets on the floor of the prison."

I roll my eyes. "Now you're just making shit up."

"He's not," Patty corrects. "Using geyser pockets as a form of defense is a long-used practice from when I lived in this realm."

I want to learn more about Patty and his life before I knew him, but we don't have the time or the privacy to share tales of the good old days.

"Is there anything else we should expect to run into?" I check with both of them.

"Just to be of great care," Kidok says. "The Hunters in Green are ruthless and greedy men who won't appreciate us trying to remove prisoners from their grip."

"Well, tough titties for them," Dillan says. "Then they shouldn't kidnap people for no reason."

*True story.*

I check with everyone to see if there are any other questions or concerns we need to address before we move out. There aren't, so I nod at Kidok. "All right, once Bruin gets back and gives us the lay of the land, we'll be ready to do this."

## CHAPTER THIRTEEN

Bruin gets back from his intel gathering in the bustling prison center of Laristar shortly after and fills us in on the missing details. "There are six wee men guarding the prison doors, and when I say guarding, I mean playing bones on the ground in front of them."

"What about HaiLe's husband and son?"

"I found a great many feline folk within the prison, close to fifty, I'd say. There was no way for me to determine who they were."

I relay that information to the non-druid members of our rescue party.

"Six guards at once?" Kidok repeats.

I hold up a hand before he gets panicky. "I know it's not ideal, but—"

His eyes widen. "Not ideal? Do you have any sense of self-preservation?"

Calum, Sloan, Dillan, and Garnet shake their heads.

*Rude.* Ignoring them, I continue with the debrief. "Does six guards playing bones mean there aren't any on patrol along the breaker wall, or there are still more walking around, ready to respond to a distress call and join the fight?"

"The first one. It seems the prospect of having a gamble with friends has won out over staying on the job."

"Does that leave any other doors unattended?" Kidok doesn't seem to follow the question, so Calum catches him up on what Bruin said about the guards.

"No. Unfortunately, there is only one entrance. If all six are there, there's no way to get around them."

"What if we take advantage of the element of surprise and immobilize them?" Dillan asks.

Patty shakes his head. "Och, no, lad. Our magic works on an entirely different wavelength than yers. It might delay their reaction a few brief seconds, but the moment they feel the magical attack, they'll break through the hold and be on their feet and rip-roarin' mad."

Well, that won't get us any farther along.

"Can we take on six Men o' Green and win?" I ask.

"If ye can get their shillelaghs away from them and destroy them, ye might have a chance. My kind tend to rely on channelin' their power through a walkin' stick. I'm an exception to that rule, Red." He answers my question before I can ask.

He chuckles at my expression but continues. "If ye remember, my ex-wife cursed my walkin' stick, so I had to get used to workin' within my own range of power. It took me a great many centuries to regain my control."

I remember. That was the shillelagh we liberated off the back wall of a witch's bar in Dublin. They'd stolen it from the old dragons' lair, forcing Patty and the dragons to move and find a new den.

"We have an objective. We'll portal straight back to the entrance of the prison cells. Immobilize and steal the shillelaghs of six Men o' Green, get into the prison, find the two feline folk we're looking for out of a group of dozens, get them out, portal back to the dragons, and get the hell gone."

"Easy-peasy," Dillan says.

"Right?"

Sloan rolls his eyes at me. "Are ye done, *a ghra?*"

"Yep. I think so."

"Wonderful. Now, I'm thinkin' Dionysus and I should work on stealin' the walkin' sticks while Garnet, Dillan, Merlin, Calum, and Patty keep them occupied. If Fi and Kidok stay out of it, maybe ye'll be able to slip into the prison unseen."

"What are you doing with the shillelaghs?" I ask.

"We'll flash them back to the dragons. Maybe they can make them into kindlin'."

Patty thinks about that for a moment and nods. "Dragon fire might do the trick, aye."

"When the guards are disabled or distracted, Kidok and I will go into the prison cells with Sloan or Dionysus. When we find HaiLe's husband and son, they can go to the dragons, and we'll meet them back there once we get everyone out."

"Sounds like a plan," Garnet says.

I chuckle. "Sounds like one, doesn't it? We'll go that route until things go to hell, then improvise."

Kidok frowns. "You anticipate failure?"

We all chuckle and look at one another.

"Failure is probably too strong a word," I correct. "We anticipate that things won't go as planned and we'll have to adapt."

"We're professional adapters," Dillan adds.

Kidok doesn't know how to answer that, but it's fine. Team Trouble is an acquired taste.

"All right then." Garnet holds his hand into the center of our gathering. "Let's flash in and do this."

Dionysus snaps us all into the interior of the Laristar breaker wall, and we materialize in two groups. The majority of the party snaps in pretty much on top of the six leprechaun guards while Kidok and I are tucked away a little off to the side.

The moment we materialize, Dionysus and Sloan portal into action and go for the walking sticks of our opponents. At the same time, Calum climbs the wall to get a higher vantage point, Garnet flashes into his lion form, and he, Dillan, Bruin, Merlin, and Patty move in for the attack.

"It's killing me not to be part of the fight."

Kidok arches a furry black brow. "You want to be part of that?"

I chuckle. "Don't you?"

"Of course, but I am a warrior."

I chuff. "So am I."

He makes no comment about that, but I get the distinct impression he doesn't believe me. Either that or he's pegging me as a self-proclaimed fighter.

*Yeah, well, he'll learn.*

Sloan and Dionysus get the first two shillelaghs without much trouble, but by the time they return from delivering them to the dragons, the wee men are on their feet and fully alert.

They have taken possession of the last four walking sticks and are wielding them against us.

One of the guards gets a solid shot of magic off, and the orange lightning bolt hits the Greek square in the chest.

Dionysus stills for a heartbeat, then becomes quite giddy and pumps a fist into the air. "That tickled. God powers for the win."

Seeing him reinstated to his full strength is a beautiful thing.

Kidok and I remain hidden behind the corner of a market stall, waiting for the guards to be drawn far enough from the entrance for us to slide in behind them to go down to the prison.

*Dionysus, watch Dillan's back.* I think the warning at Tarzan with as much power and speed as possible.

Dionysus turns, flashes to Dillan, and pulls him out of the way of the next volley of magic as a horde of creepy, furry-faced, eyeless men scramble in.

"I take it those are the mole men?"

"The Talpidae. Yes." Kidok is frowning at the scuffle before us, but the plan is the plan...until it's not.

My heart is racing as I watch my family and friends engage without me. Patty's fighting as I've never seen before. His angry leprechaun persona has always been fierce, but he's now going at things like he's physically venting a thousand years of fury.

Maybe he is.

The strike to my back hits with the force of a Mack truck and sends me sailing into the open. With no idea what hit me, I dive forward into a sloppy front roll and get to my feet, ready to rumble.

I'm still turning to face my opponent when one of the mole men launches forward with teeth bared.

I raise my arm to block, and he chomps my wrist.

I'm always thankful when my body armor holds up to a new opponent. It only failed me against two very powerful attackers under extreme circumstances. Still, I'm not as cocky about being indestructible as I was once.

The good news is...I'm in the fight now, and my armor outmatches Talpidae teeth.

Adrenaline explodes in my cells, and my defensive power unleashes. I call Birga to my palm and lift my foot to dislodge my new furry bracelet.

The asshole has the funniest look of surprise on his face. I can't help but laugh. "It's called armor, dipshit."

He releases his clamp on my wrist and sails backward as three of his friends come at me next. My hands spin and I swipe Birga through the air. My girl sings with anticipation as she slices through our foes.

The biter is back to join in with his friends.

Despite Kidok's assurance that they were hideous, if you can get over the no eyes thing, the funky extra thumbs, and the way their fangs drip with venomous saliva, they're not that bad.

I snort. No. They really are.

They're gross.

The courtyard seethes with the chaos of killing.

Birga and I fight to reclaim our position near the prison's entrance.

Dillan has his daggers out and is slicing and dicing.

Merlin is casting from within a barrier of protection, and the Talpidae and several Men o' Green are trying to break through to take him down.

Garnet's lion is a beast, grabbing opponents and shaking them into heaps of broken bones.

Sloan has his hands up and is casting like the sexy mofo he is.

*Yeah, baby.* Happy wedding night to me.

Sloan has proficiency with nature spells I still can't touch, but I've got him on power levels.

I'm a bull in the china shop kinda druid.

On that note…I slam my boot on the courtyard's stone slabs. "*Stone Spears.*"

My call ripples through the ground beneath us in a violent wave. A moment later, jagged stone spears erupt from below and skewer mole men.

I focus on the positioning of my team, ensuring no one gets poked by friendly fire, then withdraw the spikes leaving the injured and dying on the ground.

*On my mark, Red,* Bruin says across our bond. *I'm going to clear yer path.*

"Give me two secs to free up Kidok." I grunt and fight through the horde to get back to my buddy for the next part of the quest.

Kidok is fighting like a wild man, and I'm damned impressed. I can see why the Light Weavers chose men like him to secure Isilon all those centuries ago.

"*Gusting Gale.*" I thrust my hand forward and knock a couple of the mole men on their stubby little tails. I keep up the pressure of the spell and pin them to the stone of the breaker wall.

Energy rainbows shoot toward me, and I have to dive to avoid getting struck. When I regain my footing, I realize two hunters are homing in on me. "Bruin, I've got incoming guards gunning for me. Go now, or we'll miss our window."

The bellowing growl of my bear rings out, and he gets his Killer Clawbearer gripping and ripping.

The two wee men realize too late that they're about to be bowled over. They barely get their hands up when Bruin barrels through and catapults them into the air like a crushing seven-ten split.

He doesn't stop there.

With a wild roaring growl, he tramples and rams opponents out of his way as he plows our path back to the prison doors.

Dillan is already working on the locks and sees us coming. He's got his hood up, and I have no doubt the knowledge he needs to get us inside is filling his head.

"*Confusion,*" Merlin shouts, racing through the fray. His spell hits an influx of mole men, and the pause allows Calum the time to take them down from above.

Dillan whistles and pulls the door open for me. "Tarzan, you're up. Let's go."

I pick up speed again, focusing on the opening into the prison.

"Thanks, bro." I race past him.

"No problem. Safe home, baby girl."

I slow my roll as soon as I'm through the doors. Kidok nearly rams into my back, and Bruin into his back. Dillan slams the door shut behind us and the battle's noise immediately cuts off.

"Wait for me." Dionysus appears next to me and smiles. "That was tons of fun. Who knew fighting an army of tiny wee men would be so challenging?"

"Right?"

The hair on my arms rises as my shield bursts into a fiery brand on my back. "Incoming."

"On it." Bruin dematerializes from the back of the pack and solidifies in front of me, running the gauntlet.

"Here we go again." I waggle my brows at Kidok and follow Bruin's charge.

A jolt of energy bursts within me, and there's no missing that the source is the spear in my grip.

Birga loves a good fight.

Unfortunately, we're in a narrow corridor with no room to wield her. Still, with the shouts I hear coming toward us, I have no doubt she'll get her chance.

Bruin leads us straight down the passage but stops at the first junction. The air is hot, and he's frowning at the steam rising through the cracked stone.

"Is that going to erupt?"

I've barely asked the question when we're twisting back and protecting our faces from the explosion of molten fire that geysers into the air.

The hair on my arms and eyebrows singes, and I wince at the acrid stench of Bruin's fur burning. "Buddy? Are you all right?"

"Should've tucked my tail a little more than I did. Probably won't be able to shit for a couple of days fer the swelling, but I'll live."

I'm fighting between sympathy and laughter, but there's no time to focus on that. "Lesson learned. Sloan can heal you when we get back. Now, which way?"

I look at Kidok for insight.

His blank gaze tells me he's got none to offer. "I've never been captured. I don't know."

Awesomesauce. Okay... "Buddy, can you smell any stanky man grossness? Usually, dungeons reek of excrement and piss."

"Good point." Bruin lifts his black nose into the air and draws in a couple of long breaths. "This way."

We sidestep the fissure in the floor, then we're off again and racing down the corridors.

Each time we come up against a geyser, we take a beat to make sure no one else gets their privates steamed. Every time we come up against a mole man, Bruin swipes left and takes him out. And each time we come up against a Hunter in Green, Dionysus tackles him and snaps out.

I'm not sure where he's dropping them, but he's back a moment later and ready to continue.

It goes on like that until we arrive in a set of corridors lined on both sides with locked cages.

"Morok! Where are you? We're here to get you out." Kidok's call is still ringing when hands appear between the rungs of all the doors.

"Here," many shout.

"Let us out," others say.

As much as I want to avoid making things more complicated, the math of the moment says there could be fifty or sixty people here shouting for their freedom, and we won't have time to sort through them all before reinforcements arrive.

Well, crappers.

## CHAPTER FOURTEEN

As more and more hands start waving through the bars of prison cells, I take a step back. "This is all you, my man. You're the only one who can identify the guys we're looking for."

Kidok frowns, scanning the waving arms up and down the hall. "I never dreamed so many of my people would be down here. We need to free them all."

I meet the determination in his gaze and chuckle. "What's that now? We signed on for the husband and son taken for nothing more than protecting a boy with a crescent mark. We can't free everyone."

Kidok straightens and juts out his chin. "Well, I'm not leaving anyone here, so you can help me, or we'll likely get caught and killed."

*Perfect.* Give the people helping you an ultimatum during a prison break. That's classy.

Dionysus looks at me and shrugs. "What do you want to do, Jane?"

I curse, release Birga, and reach to take his hand. "Give me a power boost, Tarzan. We don't have time to open all the cells one by one. If I can open all of them at once, maybe we can get

Morok and the son and get out of here before Kidok gets us killed."

With Dionysus' power online as a power booster, I focus on the lock plate of the door closest to me. *"Open Sesame."*

I push my intention out with as much oomph as I can manage and feel the pulse of Dionysus' power as he kicks my command into high gear.

The click of tumblers sounds off and I squeeze Dionysus' hand before getting back into the game. "Thanks, sweetie. Now, find Morok and son and snap them to the dragons."

As the prisoners swing open their doors and scramble in the hall, our path becomes a mad stampede of men racing for the exits.

Or at least where they believe the exits lay.

"Morok!" Kidok shouts again.

"Here, Uncle." A teenage boy with gray fur and a white patch on his nose and chin pushes past fleeing men to make his way to us. "I can't believe you came."

"Pi, are you well, son?"

"Well enough to get out of here, for certain."

"And your father?"

He shakes his head. "He died soon after our capture."

Kidok stiffens. "Are you certain?"

"I am. They left him in our cell for days. He was most certainly dead."

That is both sad and horrific.

"Dionysus, take Pi and Kidok to the dragons. Bruin and I will get topside and notify everyone that we're on the move."

Kidok waves off my instructions. "No. Your people are here and in danger because of me. I will stay." He turns to the boy. "These people are friends, and they have aligned themselves with Zunass. Do not be afraid. Wait with the Zunass, and we will get to you shortly."

The boy scowls. "If there is a fight to wage, I want to draw blood. For my father and everything the Hunters in Green took from us."

I tap my boot on the stone floor and call Birga back to my hands. "This is a touching moment, and I hate to be insensitive, but we gotta get up there with our people. The prisoners are going to burst free any time now, and all hell will break loose."

Kidok nods. "You will go, Pi."

"No, Uncle. I will fight."

*Tarzan, snap us to the dragons. We'll dump them to have their heart-to-heart and go back for the others. Bruin, you're with the courtyard crew.*

*Got it, Red.*

I nod at Dionysus, and a moment later we're standing in the shadows surrounded by five stunning dragons. "Guard the boy and be ready to fly. We'll be right back."

Before Kidok or Pi can argue, Dionysus snaps the two of us back to the courtyard fight still in progress. "Rescue complete. Fall back and portal out."

I'm delivering my message when one of the wee men has Sloan dead to rights and looking the other way.

Every possessive and protective instinct I possess fires at once. I spin and skewer the man straight through the throat.

Garnet's lion nods at me as he rushes past to help Patty. I interpret that as high praise. Without saying it, that meant, Lady Druid, you amaze me every day with your amazeballs abilities.

Thanks, bossman.

I'd take a bow, but honestly, all I want is to gather my guys and get gone. I point at our archer standing on top of the stone wall.

Mole men are throwing flaming sticks at him, but they're bouncing off an invisible barrier and rebounding down at them.

"Tarzan, get Calum down. I'll gather the others."

I slip as I hustle to get to Sloan and hold out my hands to

steady myself. Dead bodies are piling up, and the treads of my boots are squishing and squashing in blood as I walk.

"Seriously, gross."

"Right?" Dillan is windmilling his daggers around his wrists so the blades sing. "This is one messy battle."

The prisoners I released have made it up to the door and are spilling out into the bloody courtyard like rats out of a flooding sewer.

"Time to go. Round everyone up. Where's Merlin?"

Dillan points and I catch Merlin in action. Damn, the guy might be centuries old but has moves on top of moves—like, seriously wicked, kick-ass, hokey-doodle moves.

He's a freaking phenom.

Then there's Patty…I've never seen any other Men o' Green battle, so I didn't realize how seriously badass Padraig of the Northern Hills really is.

He's beating down his opponents like a boss.

Rainbow rune beams burst from his hands in rapid succession. The colorful power tingles over my skin and I don't know whether to be intimidated or awestruck.

I choose the latter.

Having to rely on his abilities instead of a shillelagh has leveled up his game. I'm sure living with the Queen of Wyrms and absorbing her power every day for centuries has helped too.

"Are we ready?" Dillan checks the scene when the escaped prisoners have taken over the last of the foes.

"I guess so. This is more their fight than ours."

Dillan wipes the blades of his daggers on the clothes of one of the fallen before sheathing them. "True dat."

"Then let's leave them to it, shall we?" I wipe my hand on my shirt and press my fingers under my tongue to whistle. "Team Trouble, we're moving out."

Heads turn, attention shifts, and a moment later, Dionysus brings Calum down to join the huddle. When we're all accounted for, I sink my fingers into the silky depths of Bruin's thick coat and give Dionysus the go-ahead. "Take us to the dragons, Tarzan."

---

Kidok is peeved at me when we get back to the dragons, but whatevs. He was negotiating with a teenager while my team was actively battling. I won't apologize for cutting them out of the equation.

My team comes first.

When Pi sees Patty with us, he loses his shit, but not as badly as Kidok did when he first met him.

Yeah, another thing I don't care about.

Wow, am I ever cranky now that I'm a married woman.

Dionysus flashes Kidok and Pi up to the saddle on Dart's second spike, and I take my place at the first spike. Dillan and Calum join Sloan on Saxa. Patty crosses his legs and sits on Cazzie's back behind Merlin and Garnet. Dionysus flashes onto Bryvanay.

Once everyone has their feet planted, we're up and in the air again.

*It went well?* Dart says over our union bond.

*Other than HaiLe's husband being dead days before we got here, yes.*

*There is nothing you could've done. The important thing is you're bringing her son back to her.*

*I'm sure that will help.*

While I'm anticipating the dragons heading straight back to the access point to the Boundary Gate, the dragons have a detour planned.

The five of them take an assault formation and circle over Laristar.

When they're directly overhead, they exhale long streams of blue dragon fire down on the prison, torching not only the structure but as many of the Hunters in Green as they can manage.

*For our kind,* Dart says into my mind.

I'm certainly not going to argue. It's too bad they probably fried a few felines in the crossfire but maybe I'm wrong, and they were able to choose their victims with fine precision.

Yeah, I choose to think that.

Back on track, the breeze picks up my hair and cleans the cobwebs from my mind. I close my eyes and draw a few deep breaths.

Nothing seems to clear the tension in my chest.

*Why do I feel this way, buddy? What am I missing?*

*What makes you ask that?*

*I don't know. I have this sense of negativity hanging over me. It's tight in my chest.*

*Did something happen during the battle?*

*Nothing I can put my finger on.*

*Do you think it's because on the night of your wedding you have to tell a woman that her husband is lost?*

*Yeah, I'm sure that's part of it. Just thinking about that hurts my heart. Life is fragile, and families are supposed to be happy. Sometimes I wish things could be that simple again.*

*These are difficult times. You take on more than your fair share of turmoil. Perhaps, for the next few days, it will do you good to focus on love and happiness and not the pain and suffering you see every day.*

*You're a wise dragon, Dartamont Cumhaill Mackenzie. I think you're right. I need to start my honeymoon and put the last few hours behind me.*

*I'm sure a good night's sleep will give you a brighter outlook too.*

*That's true. You know how I love a good sleep.*

*I definitely do.*

We fly along, and I think about the dragons of this realm. *Why would leprechauns hunt and kill dragons? For that matter, how would they do that? Patty's people have power, but dragons have much more.*

*True, but historically, eliminating dragons is less about the slaughter of might and more about stealing and destroying eggs so new generations can't be born.*

*That's cowardly and cruel.*

*It's reality.*

*Does your ancestral knowledge give you any insight into what happened here?*

*Not specifically, no.*

*That's too bad.*

Wallowing in my mood is cut short because we're approaching the entry point where we came into the realm before long. *Dart, are you sure you can access the portal magic and reactivate the Boundary Gate?*

*I'm sure we can magically knock on the door. Whether they answer it and invite us in is another story altogether.*

I'm not worried about that. If I know Emmet and Nikon—and I do—they're pacing the security room, bugging Astrid, and studying the screen waiting for our return.

I remember being nervous like this the first few times we used the druid stones as a dragon portal.

Now, that's second nature.

*Here we go.* Dart pumps his wings and tilts, sliding sideways through the air to fall in line behind Saxa and Cazzienth. I glance over my shoulder as Bryvanay and Utiss take up the rear.

I feel the power of the dragons amp up and hope Dart is right about us knocking on the door.

I've had enough of this realm and want to go home and hug Da, my brothers, and my grandparents. I make a mental note to take the morning off all family shenanigans to play with the kids.

I haven't been paying nearly enough attention to the twins and Jackson and Meg are getting so big now. I'm missing things. Seven and four...it's hard to believe they're so big.

*Look at that. Nothing to worry about.*

Dart's words draw me out of my reverie, and I stare at the portal door glowing gold as Cazzienth passes through. Remembering at the last minute what a horror show it was coming through this way, I draw a deep breath and ready for the onslaught of discomfort.

Dart flies us through the gate, and I grit my teeth and steel myself against the discomfort of passing between realms. Is it bad like this for people who walk through?

I'll have to remember to ask HaiLe.

The dragons arch and lift us into the night sky of Emhain Abhlach. As we streak across the sky above the empty city, I take in the phosphorescent glow of the moss below.

Brendan and Emmet were concerned when it started to spread, but after learning the city is a living entity, I think it's a sign that Isilon is coming back to life.

The white lights lining the wedding tents and dance floor are still lit, but almost everyone has turned in for the night.

Nikon has snapped Emmet to the meadow, and they're waiting there with HaiLe, Sarah, and Brendan.

The dragons land and I let Kidok and Pi dismount first. They're the ones HaiLe is searching for—them and Morok.

I can't look.

I can face down any foe and fight, but I totally wimp out on this and busy myself checking the saddles while they explain to HaiLe that her husband didn't make it back. I guess it becomes obvious I'm futzing around and avoiding life because Sloan comes to check on me.

"*A ghra?* Aw, no. Come here to me, luv."

The ache in my chest steals my breath, and I'm glad he comes to me because I can't see past my tears. His arms wrap around me and the tingle of his magical signature dances over my skin as we *poof* away.

"What can I do?" Sloan's whisper warms the shell of my ear, and I cling on tighter.

"HaiLe's pain is crushing me. She lost her love…I wanted to bring him home to her."

"I know ye did. We all did."

"Can we go back to this being our wedding night? Can we pretend it's just you and me?"

"Consider it done. How does that look to ye?"

"I want to have a shower together to wash off the night. Then you'll make love to me until I fall asleep."

"Aye, that sounds lovely."

I let out a long sigh. "I love you, Mr. Cumhaill."

He chuckles. "I love ye more, Mrs. Mackenzie."

# CHAPTER FIFTEEN

The morning after the night before breaks with the golden rays of an enchanted island warming my bare skin and my husband running a gentle circuit from the round of my shoulder, down my back to the dip of my spine, and back up again.

His touch is feather-light, and I doubt I would've woken up even if I wasn't a heavy sleeper.

"Good mornin', luv." Sloan's voice is deep and raspy, and I'm not sure if it's from sleep or emotion.

"You're still here. How many hours have you been lying there waiting for me to wake up?"

"I wouldn't know. Time loses all meaning when we're alone like this."

I laugh and roll over to curl into his side. "Good answer. How long have you been saving that one?"

He meets my lips for a kiss and smiles. "Feelin' any better this mornin'?"

I breathe deeply and most of the tension in my chest has eased. "Yeah, I think so. I'll have to apologize to HaiLe for flaking out on her last night, though. I'm not proud I took the coward's road and retreated to hide."

"Ye did no such thing. Ye put the needs of others ahead of yerself in every situation on any given day. If ye need to step back to solidify yer own state of mind, do that. It's like what they say on the airlines about the oxygen masks. Even if ye have dependents there, first secure yer mask so ye can help the others."

I lay my head on his chest and close my eyes. "Thanks for understanding."

"Besides, it was yer day. I'm glad we got back to finishin' things off on a high point."

I grin and smile up at him. "Thanks for that."

He winks. "My pleasure."

Enjoying the quiet solitude of our room in the palace is almost enough peace to forget the city is holding us captive. "Do you think if we can leave through the Boundary Gate, we could reenter our realm somehow from another point?"

"I suppose it's possible, but to do that with thirty of our family and friends in tow might be more dangerous than simply trying to reason with Isilon."

Yeah, that makes sense.

"What about the idea of repopulating? Do you think that—"

The inhuman shriek of something outside has both of us jumping out of bed and rushing to the opening in the wall that leads to our balcony.

I grab Sloan's T-shirt and throw it over my head before rushing outside. "What the hell is that?"

Sloan joins me a second later wearing his boxers and frowns at the tussle of a green dragon versus a rooster-dragon creature in the sky. "I have no idea. Looks like we need to get dressed."

*Looks like it.*

The two of us make hasty work of getting clothes on and Sloan *poofs* us down to the meadow. Most of the fam jam is there with Garnet and the Greeks.

"What's happening?" I scan the faces, looking for the one who's going to fill me in.

"Sloan was right about the awakening of the Boundary Gate drawing the attention of creatures from many different realms." Emmet frowns. "We've been up all night responding to the influx of beings."

"What is that?" I point up at the volatile twisting and sparring above us. "Why is Cadmus fighting with that rooster-dragon thing?"

It's a cockatrice," Dionysus says. "I'm surprised you didn't recognize it. They're mentioned throughout history, in the Bible, *Romeo and Juliet, Harry Potter…*"

He presses a hand to his chest and straightens.

*"Hath Romeo slain himself? Say thou but 'Ay,'*
*And that bare vowel 'I' shall poison more*
*Than the death-darting eye of cockatrice."*

"That was nice, Tarzan. Still, I'm more interested in how aggressive they are. They don't seem to be sharing the air well."

"Historically, they only become overtly murderous after being mated. If they're single, they're fairly chill."

"Uh…guys?" Brendan sports a crooked grin as he points up at the two. "Maybe we read the situation wrong. I'm thinking it's not aggression we're witnessing."

I glance up and— "Wowzers. So that's happening."

"Look away, people," Emmet says, laughing. "Look away. Nothing to see here."

Da's raised eyebrows are too funny. "Well, then, let's stand down and focus on other issues. Brenny and Emmet, why don't ye turn in fer the night and we'll handle the immigration issues fer a few hours while ye get some shut-eye?"

Brenny holds out his hand. "Great idea. Someone portal me to my bed."

Emmet chuckles and stacks his hand on Brendan's. "Wake us if there's an emergency."

I snort. "There's always an emergency."

"True. How about you wake us up if there's an emergency of epic proportions?"

"Done deal."

Nikon joins the circuit of travelers and the three of them snap out. Technically, Nikon's powers have leveled up enough that he doesn't need to touch the people he's transporting. Still, hands-in has been our way for two years, so we continue to go with what works.

When they're gone, I meet Da's gaze. "Okay, give us the update, and we'll join the fun."

Da shakes his head. "Why don't ye go back up to yer room and enjoy a day of peace, *mo chroi*? We can handle this."

"I have no doubt you can, but I'm not great at checking out when there's action and adventure to be had."

"You're our little FOMO junkie," Dillan teases.

I can't deny that. "I'll save my check out and chill for our real honeymoon. For now, let's get things sorted here so the honeymoon can begin."

Da nods. "All right. Dionysus, if ye would, take Fi and Calum to the security office. Astrid has been helpin' Emmet and Brendan decide who gains entrance, but yer instincts have a magical touch to them, so it couldn't hurt to learn a bit about the folks coming through the portal doors and if there's any we need to be wary of."

Dionysus grins. "Got it, Da."

Da arches his brow at me but makes no comment.

"And be nice to Astrid," Garnet adds. "If she's the embodiment of this blasted island, stop pissing her off."

I frown. "Piss *her* off? She was pissing *me* off."

My father holds up his finger. "Garnet's not wrong. Ye tend to get yer dander up when there are other strong-willed females around ye. Let's not have any catfightin' or pissin' people off. Best behavior, Fi."

I cross my arms. "Fine. Consider me Miss Congeniality."

Dillan snorts. "We'll do that."

Nikon snaps back, and Da continues with the roll call. "Nikon, I'd like ye to take Garnet and Dillan to Boundary Gate. There's been a steady influx of people. Ye'll be our force in case we have gate-crashers and we need to push them back."

Garnet grins and rolls his fingers into fists. "Happy to be the city's bouncer. The sooner we fill these fucking buildings, the sooner we can all get home."

I'm not sure that's a given, but it's our working theory.

"Sloan and Eva, I'd like ye to tackle the Light Weavers' temple. There's still too much we don't know about what happened and why the city was locked down and went dormant. Sloan can handle goin' through the texts, but I'm thinkin' the prisms and light might be more than aesthetic. If I'm right, ye might need to light the place up fer some of the mysteries to unlock."

Sloan nods. "Agreed."

"The rest of us will integrate the folks who came through overnight. Without food and running water, we've instructed them to come to the meadow to eat and have their information recorded. Sarah's been at it all night. Aiden and I will relieve her so she can get some rest."

"Where are Gran, Wallace, and Myra?" I ask. "I would've expected they'd be down here rolling out the welcome mat and making sure everyone is well and cared for."

Da shakes his head. "It's front-line warriors only until we verify who and what we're dealin' with, *mo chroi*. Odds are, these folks are exactly who they say they are, and all is well, but I'll not risk our loved ones with unknown quantities in the mix."

"Damn straight," Garnet growls.

I press my hand against my heart. "Look at that. The two of you agree on something. It's a day after the wedding day miracle."

Garnet arches a brow. "You're late on that one, Lady Druid. We both agreed you're a pain in the ass and a reckless calamity waiting to happen from the beginning."

Calum laughs. "There you go, Fi. You're the common bond that brought them together."

"Yeah, but because they think I'm a hot mess."

Calum shrugs. "Any publicity is good publicity, amirite?"

I roll my eyes. "I don't think it works like that."

Da snaps his fingers and waves to get our attention. "If yer done, let's whip this city into shape. Plenty to do. Plenty to see."

---

Dionysus takes Calum and me to the security office and we look around. It looks different today. There are still no windows, so no natural lighting, but a line of glow along the ceiling illuminates the space.

"Where's the AI?" Calum asks.

"No idea, but I suggest you don't call her that, or she might bag you. Astrid will barely look at me since I suggested she was anything less than the real deal. Well, after she punched me in the boob."

Calum chuckles. "It's incredible that your woman repellent even works on computer females. Makes you wonder what kind of programming that takes."

"I don't have woman repellent."

"If you say so."

"Even if I don't always get along with women, it's more your fault than mine."

"Me? How did this turn around on me?"

"I was raised by a single father and five older brothers. If I have trouble relating to the feminine community, it's because I've been doused by testosterone my whole life."

"Yet we're all great with women. Sorry, baby girl, that boat won't float."

I sigh. "It made sense in my head."

"Don't worry, Jane. One of the first lessons you learn as a god is that some people will never understand your greatness and will be bitter and jealous little shrews. Cast them to the side and hold your head high. You don't need the approval of others to be your true, incredible self."

"Thanks, Tarzan. I'll remember that."

He nods and holds his arms out from his sides. "Astrid, are you here? It is I, Dionysus, God of Wine, son of Zeus, and all-around fabulous species of man."

Astrid appears and smiles at the three of us. "Here is a relative term, but yes, I believe in the sense of your question, I am."

I step toward the center console. When we were here yesterday, this workstation seemed inactive, but today, it's lit with a city map. "Astrid, if it's not too much of an imposition, could you tell us about the people who came through the Boundary Gate and show us where they are settling in?"

She strides across the floor. The movement isn't walking or hovering. It's more like she's gliding across ice on skates. It's odd but graceful.

She reaches the illuminated map and starts accessing things. "Since your party removed the warding block on the city, one hundred and sixty-seven entities have come through the Boundary Gate. That number includes fourteen species, including thirty-two petal people, a pair of mated cockatrices, and—"

"Mated? Are you sure?" I shift my gaze to Dionysus. "Tarzan, didn't you say that they only get murderous after they're mated?"

"Yes. Why do you look so worried?"

"Didn't we witness Cadmus' mid-air assault with his friendly weapon?"

"Ah, yes. I see where you're going now. You're worried about Mr. Cockatrice finding out someone else cream-filled his donut."

Calum chuckles. "The old...dipping of the dragon wick problem."

"A thrust through the Gates of Mordor."

"And tossed a hotdog down the hallway."

"Got a—"

"Nope." I hold up my hand when it becomes obvious they aren't even beginning to wind down. "Thank you for the colorful commentary. Yes, that's what I meant. Will Mr. Cockatrice take issue with his mate going outside the relationship?"

"I can't say from experience," Dionysus says, "but wouldn't it be nice if they have an open mating, and everyone can get along?"

"That would be nice, but I think I still better warn Dart to keep an eye out for trouble."

"Is poly-dragon-creature-love a thing?" Calum asks.

Dionysus grins. "Wouldn't it be lovely if it was?"

I point back to the illuminated map. "Let's get back to the immediate problem at hand. Who have we let in and how do we think they're going to get along going forward?"

---

"Okay, petal people," I say half an hour later as we run down the list alphabetically.

Astrid pulls up a picture of the little creatures.

"Ohmygoodness, they're so cute." I wave Dionysus over to look at the screen. "They're actually made out of flower petals."

Calum leans in and tilts his head. "Little upside-down flower people. Nice."

"Not nice," Astrid corrects.

I study their image and wonder how they couldn't be nice. They have bright pink and yellow flared skirts of petals, and then their bodice and arms are the green sepal leaves, and then there's a bulb with their little faces, and out of the bulb is another round of petals for hair.

"They're adorable."

"Beware their bite. They are carnivorous and have very sharp teeth. And while, for the most part, they focus on small bugs and aphids, if you try to pet one, your finger will do just fine."

I pull my hand back from the screen. "Disappointing."

Calum chuckles. "You gotta expect stuff like that coming from the fae realm. The creatures of the fae are all a bit twisted."

*He's not wrong.*

"So, how many petal people did you say we imported overnight?" I ask.

"Thirty-two."

"And what was their claim for needing sanctuary based on?"

"They were being eaten. They claim their realm is being overrun by large snails and slugs."

"That sounds like more of a natural selection process of predator and prey. How does that qualify for refugee status in the city of Isilon?"

"Their people are on the brink of extinction. The thirty-two who came through are the last thirty-two in existence."

"Well, I suppose that changes things." I tap the screen to advance to the next arrival. "Quasti. Oh, they're cute too. Tell me they don't bite."

"Not at all. They have long tongues and drink the nectar of plants."

Calum smiles at the screen. "They *are* cute."

Quasti are the size of a small, chubby cat and have six stubby legs, two large butterfly wings, a fluffy tail, and tall, scoop ears. The one on the screen is brilliant lime green with a white muzzle and tummy.

"How many of these little guys came through?"

"Two families. Eleven in total."

"Nice. I take it that if they eat nectar, they'll want to live near the meadow?"

Astrid nods. "I suggest the construction of a flower garden on the other side of the river of power. Quasti won't reside in the city. They prefer to burrow in the hillside."

I add that to my notes on my phone. Damn. So much to do. So little time.

"Okay, anymore 'Q' creatures, or are we moving on?"

"The next inhabitant is a—"

The world spins as I get a headrush from hell. I throw my hands out to the side to steady my balance, but it's no use. I've been sucked back in time and forced into astral projection moments enough to know when I'm getting hijacked.

Damn it...

## CHAPTER SIXTEEN

My knees *crack* hard on the ground, and I wait, hoping my shield doesn't flare. I don't think I can defend myself even if my life depends on it.

Which it might if my shield flares.

Movement nearby has me forcing my muscles to push me off the ground to secure a defendable stance.

It's sloppy, but I get there.

Sloan stands before me, but my momentary relief in seeing him is gone before it even takes hold. Everything in me shouts that this is not hotness.

"Who are you? What do you want?"

Not-Sloan's head tilts quizzically to one side. "Why does your energy spike with such anger, Fiona Cumhaill?"

"Because you're pretending to be my husband."

"I merely wanted to give you a comforting image so we could speak. Sloan Mackenzie's presence makes you calm and happy."

"When it's really him, sure. You need to pick another image because I won't be calm and happy while you're wearing Sloan's face."

"What face would you prefer? I know all. I can be whomever you choose."

"Let's start with who you really are."

"I am Isilon."

I draw a deep breath. "So, am I still on the island?"

"Yes, of course."

*Okay, good.* That, at least, makes me feel better. "Fine. Take the image of my grade eleven English teacher, Mr. Epema. He was a smart guy and always challenged me to a good conversation."

Just like that, Mr. Epema is standing in front of me. "Is this better?"

"Much, thank you." Now that my head isn't spinning, I take in my surroundings. We're standing in a rooftop garden, and when I step closer to the ledge, I can see the hidden city bustling below.

"Did you take me back in time?"

"No. This is simply a memory I am sharing with you."

I take a moment to watch the interactions of the citizens below. There are pseudodragons playing in the air with faeries and Quasti, and on the ground twenty-foot trees are talking and walking around like something out of *Lord of the Rings*.

"When is this memory from?"

"Right before my great slumber."

"Before everyone left?"

He shakes his head. "No one left. They were consumed."

My head twists and I try to let that little ray of sunshine wash over me. "Consumed by what?"

"Not by what."

"Fine, I'll try again. Consumed by who?"

"By the Dark Weavers."

I look out upon the city and frown. "It's a bit on the nose, but I take it they're the opposite of the Light Weavers?"

"In many aspects the opposite. In many other aspects, completely different and much worse." He gestures at the far distant part of the city where the Boundary Gate is.

In the sky, there is unnatural darkness. It reminds me a bit of how the sky darkened when Morgana tried to break free of the Neitherlands.

It occurs to me how wrong that feels here.

On this island, there has never been anything but the most beautiful sunny days with cool breezes and warm summer showers.

Dark and stormy just don't fit.

"Do the Dark Weavers bring storms and darkness where the Light Weavers brought light?"

He shakes his head. "No. The Light Weavers manipulated the very essence of energy to add light and phase things in or out of existence on this plane."

"And the Dark Weavers?"

"They also manipulate the energy of things, but instead of phasing them, they consume the fae energy."

"So, they invaded the city and ate the citizens' energy?"

"Correct. They sucked the magical essence of the fae living peacefully here in the city and broke them apart, consuming their energy. That is why I insisted we ward the entrance to the city and bar entry. You should have listened to me."

I can't even wrap my head around that.

"Why are you telling me this? Emmet is your champion. Why aren't you coming to him with this?"

"I spent time in your sibling's mind. While he holds power and good intentions, he has yet to understand his abilities and lacks confidence. He believes in you. He looks at you when difficult decisions must be made."

"What decisions need to be made?"

"I insist you stop bringing people into the city. I made my intentions clear to them when I ordered the Boundary Gate sealed, and yet, more new inhabitants flood in by the hour."

"That's *your* doing."

"Mine? It most certainly is not."

"It absolutely is. If you had been honest and communicated your concerns instead of keeping this to yourself and holding us prisoner, we wouldn't have taken things into our own hands."

"But now that you understand, you will stop the immigration?"

"No. I didn't say that."

His expression makes me think he's warring between confusion and the urge to smite me. "The Dark Weavers will come. They will sense the island is once again accessible, and they will invade our streets and consume everyone."

"I understand the risk and the fact that you are concerned about the well-being of the citizens and going through that kind of traumatic loss again, but making decisions based on fear isn't a good enough reason to deny people the help they need."

"It is more than fear. It is knowing what will happen."

I watch the inhabitants of the realm going about their daily lives, and my heart aches for them. "What happened was tragic—I'm not saying it wasn't—but the people banging on the portal door, begging for refuge can't be turned away based on what you worry *might* happen."

"*Will* happen."

"Why, if you don't want the city repopulated, won't you let my friends and family portal home?"

"You didn't come through the Boundary Gate, so that energy isn't being released into the ether. Also, your friends and family are very powerful. They have revived me more in the past two days than I believed possible."

"Keeping them here against their will is wrong. If you know all...you know that."

Isilon has the decency to look conflicted. "I don't want to slumber anymore."

"Right, so allow us to repopulate the city. You can't have it both ways. Either we repopulate the city, and you awaken and grow strong and vibrant again, or we all leave because we can't trust you'll let us go, and then you'll go into hibernation again."

"No. I can't take the darkness again. I won't."

"Then help us welcome new citizens into your streets and we'll plan our defense for if the Dark Weavers come."

"For *when* the Dark Weavers come."

"All right...*when* they come."

Isilon frowns. "I don't like it. You don't understand the force of what you will come up against."

"Then explain it to us, and we'll be that much more prepared."

He considers that for a long while and nods. "Very well, Fiona Cumhaill. I will consider your counsel."

---

"Fi? What the hell, baby girl?" Calum has my shoulders gripped tight and is staring hard at me. "Where did you go on me?"

"*A ghra?*" I turn, and Sloan is rushing forward with Dionysus and Eva behind him. "What happened?"

I give myself a little shake and snap out of it. "S'all good. Isilon and I had a little *tête-à-tête* in one of his memories, so I guess he pulled me out of my body for a bit."

"Mr. Epema?" Calum is staring at Isilon standing there in our teacher's likeness.

"Isilon," I correct. "He wanted to take the physical likeness of someone I could converse with but who wouldn't weird me out."

"Oh, cool. Mr. Epema is a great choice. That man was really freaking smart."

*True story.*

Sloan looks less amused. "Are ye well, luv?"

"Perfectly fine. The important point is that we chatted about how it's not nice to hold us prisoner here to populate the city while he expects us to ignore the people pleading for sanctuary."

Sloan turns his attention toward him and frowns. "Ye see the hypocrisy in that, do ye?"

I pat Sloan's arm and shake off the last of my ordeal. "It's not so much hypocrisy as it is fear."

I spend the next few minutes updating Sloan, Calum, Eva, and Dionysus about the invasion of the Dark Weavers and Isilon's fear that having people arriving through the Boundary Gate will somehow signal to them that the island is once again ripe for attack.

"Och, well, we've fought powerful foes in the past," Sloan says. "Given the chance to study the danger they pose, I have no doubt we'll come up with a plan for how to keep history from repeating itself."

"I told him as much, but he's not sold."

Calum waves that away. "If you give us the intel, we'll devise a plan. In the meantime, don't brainsuck Fi anymore. I hate it when shit like that happens."

I chuckle and hug my brother. "I'm good. Thanks for loving me enough to be freaked out."

"I was freaked out too." Dionysus holds out his arms. "I went and got Sloan."

I chuckle and hug Dionysus as well.

When I ease back, I check in with Sloan and Eva. "So, how did you guys do at the Light Weavers' temple?"

Sloan waggles his brow. "Come. We'll show ye."

---

Sloan *poofs* us to the inner sanctum of the Light Weavers' temple, and I smile at the orderly stacks of tomes on the table. I doubt even Sloan could've gotten through this many in the hour since we split to work on things.

The piles must each mean something.

"Got your system all worked out, do you?"

He flashes me a sheepish grin. "Sorry, ye know how I can get."

I chuckle. "I do, and don't apologize for it."

The grin he flashes me catches me off-guard. He still doesn't understand how incredible he is. It's not like it's an effort to think he's amazing…anyone who sees him in action on any one of a dozen fronts will see he's amazeballs.

"Okay, show me what you've got going on."

Sloan waggles his brow and takes me to a glass podium in the center of the space that wasn't there the other night when we were here. "Eva was examining the space and found a faint impression of a square in the center of the mosaic. By trial and error, we found that this podium fit like they intended it to be here."

Eva grins. "We think it likely was always here, but when the danger of the last days was upon them, they moved it so it wouldn't be immediately evident why it was there."

"Cool. So why was it there?"

Sloan nods at Eva, and she launches into the air above us in her dove form. While she flaps her ivory wings, Sloan checks the positioning of a book lying open on the platform of the podium. Then he picks up a yellowish-green crystal. It's about six inches long and cut in a triangular prism. "This is prasiolite. As you know, quartz is used for manifestation and to help create focus and clarity."

"Uh-huh."

"So, we wondered why this polyhedron wand was sitting on a podium in the corner. Then we discovered this." He holds the chunk of crystal over the writing on the text, and Eva does her heaven's light, dove radiance thing above.

The golden light she gives off beams through the prasiolite, and when the diffused light hits the open pages of the book, Kyna appears five feet away from us.

"Holy shit. You're alive!"

"Not exactly, luv," Sloan says. "She's left a hologram for us to find, but so far, I haven't figured out why."

"Well, her lips are moving. Can we turn up the volume so we can hear what she's trying to tell us?"

"I haven't figured out how to do that yet."

"Help me, Obi-Wan Kenobi. You're my only hope." Calum grins at me and shrugs. "There's no way you weren't thinking the same thing."

I giggle. "Oh, one hundy percent."

The two of us chuckle for a moment, then I'm back to Sloan and his discovery. "This is amazing, hotness. Well done."

My phone buzzes in my pocket and I pull it out to read the incoming message.

It's from Benjamin.

**Fi, we've got trouble. Our suite. Please don't say anything. Bring Sloan.**

Well, crap on a cracker, that doesn't sound good.

"Problem, luv?"

"Maybe." I slide my phone into my pocket and think about how best to handle that cryptic message.

If Sloan and I abandon our jobs to return to the castle, Dionysus will want to tag along too. If Benjamin wants discretion, I can't have Dionysus interested in what it's about.

"Hey, Tarzan. Since Sloan's going to be stuck here going through books and doing boring stuff, if you want to take Calum to the meadow to help Da with the new citizens, I think he'd appreciate it."

"You do?"

I nod. "Oh, for sure. Maybe you can make some of the new arrivals feel at home too."

"Can we have a 'Welcome to the Island' party?"

"Yep. I think that's an excellent idea. Can you take lead on that?"

He straightens and presses a hand to his chest. "Jane. Who else could do an event like this justice?"

"No one I can think of. You're the man, sweetie. Thank you. I don't know what I'd do without your help."

That's true, so I don't feel bad about my diversion.

Calum's watching me with a knowing look, and I shake my head. "Can you go with him and make sure things go smoothly?"

"Whatever you need. We'll catch up on things later?"

"Yep. Looking forward to it."

With the promise of filling him in later, Calum clasps Dionysus' shoulder, and the two of them snap out.

Sloan looks down at me. "Do I want to know?"

"I got a text that we need to *poof* back to our suite to take care of something private."

He sets the crystal down and frowns. "Should I be worried?"

"I don't really know yet." I take my phone out and let him read the text. "I would like to respect their privacy."

A crease of worry pinches Sloan's brow. "All right, let's go see what it's about. Eva, we're goin' to take a break. Can we circle back to things later?"

Eva's dove glides down, and my sister-in-law takes form beside us. "Sure. I've been missing my guy anyway. Let me know when you need me."

## CHAPTER SEVENTEEN

Sloan *poofs* me up to our suite in the palace, and after I make a quick pitstop in the bathroom, we strike off down the hall to the stairs.

"Knowing Xavier's mood last night after being trapped here, Brenny told me he put the vampires as far away from the other guests as possible. He didn't want the chaos of squealing kids, crying babies, or Dionysus to set them off."

Sloan chuckles. "I love that Dionysus has a category among squealin' kids and cryin' babies."

"Don't tease. He tries so hard."

"Aye, that he does."

I don't think Xavier or Benjamin would go off on a vampire rampage of slaughter, but having a vamp lose their temper is never a good thing.

"Knock, knock," I say as my knuckles rap on the door. "It's Fi and Sloan."

Benjamin opens the door and draws a deep breath. "Come in."

The two of us join him and Laurel in the common area of their two-bedroom suite, and I glance around. Benjamin texted me that we've got trouble, but the place is in order, and the two of them look fine...well, other than looking like a bomb is about to go off.

Vampires are never chill, but Benjamin and Laurel both seem unusually anxious. "What's wrong?"

Laurel steps forward and hugs me. "Is there any progress on getting us home, Fi?"

I shrug. "I spoke to Isilon, the city's consciousness, and impressed upon him how important it is to let everyone return to their lives, but he wouldn't lift the lockdown. He did say he'll consider my argument, but I'm not holding my breath for him to suddenly be struck with a need to right his wrong."

"Fuck." Benjamin runs his fingers through his hair and exhales heavily.

"What is it, sham?" Sloan asks. "How can we help?"

"Benjamin, you need to tell them," Laurel says.

"He's going to fucking end me if I do."

My instincts are firing up a dozen different scenarios, but they all come back to one thing. "What's wrong with Xavier? What's happened?"

Benjamin scowls. "Getting stuck here for days was never the plan, Fi."

"I know that, and I'm sorry."

"We know you are." Laurel throws Benjamin a look. "It's really bad timing because Karuna's been unwell this past week."

"I'm sorry to hear that. Is it serious?"

Laurel shakes her head. "No, just a flu, but she's been throwing up and running a fever."

"And he's worried about her? I'm sure the other members of your family will take good care of her in his absence."

"Yes, they will. That's not it."

She draws a deep breath and looks at Benjamin, but the guy has pretty much shut down.

"Seriously, you guys. Tell me what the problem is, and we'll get it sorted."

Laurel frowns. "Xavier hasn't fed. He was away for almost a week. Then he came home, and Karuna was sick. He refused to feed from her and drain what strength she had."

"Now he's trapped here and can't get to her."

Laurel nods. "Him feeling cut off from her isn't helping either. It's all culminating into a giant snowball of 'we need to get him home really damn fast.' Normally, if someone in the family gets this bad, another of the feeding companions will step in, but as you both know, I'm no good to him."

No. She wouldn't be.

The ring Merlin fashioned for her granted her the gift of a corporeal form, but in reality, Laurel is still a ghost.

The weight of the situation isn't lost on me. Neither is the unspoken question hanging in the air.

"All right. I'll feed him."

"Like hell ye will. The last time that man got his mouth on ye, he nearly crushed yer windpipe and took so much blood ye nearly died."

The memory of that horrible night flashes back, and I raise my hand to my neck. The scars Xavier left that night have faded to the point that no one who didn't know what happened would notice.

There are still moments in the dead of night when I wake in a cold sweat panic, and struggle to remind myself it's over and I'm safe.

"That wasn't Xavier's fault." I hear the words coming out of my mouth, and they don't even sound convincing to me. "He was under the influence of heightened bloodlust brought on by a conniving bitch."

"Xavier would never have lost control otherwise," Benjamin agrees.

"I believe that."

"It's a lot to ask," Laurel says.

"It's too much," Sloan snaps.

I take Sloan's hand and squeeze. "This time will be different. You're here and so is Benjamin. Neither of you will let Xavier lose control. It'll be fine."

Sloan curses and pulls me a couple of feet away to turn me to face him. "Look me in the eyes and tell me ye believe that."

I see his panic, and in the reflection of his pale green eyes, I see mine as well.

My speech to Isilon from an hour ago comes back to haunt me. *"Making decisions based on fear isn't a good enough reason to deny people the help they need."*

*Dammit.* Why do I have to be so damned wise?

"Why are you smiling?" Sloan asks.

"Just laughing at myself and the irony of life. Yes, of course. I will feed Xavier. I assume that's why you had me bring Sloan?"

Benjamin nods. "We hoped the issue is being resolved, but failing that, yes, we thought it best that both of you are involved in the decision.

"I still don't like it," Sloan snaps.

I offer him a look of apology. "I understand that, and I value and respect your opinion. You're protective and worried about what happened last time, and your concerns are valid. But if you're honest with yourself, you know this is an entirely different scenario."

"It is," Laurel concurs. "I would never have suggested it if I thought you would be in danger."

Benjamin raises his hands. "It's just... given the situation and who is here, there is no other choice. Feeding is personal, and Xavier has never forgiven himself for what happened and how it happened with you the last time."

"I told him we were okay."

Benjamin shakes his head. "That's not what I meant. He never forgave himself for betraying Karuna. I think knowing Karuna likes you and the two of you are friendly, you are the only one he'll even consider."

"And the fact that you are hopelessly in love with Sloan," Laurel adds.

"That's why we wanted him here with us. So, there's no mistake in anyone's mind that this is anything but a friend helping out a friend in a difficult and dangerous situation."

"Just how dangerous is the situation?" Sloan asks.

"If he feeds now, there are safety concerns but nothing we can't mitigate. If we wait even another few hours, the people in this building will be at risk."

"That will humiliate Xavier and traumatize the person unlucky enough to be in his path," Laurel adds.

I know too well what it's like to be the unlucky person in his path when he's suffering from blood lust. "All right. Let's get it done. The sooner the better."

Laurel rushes forward and hugs me. "Thank you, Fi. I'm so sorry it came to this, but no one anticipated being stuck here for days."

"No, I know. And I couldn't be sorrier about that."

Laurel waves that away. "You had no way of knowing that a sentient city was going to hold us hostage. Totally not your fault."

"Thanks." When the conversation dies down, I look around the room. "So, where are we doing this?"

Benjamin frowns. "I don't think he'll come out here voluntarily. I'm thinking us going into the bedroom is the only way."

*Right.* The five of us in Xavier's bedroom while he's in bloodlust and going to feed on me.

That sounds super cozy.

"Yeah, okay. Good times."

---

My mental hamster is still tripping over all the ways this could go sideways on us as we enter Xavier's room. Benjamin takes the lead and doesn't bother with the lights as we step inside. It's midday and even with the drapes pulled, there's enough diffused light to allow us to see.

"Xavier. You're not going to like this but—"

"I don't. I hate it." The hissed words come from the shadowed corner, and I blink, waiting for my eyes to adjust so I can see him more clearly. "But I'm not a fool, and I'm not deaf. I heard everything you were speaking about."

I take a slow step toward him and release Sloan's hand. "Then you know I'm okay with this. You know how I am with people I care about. If I can offer help to anyone, I will."

"You shouldn't have to. This is not your problem and after the last time..."

"Forget about the last time. That wasn't you."

"Oh, Lady Druid, don't for a second think that wasn't me. Just because I wear an expensive suit and hold my family to a higher standard doesn't mean I'm not the monster from every horror story ever told."

"I'm well aware you're capable of being that monster, but I know you better than that."

"Then you're a trusting fool."

I chuff. "Is this how you sweet talk the ladies? You need to work on your game."

The throaty growl that comes out of the darkness sends a spear of icy chill down my spine. I can't help the trembling of my hands or the dryness of my throat—those things are etched into the DNA of a person's survival instinct.

What I can do is make a calculated choice to conquer that fear and do what's right.

"How do you want to do this?"

"I don't."

"Xavier—"

Benjamin starts but I hold up my hand. "It's fine. We're fine. Would you and Laurel please wait in the next room?"

"What? No," Laurel says, her eyes flaring wide.

I wave off her objections. "This will be easier with fewer eyes on us and if anything goes wrong, Benjamin will hear it and can rush in here at lightning speed."

"They will stay," Xavier counters, his words more command than a statement of fact. "When I'm forced to explain this to Karuna, I can only hope it gives her some comfort to know Benjamin and Laurel were here to oversee things. Then there will be no doubt."

"No doubt about what?"

Xavier doesn't answer, but he lifts his gaze to Sloan. "I offer you my sincerest apologies for the monster I am by nature."

I shake my head. "I'm getting lost. It's a feeding. Easy-peasy. Let's not build it up to epic proportions."

Sloan places a gentle hand on the small of my back and nods. "I understand. We'll deal with anything more that comes of it without insult. You've made your intentions clear."

I look from Xavier to Sloan and back again. "Comes of what? What am I missing?"

Xavier looks away, and it's Sloan who meets my gaze. "They mentioned vampire feedings are an intimate exchange, luv. I believe Xavier is concerned there might be a pull between the two of you beyond his hunger for your blood."

I blink and scan the faces of the others. "Oh. Okay. I didn't realize that's a thing."

"That's why Sloan is here," Laurel says. "When Xavier fed on you when he was possessed, nothing sexual happened because he was in a frenzy, and you were fighting for your life. This won't be like that."

Xavier curses and I'm pretty sure he's about to call the whole thing off.

"We're all adults. Sloan's here to protect my interests, and Benjamin is here to protect yours. Take what you need from me and when you've fed and withdrawn your fangs, Sloan will *poof* us out of here. If I'm wound up, he'll take care of me. If you're wound up, you'll have the privacy of your room."

Benjamin steps forward. "It's the best for everyone. I can't see any other scenario working."

Xavier commits to the idea because after a muffled sigh of his speaking ancient Korean, he girds himself and nods. "Very well. I thank you for what you offer and regretfully accept."

---

Once the decision is made, everything happens quickly. Laurel has me lie on the edge of the bed, and Benjamin moves a chair to sit beside the mattress.

"Sloan, if you'll lay next to Fi, you can keep her distracted while Xavier feeds." The look he sends us is filled with regret and apology.

"What? What aren't you telling us?"

Benjamin straightens. "Nothing...honestly. It's just...this will be intense for you. It's perfectly normal for us, so please don't be embarrassed if your reaction becomes overtly amorous."

Laurel chuckles. "What he's trying to say is that the feeding will kick off your sexual endorphins, so if you start moaning and stripping your clothes off, it's nothing we don't see happen every day in our lives."

*Seriously?* I look at Sloan and if I said the word he'd have me out of this room and this situation in a racing heartbeat. But then we'd be back where we started and delaying Xavier's feeding puts everyone I love at risk.

I swallow and force a smile. "What happens in the hidden city stays in the hidden city, I guess."

Laurel winks at me. "That's the spirit, girlfriend. Honestly, Fi, there's nothing to worry about. Trust me. You won't be suffering."

She sends a longing gaze toward Benjamin, and he blushes. "You'll be fine, Fi. I promise you."

For the number of times my friends and family have seen me in an embarrassing and compromising situation, this is just par for the course. "All righty then, consider me warned."

I settle into position and Sloan crawls beside me and drapes his arm across my hips. I see the question in his gaze, and I nod. "It's fine. S'all good."

Xavier is there a moment later, sitting in the chair at the side of the bed. He moves slowly as he collects my arm and brushes a gentle finger over the pulse in my wrist. "I thank you for what you offer, Lady Druid."

"Do what you need to do. Get yourself right."

Another stroke over my wrist and I'd swear my blood is buzzing in my veins. Is that an effect of his intentions or my imagination?

He breaks eye contact and turns away, shifting so the back of his head cuts off my vision. The strike of his fangs through my flesh is intense, but a moment later, I'm washed with the most incredible sense of feel-good hallucinogen.

"Wow, you should market that serum of yours, dude. It's incredible."

I let my mind float around for a bit, enjoying the high. In a distant part of my mind, I register the gentle suckling of his mouth against my skin.

*This isn't so bad.*

"Lemon squeezy," I say, smiling up at Sloan.

He nods, but his expression is still tight and concerned. "How long will the feeding last?"

"Normally, with a human companion, it takes about twenty minutes," Benjamin says quietly. "With the power Fi's blood holds, likely half that."

*Ten minutes?* "Bah, no probs. S'all good." I hear my voice warbling in my ears, and I sound drunk. Am I?

For sure I'm buzzed, but—

"Oh, I...uh, okay, wowzers." A rush of intensity hits, and my heart pounds faster. I swallow as my cells ignite and all my girlie parts start to weigh in.

Still, it's not too bad.

I'm an adult after all. I can control my urges.

Especially in mixed company.

Xavier growls, and the predatory sound zings through me and does all kinds of damage to my self-control. He shifts position and clutches my arm tightly, securing his hold like he owns me...or at least my vein.

I groan and arch my back off the mattress. It strikes me too late that I'm supposed to be fighting the sexual impulses firing inside me. I open my eyes and focus on Sloan's beautiful face inches from mine. "I'm sorry. I'm trying."

"Don't be sorry, luv. I'm right here, and ye've done nothin' wrong. Feels good, does it?"

"So good."

"Then all is well. Yer safe and not sufferin', that's all I care about."

Does he mean that?

"I love you, Mackenzie." I lift my head to kiss him.

The contact of his lips on mine releases another powerful wave of desire. What I meant to be a gentle reassurance of my devotion becomes more.

Much more.

Xavier growls again. Then Laurel is standing beside the bed holding my arm down. "Try not to move your arm."

Yeah no. I don't care.

Laurel can be in charge of that arm if she wants. I've still got my other arm, and it's currently wrapped around Sloan's back ensuring he can't get away.

The kiss is crazy hot, and I'm trying to focus and keep things presentable for the others in the room, but it's hard. I want more. I need more.

"You're doing great, Fi. Just focus on Sloan, and it'll be over soon."

I shift my hold and go for the back of Sloan's pants. I can't get at anything better with the way we're positioned, but at least I can grab his very fine ass.

Sloan breaks from our kiss and eases back to look at me. His expression is warring between concern and amusement, and I don't like the conflict.

"I'm good, hotness. But you know what would make me even better?" I whisper into his ear all the truly carnal things I want to do to him.

Xavier growls, and Benjamin moves in quickly, gripping his king's shoulders to force him to remain seated.

Sloan makes a face, and I realize that two of the three people in this room have heightened hearing…and Xavier is likely turned on too.

*Oops.*

To keep from dirty talking myself into a vampire battle, I reclaim Sloan's mouth and focus on not saying anything more.

I'm enjoying the connection with my guy when the suckling eases, and I get the sense the feeding is coming to its end.

Now it's Benjamin growling. "No. Don't be a fool. I've got you. Finish the fucking feeding."

"What's wrong?" I can barely make sense of the words, but the tone is definitely not good.

"It's too soon for him to withdraw and stop the feeding," Laurel says. "If his system doesn't get what he needs, his cravings will grow. It'll make him almost as dangerous as if he hadn't fed at all."

"Then finish," I say, only half caring. "Don't be stupid. I'm good."

"You won't be," Xavier growls against the flesh of my wrist.

I haven't got the mental capacity at the moment to figure out what that means but Sloan does. "Finish the feedin'. Nothin' will happen to compromise my wife. I promise ye that."

*Hubba-wha?*

"I've got you," Benjamin says, getting a better grip on his king. "Finish the fucking feeding."

A huge rush of feel-good sexy hits and I'm squirming on the mattress, lost to whatever is going on with Xavier. At this moment...I don't even care.

I fall back into my erotic haze of kissing Sloan and grabbing his butt and trying to grind against him but having no ability to free myself to do it.

The buzz in my cells is getting more intense, and Xavier's growl is more like one long rumbling promise of something dark and deadly.

*Whatevs. Not my problem.*

Releasing my hold on Sloan's ass, I move my free arm, trying to grip or grab something that'll get me closer to where I want to be. Hot and bothered doesn't even begin to describe where I am right now.

"Hotness, please. I ache."

"Just a little longer, *a ghra*. I promise."

"No, now." I call *Bestial Strength* and my power surges.

Sloan curses and his powers surge too. "I won't be able to hold her off long, boys. Finish this."

Xavier growls, standing curled around my arm.

"No!" Benjamin snaps. "She is not yours, Xavier. Karuna is yours."

The release of his fangs from my arm is a painful pleasure and I cry out. Xavier turns and his eyes are glowing red.

"Out, now!" Benjamin shouts.

Sloan portals us so fast my head spins. One moment I'm on the bed in Xavier's room and the next, I'm on the mattress in ours.

"Finally," I grope at Sloan but he's off me and rushing to the door, pressing his hands against the portal, raising wards. "Fiona, release Bruin!"

*What? Why? Yeah no, I don't care.*

*Bruin, Sloan wants you.* I release my battle bear and start stripping off my clothes. "You better get back here, hotness, or you'll miss the party."

Sinking back onto the mattress, my head spins as my body continues to make demands.

Geez, feeding Xavier was amazing.

Why was everyone so worried?

# CHAPTER EIGHTEEN

It's close to dinner when I'm finally feeling enough like myself again to risk being in the company of my family and friends without worrying I will embarrass myself. Between Cadmus' morning escapade pulling us out of bed, then getting straight to work, feeding Xavier, and getting waylaid by the aftermath of his vampire sexy serum, we've missed all the meals today. I'm ravenous.

The voices of people in the Great Hall make me second guess my decision to be out in public, but my hunger overrules.

"Hey, Fi. Where have you two been all afternoon?" Dillan waggles his brow and gives me a sly grin.

"Nunya." I stride in and beeline for the banquet table set up for the taking.

"Nunya?" Eva asks.

"Nunya business," I finish for her. "Sorry, the attitude is directed at my brother, not you. You're lovely. He's the pain in the ass."

Dillan chuckles and holds up his hands. "Someone's pissy. Usually, after an afternoon of sex, you're nicer."

I flip him a middle finger salute and start filling my plate. "I haven't eaten yet today."

"Oh, that explains it," Calum says, coming in from the balcony with Kevin. "Hangry Fi is no one you want to mess with."

"Then let me warn you, hangry Fi is in the house."

My brothers chuckle, grab a few pieces of yesterday's cakes and retreat to the safety of their corners.

Kevin opts for carrots and dip instead and I notice the stain of pink paint on the thigh of his jeans. "You got tagged?"

"Yep. Your brother is an ass."

"True. Which one?"

"Emmet. I went to take him some food, knowing he'd been up all night and was likely starving, and while I was setting the tray down in his room, he nailed me."

Emmet laughs. "It was too easy."

"Technically, we said no game while the guests are here," Kevin gripes.

Emmet holds up a finger. "Technically, we said there would be no shooting or causing mayhem during Fi's wedding day. That was yesterday. Also, no guests were disturbed by your assassination. No fault. No foul."

Kevin rolls his eyes and comes over to dip carrots and stand at the food table. "Like I said. He's an ass."

"Aw, muffin. Sorry not sorry."

Kevin flashes him his middle finger and points at the leather bracer on my wrist. "That's cool. Is it new?"

"Yeah. Do you like it?"

"Yeah. It might be a bit wide for your wrist. Are you sure you got the women's one?"

I got the one that was big enough to hide the puncture marks on my wrist. Sloan and I tried to heal the marks, but it seems vampire serum doesn't respond to druid healing as we hoped it would.

"With a citywide lockdown, it's a case of taking what we can get. I'll sort it out when we get back home."

I might've put a little too much edge on that comment because Kevin takes a beat and shrugs. "Sorry. It's cool. I didn't mean to offend."

*Dammit.* "You didn't. I'm cranky and feeling out of sorts. You're fine. It's me."

Da is watching from the table in the corner. I can't let him know about me feeding Xavier, or he'll lose his mind. He barely tolerates Garnet. The vampires in my life take up an entirely different realm of unwanted as far as my father's concerned.

Especially after Xavier attacked and almost killed me last summer.

To avoid the scrutiny of my father gleaning too much, I take my plate out onto the balcony and set it on the wide stone railing.

This.

This is what I need. Sunshine, fresh air, and playful dragons doing aerial acrobatics.

"Are ye all right, *a ghra?*"

"Yeah. Just a little amped up."

"Still?" His dark eyebrows arch as he pegs me with a quizzical look.

I wave away his surprise. "Not like that. All my impulses have been sated. It's just...I don't know. I'm off."

"Well, ye've had a day. Between last night's emotion, then getting taken by Isilon, and the other thing this afternoon, it's been a lot, I'm sure."

*It has.* I just wish I believed that's all it is.

I focus on my plate and practically inhale my breakfast, lunch, and dinner all in one meal. "I suppose, as the hosts of this lockdown fiasco, we should make our rounds and check in with everyone."

"I'm sure they would appreciate it."

Giving up the serenity of the view from the palace balcony doesn't appeal to me, but can't be helped. Eventually, I have to pull up my big girl panties and face my family and friends.

I finish the last few forks of food and check in with Sloan.

He's finished too, so I guess there's no putting this off. "Are you ready for this?"

"Baby, I was born ready," he says with more Cumhaill sass than he's ever displayed.

I laugh. "Yeah, I'm quite sure you were."

Sloan takes my dirty plate, stacks it with his, and gestures for me to lead the way inside. "Yer Fiona-feckin'-Cumhaill-Mackenzie. Yer a force to be reckoned with. If ye need me to get a set of pom-poms to be yer official cheerleader, I'll do it."

I laugh at the image that paints in my mind. "Let's leave that to Dionysus. You can be my handsome hubby and tall, dark, and dangerous right-hand man."

"Even better. I don't think I can pull off a mini skirt."

"I look fucking awesome in a mini skirt," Emmet says, lifting his head from the food line and horning in on our conversation.

"I don't think yer supposed to be quite so proud of that, Em," Da says. "Not unless yer makin' a statement of choice we don't know about."

Emmet waves that away. "Nah. Little Emmet is straight as an arrow, Da. But I get your point about the skirt thing. We can keep that in the vault."

Da gives me a look, and I laugh, my heart a little lighter. Thank the goddess for my family.

"Ye look like yer sufferin' under the weight, *mo chroi*. Is there anythin' I can do?"

Da's arms are open, and I step into his hug without hesitation. "This is good. Do you mind if we stay like this for a bit and let the world sort itself out?"

"Fine by me."

I accept the extra squeeze and draw a steadying breath. "Thanks, Da."

"Forever and always, baby girl."

I step back. "Now I need to go solve the problems of the world. Thanks for the hug."

"If ye need another, ye know where I am."

*I do.* Right beside me every step of the way.

Stepping back, I kiss his cheek. "Thanks, oul man. I might take you up on that."

---

The strumming of guitar chords draws me down the main stairs and into the room of heads. Technically, they're carved busts, but Emmet calls it the heads room. I'm singing as I enter, smiling at Niall Horan on one of the sofas playing his guitar and singing to the kids.

I press my hand against my heart. "And I love him a little more."

Sloan chuckles. "She says to her groom of twenty-four hours. The man who excised all her deviant sexual cravings for the past three hours."

I laugh and bump shoulders with him. "Deviant? Rude. I didn't hear you complaining."

Now he's laughing. "No, ye didn't."

Didn't think so. "Don't worry. I'm a no returns kinda bride. No buyer's remorse here."

"That's a relief."

Niall finishes his song and stands to come over. Nikon takes a turn with the guitar and sits to keep the jamboree going, and the feline folk's kids occupied.

"Howeyah, sham?" Sloan extends his hand.

"Och, grand. Yer family is lovely and spendin' time with them has been no hardship."

"That's very generous of you." I step in to hug him. "I'm so sorry life went off the rails, and you got stuck here."

He waves that away. "I got to sing at the wedding of a super fan. I got drunk with Dionysus, an immortal Greek, and a Man o' Green last night. Calum took me up on a dragon this afternoon. Aye boy, when could I ever have had such a time if not for bein' stranded here?"

"So, you're not mad?"

"Not a bit. In fact, if we're not free to leave by tonight, yer brothers are promisin' a riotous time involvin' flip cup slip n' slide."

I laugh. "That's a great game."

"Will ye be joinin' us then?"

"If we're not needed, maybe. For now, we're doing our best to appease the city to get it to let us go home."

He shrugs. "Well, don't rush on my account. As yer brothers' say, *s'all good.*"

"That's a relief." HaiLe notices our arrival and stands, looking expectantly at me.

"Excuse me for a moment, will you, boys?"

Sloan pieces together my intention and nods. "Aye, luv. Take yer time."

---

I meet HaiLe in the middle of the room, and I stumble over what to say to her. "I can't begin to process the grief you must be suffering. I'm so sorry we couldn't bring your husband back to you."

She runs a hand up and down the gray fur on her arm. "Except, in a very important way, you did. You brought Pi back to us and with him the understanding of what happened once we were separated. My mate died protecting his family. He was at peace knowing he did right by us."

"It sounds like he was a brave and loving man."

"He was, and I was lucky to have him for the years I did. In the end, I still do have him." She turns back and smiles at her five kids. "There is no looking at them without seeing Morok. They are his legacy, and as long as I have them, their father will never be lost."

I rub the tension in my chest, but it doesn't ease. "I'm sorry I didn't check in with you last night. I got a little overwhelmed and…"

HaiLe shakes her head. "Don't for a moment feel bad about anything that happened last night. You and your family and friends had gathered for your mating celebration, and you left it all to fight my battle and risk your lives. Of course, you were overwhelmed. I'm sorry for the disruption to your day."

I wave that away. "Having an emergency and ending up on a battlefield is likely a more appropriate reception than drinking and dancing anyway. Thankfully, both of us know what we signed up for."

"Still, I thank you both for your sacrifice."

I smile at her little kittens and Dionysus lying on the floor playing with the smallest ones. He's wanted kittens, but I'm not sure feline folk children count.

"Dionysus seems to be having fun."

HaiLe chuckles. "I'd swear he has more energy than my young do. He never tires."

"True story. He is especially fond of children and having had a difficult childhood, does his best to help keep little ones happy."

"He's a very sweet man."

"He is at that. Honestly, I was worried that—"

A scream rings out from above and echoes through the halls. I rush toward Sloan. "That's Kinu."

Sloan grabs my hand and we portal upstairs.

We *poof* to the third floor where my family has claimed

rooms. We race up the hall, unsure where the cry came from as Dillan and Eva emerge on our right.

At the same time, Da flies out of his room farther down on the left. "What's wrong?" he asks.

"No idea."

He leads the way, and we follow closely.

Calum and Kevin are running up the hall from the opposite direction, and we break into the third-floor gathering room together.

I scan the room, searching for the source of the panic. Aiden is hugging Kinu, Kevin is playing with Bizzy, and Myra and Garnet kneel next to Imari and Jackson where they're coloring.

"What happened?"

Kinu pushes away from Aiden, tears streaming. "*You* happened, Fi. You opened this bloody can of worms, and now my kids will never have a normal life. Did you think of that when you volunteered everyone to be magical heroes in a world you didn't understand? Did you think about the danger you were putting my children in?"

Aiden is pulling Kinu back, trying to reason with her but I'm still not tracking.

I scan the room. Gran and Granda have the twins. Meggie's sleeping on the couch and Jackson's with Imari. "I don't understand. What happened?"

"It's my fault, Auntie Fi." Jackson gets up to come over to me. He lifts his hand and sweeps his floppy brown bangs off his forehead. "I showed Mommy I have a moon mark like Imari and now she's mad at me."

I kneel to hug him. "Oh, no, sweetie. She's not mad at you. She's super surprised. Mommy loves you so very much she bursts with emotion sometimes."

"I don't think so."

If Kinu is mad at anyone, it's me, but I have nothing to do with the crescent marks.

At least, I don't think I do.

No, I'm pretty sure I don't.

"It's fine, lad," Sloan says. "Why don't Uncle Kevin and I take ye down to the room of heads and ye can join the feline kids singin' songs? There's a boy there named Binx who has a mark too."

Kevin scoops Bizzy over his shoulder and holds out his hand for Jackson.

"Can I go too, Daddy?" Imari asks.

Garnet scowls. "You're not leaving the palace?"

Sloan shakes his head. "No, only to the room with all the busts. That's where the feline folk kids are playin'."

Garnet nods, turns to Anyx, and tilts his head toward his little girl.

"Come on, little bear." Anyx holds out his hand. "We'll go too. It's always fun to make new friends, isn't it?"

Imari nods. "Why was Jackson's mommy yelling at Auntie Fi?"

"It was a misunderstanding, sweetie," Myra says. "You know how Daddy gets all growly and gruff, and I tell you sometimes adults need a minute to sort out their grumbles so they can find their happy faces again?"

"Uh-huh."

"Well, it's sort of like that. Nothing for you to worry about. You go ahead and play with the kids. Anyx and Uncle Sloan are in charge. Don't wander off."

"Okay, Mommy."

The three of them flash out with Jackson and Imari, and I turn back to Kinu. "I'm sorry you're upset, and I'll take the heat for opening up the family druid stuff, but I didn't expose magic or drop the veil or cause the crescent marks to start appearing on kids. That's not fair."

"Isn't it?" Kinu snaps.

"No, it's not." Aiden turns Kinu toward the door. "But as Myra said, sometimes adults need a minute to sort things out. If you'll excuse us. Gran, do you mind?"

"Of course not, luv. Take as much time as ye need. We've got the wee ones covered."

Aiden frog-marches Kinu out of the room, and I'm left standing there with my mouth open.

"Am I to blame? Is it my magnet for mayhem?"

"No, it's not," Garnet says. "I've seen a lot of bizarre events fall at your feet, but legends of crescent marks appearing have been recorded in books dating back six centuries. Even you aren't that much of a hot mess."

I chuckle. "Thanks, bossman."

Myra hugs me and leans back. "As a mother of a child touched by the same destiny, I can tell you how frightened I was and how powerless I felt. Kinu targeted you as the recipient of that panic."

"Lucky me." I draw a deep breath and meet Da's gaze. "Da? What do you think?"

"I think Myra is a smarter woman than me and she knows best how Kinu is feelin'. I'd bet she feels bad about callin' ye out like that."

"She spouted off," Dillan agrees. "As the king of blowing his top and spewing shit, I can tell you from experience she's likely embarrassed and sorry she laid into you."

I draw a deep breath into my lungs and exhale. "We still don't know what it means or how these marks will affect the kids."

Garnet shakes his head. "No, we don't, but we learned an important lesson last night."

"Yeah? What's that?"

"That it's not only our realm being affected. Binx was marked, and he lives in another realm altogether."

*That's true.*

"We know the crescent marked are destined to lead the people through troubled times."

I draw a deep breath. "That's a lot of responsibility to put on kids who aren't even ten years old."

Myra nods. "Well, maybe what they're destined for isn't going to happen for ten years, and the crescents are a sign for us to train and prepare them."

"I like that theory a great deal more than it affectin' them now," Da offers.

"You and me both," Garnet agrees.

"It's not a full moon," I say. "Binx and Imari both got their marks on the full moon but that was on Wednesday."

Garnet shrugs. "Maybe Jackson's a late bloomer, or maybe the full moon has nothing to do with it. We're all still talking out our asses here."

*I know, and I hate that.* "We need to start putting real facts together and figure out the connection between the kids."

"Do you think there is a connection?" Myra asks.

"There has to be, doesn't there? If not, why would Binx get a mark in another realm? Is it for a different destiny or are they supposed to join together somehow?"

Da grunts. "I don't suppose there's any answerin' that yet, *mo chroi*. We don't know enough."

"Then we need to know more. We need to talk to people who have lived through the past six centuries who might know about the other instances when they appeared."

Garnet nods. "Well, we have a few of those people here. Perhaps we start with Nikon and Andromeda, Dionysus, Merlin, and Patty."

"It couldn't hurt to talk to Isilon too. He claims to know all. If he's had people within his city for millennia, maybe he knows about the crescent marks of old."

Da nods. "That's smart thinkin'. Let's gather the group and see what we can learn. The sooner we know what we're dealin' with, the sooner we can safeguard these kids."

Garnet nods. "It can't be too soon."

"I agree with ye, Grant. It can't."

## CHAPTER NINETEEN

Twenty minutes later Da, Garnet, and I are in the Great Hall waiting to meet with Merlin, Dionysus, Patty, Nikon, and Andromeda. Despite Kinu's reaction to the appearance of Jackson's mark, I'm not the bad guy.

I love the kids and will fight and die to protect them from harm.

I know she knows that, but her accusations still hurt.

"Oh, there's still cake." Dionysus brightens, holding up the lid of the cake cover and pointing at his discovery. "Anyone want some?"

"Yeah, I could use a sugar hit. Thanks, Tarzan."

"How big?"

I give him a measure with my fingers and look up to find Da studying me. "What?"

"Ye can't take it to heart, *mo chroi*. Ye know she didn't mean it."

"Didn't she? Maybe I'm not responsible for the crescent marks, but she still blamed me for taking away the kids' normal childhood...and it's not the first time she's hit me with that."

"Still. Even beneath her fears, ye know she realizes it's not yer fault."

I shrug, not sure of anything.

A couple of years ago, I would've said with confidence Kinu and I were as close as sisters. Now? I don't know. "There's a bit of truth in everything people say. She's obviously got hostility toward me bubbling to the surface, or else it wouldn't come out like that again and again."

"It's been a stressful time. I wouldn't worry too much. She'll come around."

Dionysus is back with two plates in hand. He hands me my piece, and I laugh at his. "You're lucky you've got your godly physique back."

"I know, right? I never appreciated my fine form enough before I was human."

I chew my first bite and bark a laugh. "You're hilarious. All you do is appreciate your fine form."

He waggles his brows and grins. "No, I allow other people to appreciate it."

Da grumbles. "All right. How about we get on topic and get back to the problem at hand?"

"Fine with me." I glance around to see who's joined us. Garnet and Myra are chatting quietly on the balcony. They haven't been alive long enough to have lived through any cycles of crescents before but have a vested interest in what we learn.

Also, Myra being a Fae Historian gives her knowledge of any books or texts that might be mentioned, which could be helpful.

Nikon had already rounded up Patty and Merlin and went searching for his sister. When they snap in, we're ready to tackle the mystery of the crescent marks.

---

By the time I've finished my cake, we've finished what we know, and Da asks if anyone has any firsthand or hearsay information on the appearance of crescent marks that might be helpful.

The answer, disappointingly, is no.

Myra is still the one with the most information, and that's only because she knew of the whispers of others in the past who received the mark before a time of struggle.

It's generally agreed that the kids are supposed to act as guides through a troubled time, but whether that time is now or ten years from now, no one knows.

"Considering four children you're connected with or crossed paths with have been marked within a few months, I'd say there is a tie to you, Fi," Merlin says.

My stomach squirrels. "Is it my fault?"

"It's not," Myra insists, waving my concerns away. "If anything, the universe has put the children in your path because you are well-suited to figure things out and protect them as they set off on their journey."

"I'm still hopin' it's a train for ten years scenario," Da says. "Then, at least we can ready the wee ones and help them prepare fer their destinies."

Garnet nods. "Agreed."

"What if they're not supposed to be involved in the battles to come?" Dionysus suggests. "What if them being 'guides' through troubled times is an accurate account of their part to be played?"

"How so, Tarzan? What are you thinking?"

"I'm saying maybe the foe we're facing might come at us in six months. But the children, either when gathered together or individually, are here to give us the insights or advantage we need to win the fight."

We all like that theory much more.

"They are referred to as the guides through troubled times," Myra reminds us. "It's certainly possible."

"Maybe they should play together and get to know one another, and something will reveal itself," Andromeda suggests.

"We can't be sure it's only the four we know of," Merlin offers.

"We should put out feelers into our communities and make it known we need to be informed if other children are marked."

"If I'm right about the magic of the universe setting them in Fiona's path, I think that will happen organically," Myra says. "But, of course, it doesn't hurt to send out the call for information."

Garnet clears his throat. "When the island lockdown lifts, I'll contact Clarissa Tremblay in Montréal and see if she'll allow us to bring Bella to meet the other children."

I imagine she will.

After keeping her daughter safe during the vampire attacks in Montréal, I think we've proven we'd never let anything happen to Bella.

"I'll continue to search for any mention of the crescent marked in ancient texts and legends," Myra says. "I had already sought out several tomes I've been trying to locate. I'm sure, given a few more days or weeks, I'll be able to find them."

Even though we don't officially know more than we did an hour ago, I think everyone feels a little better about the situation.

I meet Merlin's gaze across the group. "Wallace is examining them for any physical indicators of what might be happening, but maybe you should examine them for any magical changes."

He nods. "Consider it done."

Myra draws a deep breath, gathers Garnet's hand in hers, and beams a warm smile onto the group. "Thank you all for helping us with this. It means so much that we're not trying to figure this out in isolation."

It's Da who answers. He takes my hand and sets his other palm on Dionysus' shoulder. "That's what family is all about. The good times are fun, but it's durin' the times of trouble when family counts most."

I nod. "We'll figure this out. There's no other option."

After our meeting adjourns, I leave Da to chat with Myra and Garnet while Dionysus and I go down to the heads room to catch up with Sloan and to talk with HaiLe about our theories.

"Hey, Fi." Kevin jogs over to greet us. Bizzy is playing with the younger feline kids, and Jackson and Imari seem to have made friends with Binx.

"Where's Sloan?" I scan the room.

Kevin laughs. "He's in the washroom cleaning up."

"Cleaning up? Did one of the kids barf on him or something?"

"No, they didn't." Sloan steps back into the room with a cloth in his hand, wiping the shoulder of his shirt free of pink paint. "Dillan asked me to help him move a cabinet up to his room, and when we portaled in, he shot me."

"Rude. He 'Good Samaritan'd' you. He suckered you in with a plea for help and shot you."

"That sounds more like he 'Boy Who Cried Wolf'd' you," Kevin says.

I see how that works.

Sloan doesn't seem to care. "Either way, he assassinated me and knocked me out of the game."

I hug him and wave a hand over the paint, removing it with a spell Fionn taught me to remove blood. "There, now you're perfectly presentable again."

Sloan glances down and smiles. "Better. Thanks."

"What's a wife for if not to clean her hubby's clothes and make him look good?"

Sloan laughs. "I can think of a dozen things I'd prefer ye to focus yer skills on."

I grin and start counting off my fingers as I think about that. "I bet I could guess the first five."

"Or not." Kevin raises a hand between us. "Let's leave some things to the intrigue of mystery, shall we?"

I give him that and head over to speak with HaiLe about everything we discussed upstairs.

"Guides through a troubled time," HaiLe repeats, worry clouding her golden cat's eyes. "You think the children are tied to one another somehow?"

"It's only a theory at this point, but we believe so. Magical chaos tends to find me, so we're working under the assumption that you arrived when you did by the guidance of fae destiny or the magic of the universe or whatever guiding force you believe in."

"As much as I hate that it's happening, I'm so very grateful to have found you and your friends. I honestly don't think we would have survived another week with the Hunters in Green tracking Binx."

"Did they give ye any idea why they wanted him?" Sloan asks.

HaiLe shakes her head. "No. Just from the moment one of them spotted him in the street, they were after us and wouldn't stop."

"Well, you're here now, and you're safe. My brothers and Sarah will ensure you stay that way."

She reaches forward and takes my hand. Her charcoal fur is so incredibly soft, which is a contrast to the calloused pads of her paw. "Thank you so much."

Merlin steps into the room and waits by the door. When he looks at the kids, I understand why he's here.

I turn to HaiLe and broach the subject. "We plan on having Jackson and Imari examined by Sloan's father for physical clues as to what the mark might mean and by Merlin to gauge if there are any magical changes. We'd like to have Binx checked over too, so we can get a baseline of information as early as we can."

She glances at where her boy is laughing and playing with Imari and Jackson. The three have become fast friends and are making the most of a strange time. "What would they do to them?"

I wave Merlin closer. "How will you be checking for magical changes?"

"For now, I thought I'd simply sit with them and get a sense of their powers as they play. We have a human druid, a Moon Called shifter, a fawn, and a member of the feline folk. There must be a reason for such a diverse group. I'm hoping simply spending time with them and registering their natural magical abilities might tell me something."

I check with HaiLe. "So, nothing invasive. Just him sensing and observing."

HaiLe brushes a paw over her whiskers and nods. "All right. That sounds harmless enough."

Merlin extends his hand, and when she reciprocates, he clasps her wrist as she grips his. "I am Merlin. Your boy couldn't be in better hands than here with us, I promise. We'll figure out what's going on and help them get through whatever comes."

HaiLe sighs. "Thank you."

---

We leave Binx, Jackson, and Imari to play magic tricks on the floor with Merlin. Sloan *poofs* us upstairs to gather Da and Garnet to return to the security building so we can chat with Isilon.

"Ye understand what I'm sayin' though, aye? If Isilon is the city, he can project himself anywhere within the boundary walls. We don't need to come here."

"I get that, but I'd rather not invite the sentience that possessed Emmet into his home or worse, into our private space where our family is staying. I like the idea that we keep this a working relationship."

Garnet arches an ebony brow and gives me a look.

Sloan chuckles. "Far be it from me to bust yer boundary balloon, *a ghra*. Whatever helps ye get through the day, I'll play along."

Awesome. Who could ask for more?

I step away from the three of them and glance around at the ceiling. "Isilon? Will you speak with us, please? We have a question and hoped you might be able to help."

When the likeness of Mr. Epema appears in the security office, Da frowns over at me. "Isn't that one of yer high school teachers?"

I grin. "Yeah. I asked Isilon to do that so he doesn't creep me out."

"Him embodyin' someone ye know doesn't creep ye out?"

"Not as much as when he tried to talk to me wearing a Sloan suit, no."

Sloan makes a face. "Ye never mentioned that."

"Yeah, well, busy busy."

Garnet waves the conversation along. "With that in mind, can we get to it?"

"Yeah, sure." I address Isilon and consider what I want to ask him. "We've encountered four kids branded with a crescent moon on their foreheads over the past months. From what we know, this happened before. Can you tell us anything about that?"

"Of course, I can."

When no information is forthcoming, I go over my question again. "Will you please tell us about that?"

"Of course. To my knowledge, crescent moons spontaneously appearing on beings has occurred three other times in this realm and six times in other realms."

"Oh. That's more often than I thought."

Da shrugs. "Likely because we wouldn't know about it happening in other realms."

*True.* "What can you tell us?"

"The phenomenon is known as being Crescent Called, and it occurs when a dangerous time of uncertainty is approaching."

Garnet growls. "What are four children supposed to do to negate that danger?"

"Nothing. The children marked by the crescent moons are the guides to overpower the conflict, not the tools to battle it."

Well, that makes all of us feel a little better.

"How do they guide us?" I ask.

"In different ways. As time passes, each of the children will develop a unique skill. When combined with the others, it will pave the way for success in the battles ahead."

"What kind of powers?" Garnet asks. "Each of the children, so far as we know, is already a member of the empowered community. Is their power based on their species traits or something more?"

"Something more."

"Can you tell us more than that?"

"I cannot. Their gifts will manifest based on the danger approaching, their innate abilities, and their personalities. It would be impossible to try to guess what might manifest. The possibilities are endless."

I draw a deep breath and consider that. "What's the timeline? How soon will these abilities manifest and need to be tested against the incoming foe?"

"I cannot say."

"Yet you claim to know all," Garnet grumbles.

"All of which is past and present. I cannot predict the future."

"Okay, well, you've been helpful anyway. Thank you. Now, since we've worked for two days bringing guests into your streets and getting them settled, will you please release our friends to return home? If there is danger approaching, we must make preparations."

Sloan nods. "One of the children is living unaware in the human realm. We promised her mother if we found out anything, we would notify her and help keep the child safe."

"The little fawn in Montréal." Isilon nods. "Yes, you should notify her mother. Although, there is another great source of protection building in Isabella's circle of friends. It is not your protection she needs."

"Then whose?" I ask.

"That is not for me to say. Let me assure you, though, the energy awakening in Montréal is formidable. Look to develop allies there."

"Yes, the tributaries there have created a natural collection of prana energy larger than anywhere else in Canada," I agree.

"I speak not of the power awakening but the beings harnessing those powers. Develop your allies from that pool of strength."

I meet Garnet's gaze, and he nods. "Whatever we need to do to help these kids—consider it done."

"What about—"

An alarm goes off, and Nikon hurries over to the view screen. "We've got someone at the portal door, but they aren't trying to hail entry. They're trying to force their way in."

We all rush over to see what we're dealing with.

All except Isilon. "They are Dark Weaver initiates. Scouts, you would call them."

"Will they be able to force entry?" Nikon asks.

"They managed it in the past, yes. That is exactly why I wanted the Boundary Gate sealed shut and left inactive. Opening it so many times has notified the enemy my city is once again occupied."

The cold bite in Isilon's tone is petulant. He might be a sentient wonder and a magical mystery, but he's also a spoiled child.

"We'll take care of it." I hold out my hand. "Garnet, take Da and me to the gate. Sloan, portal back to the palace and get my brothers, Merlin, and the Greeks to join the fight."

Everyone nods, and we flash out.

## CHAPTER TWENTY

We arrive at the gate too late to stop the breach but in time to catch the invading force as they push through into our domain. I call my armor forward, release Bruin, and call Dart. *We have Dark Weaver minions busting through the Boundary Gate. Care to join?*

*On our way.*

"The dragons are coming." I call Birga to my hand as Dionysus arrives with the second half of our team. "Welcome."

"Thanks for the invite," Dillan says, still buckling the toggle of his cloak.

"Greek, can I get a boost to higher ground?" Calum points at the roofline opposite the gate and Dionysus nods. The two of them are gone in the next moment.

Da has his staff in hand and is advancing with Dillan. Merlin and Sloan are our strongest casters and attack on a magical front. Garnet has shifted to his lion form and is currently shaking one of our opponents by the neck. Eva has her scythe out and is grinning so wide her dimples are showing.

Birga and I jump into the fray next to Bruin and start to play our part.

The two dozen invaders seem surprised to be met with such resistance. After the devastation they caused last time, they should expect a strong opposition.

They're good fighters but don't have the same will to win as we do. In battle, motivation is key. If you don't know what you're fighting for, there's no sense fighting.

Fionn taught me that.

I join my battle bear, and we get our groove on.

There's nothing quite like battling with your brothers-in-arms, which in my case are mostly my brothers-in-life.

"Fi, down!"

I duck and roll to the side as a bolt of black energy passes through the air where I'd been standing. It hits the wall of the next building and spreads like a creepy shadow up the stone wall.

"I suggest not getting hit by that black magic." I get back to my feet and spin Birga in my hand as I go after the caster.

The street is in a state of full riot when Dionysus rams a metal bar through the stomach of one of our opponents. It bursts through his back, and I wince. "That was brutal, Tarzan."

"He hurt Nikky. He deserves to suffer."

I turn to check on Nikon and scramble to get to him. He's on one knee but curled over like he is I can't see what's wrong.

*"Impenetrable Sphere."* I throw the bubble of protection around him, then Bruin and I cut down the men in our path to reach him.

"Are you okay?"

Nikon spits blood on the cobbled ground and stands, wiping more blood from his face. "I turned exactly the wrong way at exactly the wrong moment. I'm good. My head's just spinning."

He moves to take a step and staggers to the side.

I release Birga to use both hands to catch him and help him back to the ground.

"Shit. I don't feel so good, Red."

When he looks up at me, I can see why. "You've got one helluva gash to the head, sweetie. I'm pulling you from the game. You need that looked at."

"I don't think I can portal."

Straightening, I search for someone who can. Sloan and Merlin are essential. They're holding the advance. Garnet's lion isn't easy to corral. The choice is clear. "Tarzan, take Nikon to Wallace in the palace. ASAP."

Dionysus snaps the neck of the guy he's fighting with and disappears at the same time Nikon is gone too.

"You've got a runner!" Calum shouts from above. "Sketchy dude headed out of the courtyard that way." He points.

"On it. Emmet, you're with me."

---

Abandoning the battle at the gate, I launch into the nearest alley and gun it. Emmet's footfalls thunder tight to my heels, and the sound is a comfort. My stride eats the distance as my heart races inside my chest.

"This guy goes down, Em. No way we're losing him in this city with innocents living here."

"Agreed."

As the commotion of the Boundary Gate grows faint behind us, we cut through a side street. The rhythmic sound of footsteps connecting with stone echoes hollowly on my right.

I check with Em, and he nods. He hears it too.

We race on.

A shadow overhead blocks the sun and casts the magnificent silhouettes of dragons onto the stone streets. *We've got a runner, Dart. See if you can track him. I think he's one street over.*

*Got him. Yes. One street to your right, heading toward the city pond.*

*Don't lose him.*

*We won't.*

"The dragons have him. I'll cut over on the next street."

"I'm with you."

I lean right at the next side street and pump my fists. The city really is charming. Not that I'm sightseeing at the moment, but it's hard not to notice.

*Fi, you're going to crash right into—*

The collision is epic and lifts me off my feet. I flip, flailing mid-air and faceplanting into the pond.

Water invades my nostrils at a violent speed, and I resurface sputtering and choking.

Hacking for air, I'm thankful Emmet is with me because he's taking control of our runner.

That leaves me free to gag on pond water and get to my feet. Who are we kidding? The pond in a magical oasis is turquoise blue and magical. It's not the least bit boggy or gross.

Thank you, Mother Nature, for small miracles.

Struggling to drag myself back to the low stone retaining wall around the pond's edge, I choke my lungs clear.

Emmet is struggling to get our perp back to solid ground. I'm worried about him and that dark magic the other one used on Nikon.

Dart and his siblings are circling, and I have a better idea. "Em, back off and leave him to the dragons."

Emmet backhands the guy a good one and lets him flop on the surface. My brother drags his legs through the water over to me, and I signal for the dragons to take over. *Crunch and munch, buddy. He's a Dark Weaver, so be quick about killing him before he magics you in any way.*

Dart dives with talons extended and snatches him out of the water like a massive eagle on a fish. The crunch of bones is immediate. Then he tosses the body in the air.

Saxa swoops in, bites off his head and most of his shoulders, and tosses him again. The blood spatter is impressive, but not as impressive as when Dart and Bryvanay each snap an end and pull him into two.

When Dart tosses his head back and chews, I catch Emmet's grimace.

I laugh. "Hey, dragons' gotta eat."

"Yeah, I know, but that doesn't gross you out even a little?"

I shake my head. "Nope. It's only the bone-crunching I don't like. But I didn't hear a thing that time."

We hear the scuffle of a vicious fight coming our way. Cursing. We pull ourselves out of the pond and start sloshing our way back to the fight.

There's a sharp crack of impact and then the raining sound of stone debris.

There's a grunt, a crash, then Dillan is chuckling. "Fuck you, assholes."

Emmet and I run, searching for where the hand-to-hand is happening, but the hits echo off the stone and bounce at us from all angles.

I don't know which way to go. "Where is he?"

The sounds of the battle tighten in my gut. Rory is screeching, but that doesn't help either. *Bruin, where's Dillan? He needs help. Dart, help us find Dillan.*

"It must be a spell to throw us off," Emmet says, his head on a pivot as he tries to figure this out.

I focus on clarifying my vision of what's happening around me. It doesn't feel like a confusion spell. My mind isn't muddled.

"See the Unseen," I call, focusing on anything that might be boggling us. *"Dispel Magic."*

Emmet is casting too.

I'm not sure which one of us got it right, but the effect is immediate and far more powerful than I expected.

It's also timed at exactly the moment when an incoming blast of black magic is about to hit me. I shove Emmet and don't get completely out of the way. The stone of the walkway comes up hard and fast. I tuck but barely save my head from cracking on the cobbled stone.

My shoulder hits and my arm bends awkwardly behind me. White-hot pain shoots down my right side and I blink, my vision spotty.

The guys attacking Dillan are there. Not twenty feet away, they're beating on Dillan like a dog in the street. Rory is down and laid out on the stone.

I scramble to my feet, ignoring the lethargic response of my right arm. Fuck, I can't even flex my palm enough to call Birga.

Hand-to-hand is out.

*Bruin, I need you, buddy.*

The fact that he hasn't come already has me worried. Even if he can't get to me, he always answers.

*Dart, are you guys up for another round?*

*Happy to join in.*

*Emmet and I need to get Dillan clear. Then you can eat this one raw, fried, or however you like.*

*You're the best.*

Holding up my left palm, I call what power I can. *"Impenetrable Sphere."* I throw the protective bubble over Emmet and me as we rush this asshole.

"The dragons will take care of them. Em, you gotta get Dillan. I'll get Rory."

"You've got a gimpy arm there, little sister."

"Yeah, I decided we could beat these guys with one hand behind my back."

Emmet snorts. "Such a show-off."

We move in, and I've got my left hand up and am conjuring everything I can think of to get the job done. *"Fire Storm."* I throw the roaring flames at the two Dark Weaver minions and have never been so happy to be dive-bombed by dragons in my life.

The dragons take the two by surprise and their attention shifts.

Their distraction isn't long, but it costs them. Emmet and I get in close enough that he blasts them with a pulse of energy. They're knocked staggering to the side and whirl around.

The instant they're spun, I grab Rory's talons and retreat fast while Emmet grabs Dillan.

*"Bestial Strength."* I'm getting away when a hard punch to the back of my right shoulder steals my breath, and I go down in a rush. Struggling in an all-out brawl isn't something I'm equipped to do at the moment, but I'm not getting a choice.

The men are speaking a language I've never heard before, but I like to think they're saying, "Holy shit, we should never have come here to take on these people. They are way too much awesomeness for us."

"That's right, dickwad. Way too much." Being on my back gives me the distinct advantage of timing. As Utiss comes in, talons outstretched, I let the man attacking me stand and hover over me.

When I get really flat to the ground, he realizes too late he's the next dragon snack.

Too bad, sucker.

His friend straightens, watching my guy get carried off, which is very helpful because Cadmus snatches him up without effort.

Emmet drops to the ground, and I scootch over to see the damage done.

"Damn, Dillan's in rough shape."

Emmet sinks to the cobbled ground beside me. "He ain't the only one, sista. You're not doing much better."

I wave that away with the hand I can move. "Meh, at least I'm still conscious."

I'm third in the triage of injuries, and it becomes apparent that the hidden city of Isilon is woefully ill-prepared for medical emergencies. We set up in the Great Hall, and it's a bloody mess.

Wallace is a champion and dives in regardless of having no clinic, no supplies, and no staff to help.

Sloan is able to back him up to a certain extent, but the crisis then becomes the fact that we've got no medical tools, no sterile wraps, or anything they need to staunch bleeding, treat poisoning, or combat dark magic.

"Isilon," I shout, half slouched over in my chair. "You need to lift the lockdown. I swear we'll continue to work to fortify the city and we'll be involved in assuring the people who come here aren't consumed by the Dark Weavers, but now you're endangering us."

Da snaps, glaring around the room, "If ye haven't clued into it yet, intentionally causin' one of us harm will mean the end of our loyalty to this city. Ye can rot in hibernation fer eternity fer all we care."

Mr. Epema appears before us looking vexed. "Threatening me to get your way doesn't win over my goodwill, Niall Cumhaill."

"Aye, I'm well aware, ye selfish fuck. It's what ye've done to us the past two days. Keepin' us here against our will at the cost of our lives both back home and here hasn't warmed us up to the idea of helpin' ye. In fact, perhaps I'll speak to Mother Nature and remove my sons from their duties here altogether."

Isilon's expression falls. "You would take my champion away?"

Da snaps his fingers. "Like that, I would. If ye can't be trusted to put the lives of the folks within yer city ahead of yer selfish needs, yer not the city that deserves my family's loyalty."

The idea of that seems to take him completely off-guard. "I only wanted to ensure—"

"We don't have time fer yer justifications. We've got injured people here who need proper medical care. Lift yer fuckin' lockdown so we can take them to Wallace's clinic."

Isilon straightens. "I don't appreciate your tone, Niall Cumhaill, but I will comply. Consider yourselves free to travel beyond the city's boundaries."

"Thank you, Isilon." I wave at him. "You made the right choice."

The moment Isilon leaves, I find myself on one of the gurneys at Wallace's clinic. Sloan is there, tending to Dillan, and Wallace is calling for his staff to get in there to assist.

There's a moment of triage chaos, and I tell them to focus on Nikon and Dillan.

"I'll be fine," I assure them. "Maybe broken. Maybe dislocated. Whatever it is, it's more painful than dangerous."

"Take this, and we'll get back to you." The brunette nurse hands me a gummy bear. "It'll dull the pain."

I chew on the little purple bear and swallow it. Mmm, grape.

"Da really chewed Isilon a new one." Dionysus pulls up a chair to sit with me. "When he's all fired up, he's a scary man."

I chuckle. "Never threaten the well-being of someone in Clan Cumhaill. It won't end well."

Dionysus crosses his arms on the mattress of the gurney and sets his chin on his arms. "I wish healing was one of my powers. If it was, I'd make sure none of you ever had to hurt."

I reach over with my left hand and squeeze his elbow. "There's only so much we can do to insulate our lives, sweetie. Part of being human is being reminded of how precious our lives are. We need to get a few knocks and bumps for that to happen. Besides, you have lots of other gifts to offer."

He sighs. "My gifts aren't useful to your family. Most of you are monogamous and married. Calum and Kevin are the only ones who partake in my kind of magic."

I laugh. "That's not what I meant, Tarzan. You have more strengths to offer than your sexual awesomeness."

"You're right. I also throw a damn good party."

"More than that too."

"You think so?"

"I know so. You're loyal, protective, fun, and bring joy to our family. You're a skilled fighter with a sharp mind and you portal us all over the world without complaint or hesitation. Your gifts are many and appreciated."

He moves his hand to squeeze my wrist. "I don't like you to hurt...or Nikky...or Dillan."

"I know, but now that we're here, Wallace and his team will patch us all up, and we'll be good as new." I yawn and close my eyes. "Hey, Tarzan?"

"Yeah?"

"My gummy bear is taking hold, and I'm getting floaty. If I fall asleep, don't panic, 'kay?"

"Promise. Let the floaties take you, Jane. I'll be here when you wake up."

# CHAPTER TWENTY-ONE

I wake sometime later, and Dionysus is, indeed, there waiting for me. I'm on a recovery bed, and he's stretched out beside me snoring while Sloan sits in one of the cushy recliners in the corner.

"Nikon and Dillan?"

"Both recoverin' and sleepin' it off. Da will stay here with them and let us know when they wake. I'm assumin' Nikon will be well enough to portal himself and yer brother back to the palace when they're back on their feet. If not, I'll come get them, or yer bedfellow can stay and take care of transportation for us."

He lifts his chin and gestures at Dionysus sleeping beside me.

"What's wrong with this picture?" I whisper, giggling. "Isn't it you who's supposed to be there?"

"I'm there when it counts."

"For the good stuff, for sure."

His smile sobers. "It bothers him to see ye hurt."

I glance at Dionysus sleeping and can't help loving him. When he's at rest, all the tension and mistrust he tries to hide from the world dissolves, and he looks innocent and happy.

"I love seeing him like this."

"Quiet and still, ye mean?"

I grin. "At peace with the world."

"Aye, I see it too. Now, would ye like to get back to things?"

It all rushes back to me, and I realize I can move my arm. "I'm fixed."

"Ye are. Everythin' is back where it's supposed to be, and there are no lastin' effects."

"I missed it all."

"Seems so."

"Those purple gummy bears pack a wallop."

He chuckles. "Aye, they can. Ye don't see it comin' when it's in a sweet treat. I used to nick a few now and then in my uni days and send myself off if I needed to settle the storm in my mind."

"Drugs and stealing. I'm shocked. I've married a hoodlum."

He shrugs. "Yer stuck with me now. Like ye said. Yer a no returns bride."

"I did say that, didn't I?"

"Ye did, and I'll hold ye to it."

"Please do."

We sit for a moment taking in the completion of another adventure. Then, I ease to the edge of the bed and sit up. Rolling my shoulder, I test my mobility.

"Jane? Are you awake?"

I twist to look behind me. "Yep, and I'm all fixed. I'm going to check on Nikon and my brother. Do you want to come or snooze some more?"

"No. I'll come. I want to check on them too."

The three of us move to the room next door and find Dillan out cold with Eva sitting in the chair next to him holding Rory.

"How are the patients in here?" I move over to check on the little purple dragon.

Rory is curled up in Eva's arm with her head tucked into her ribs, hiding from the world. "She's still upset, but I think she'll be fine once she heals enough to merge with him."

"How's D doing?" I study my brother.

Most of the bruises have been taken care of, but he hasn't been able to shower yet, so dried blood mats his hair.

"I have it on good authority that he'll make a full recovery."

"I suppose you would know."

She grins. "You can take the angel out of reaping, but you can't take the reaper out of the angel."

I bend and stroke Rory's purple spine. "Rest, little one. Your daddy is tougher than anyone I know. He'll be fine."

Eva nods, and I leave her to sit with them in peace.

"Nikon's room is across the hall." Sloan points the way.

We cross to his room, and he's sleeping it off too.

"Tarzan? Will you stay with Nikon? I don't want him to be alone, but I also need to get back to the palace and check on things. Do you mind?"

He steps over and sits in the recliner beside the bed. "Done deal. I'll keep you posted and bring them both back when they're ready."

"Thanks, sweetie." I take another look at Nikon and am thankful everyone came out of the battle in one piece.

I can't exactly say unscathed but patched back together at least.

"Let's say goodbye and thank you to your father. Then, I want to go back and assess the fallout of what happened."

Sloan places a gentle hand on the small of my back and leads me out to the clinic proper.

---

"Good. Yer back." Da comes over to hug me when we arrive at the Great Room of the palace. "How are Nikon and yer brother?"

"Both out of danger and sleeping it off. Dionysus and Eva are sitting at their bedsides and will bring them back when they wake."

"That's good news."

"Fi, my girl, howeyah?" Gran rushes over to hug me, and Granda follows. "Ye look well enough."

"Yeah, I'm fine. Wallace patched me back up as always. No harm done."

Granda hugs me and kisses my forehead. "That's good to hear."

"Who all is still here? Now that Isilon lifted the lockdown, I assume most people have gone home."

"Some fer sure," Da confirms. "Fionn sends his love, but the Hunter-gods couldn't hold him here any longer. Anyx took Aiden, Kinu, and the wee ones back to Toronto. Garnet took yer musician back, but I think the lion and Myra were waitin' to see that ye arrive safe home."

I make a mental note of whom I need to reach out to and point at the stand-up whiteboard against the far wall. "What's all this?"

Brenny turns from where he's writing on the board and puts the cap on his marker. "With more and more people here, it's becoming apparent we need to whip this city into shape. This is the beginning of a hidden city To-Do list."

I move in to get a better look and read off some of the tasks.

Create a flower garden for the Quasti on the hillside on the other side of the prana river.

Resurrect the old healer's clinic and stock it for emergencies.

Ensure the aqueducts are clean and deliver water to the first quarter.

Prepare more homes to be ready for incoming citizens.

Create a community job list after reviewing intake information.

Revive the tavern and arrange live music once a week.

I laugh at that last one. "Who is in charge of live music for the tavern inn?"

Emmet laughs. "We've volunteered Dionysus. He said you put

him in charge of the 'Welcome to the Island' events, so we went with it."

Right. "Yep. I said that. Okay, cool, let him run with that. He'll have tons of fun."

"I can help get the tavern up and running," Liam offers. "On one condition."

Brenny looks over and shrugs. "What's that?"

"Your sister has to tend bar with me once a week on the event nights."

I look at him. "Once a week? Can you spare that kind of time from Shenanigans?"

He nods. "Honestly, since Mom and your dad moved to Ireland and you guys all got busy with wild empowered stuff, and Brendan died…running Shenanigans isn't as much fun as it used to be."

I know exactly how he feels.

The idea of reclaiming a bit of that part of my life gets my blood buzzing in my veins. Could we do it? Can we recapture that and have some family fun again?

Why the hell not?

I look at Sloan to see if he'd like to weigh in. Another commitment means more time when we're not alone or focused on us.

Sloan smiles and shakes his head. "I know exactly what yer thinkin' and if it brings ye joy in yer otherwise stressful life, I'll happily take up a barstool and drink a few pints watchin' ye do yer thing. I'm all for it."

Man, I love that guy.

"Monday or Tuesday nights could work. Shenanigans never needs two on the bar at the beginning of the week. I'm sure they can handle it. Sure, we'll have to work around my liaison duties, but I'd love to pour drinks with you one night a week."

Liam waggles his brows at me. "Look at us, getting the band back together."

I love the idea. "Yeah, Liam and I will tackle the tavern."

"I'll take on the task of getting the clinic up and runnin'," Sloan volunteers.

Emmet beams and grabs a marker, writing our names beside the jobs we're claiming.

"I'll nurture the flower garden for the Quasti," Gran says. "If someone will portal me over the river."

"I've got you, Gran," Dionysus says, joining us with Nikon at his side. "Those little green fuzzballs are too cute. I'm happy to help them build their home."

"Welcome back, son." Da goes over to pat Nikon on the shoulder. "Glad yer back on yer feet."

He touches the side of his head, which is still a matted bloody mess. "It looks worse than it was. You know how head wounds bleed."

"Merely a flesh wound," Brenny quotes, his Monty Python impression spot on.

"I'm not dead yet," Calum adds.

"Yes, you are."

"I'm getting better."

"No, you're not."

Da chuckles. "Ignore them. Sit. Get yourself something to eat and drink."

"Where's Dillan?" Emmet asks.

"He and Eva are going to enjoy his convalescence in private," Dionysus says.

I don't blame them. "Well, this is their wedding weekend too."

"Right you are, Jane."

"Okay, so back to the jobs list," Brendan says. "Have we got any other takers?"

Sarah comes in holding Ireland in her arms. "I'll take on the preparation and assignment of houses...if maybe Nikon wouldn't mind snappin' me back to civilization fer housewares and supplies when needed?"

Nikon sits at the long table in the center of the room and

pours himself a drink. "Sign me up. I'll even finance the shopping."

"Really?" Sarah's grin widens as her eyes twinkle with mischief. "Ye'll be my sugar daddy, will ye?"

Nikon chokes on his drink and sputters before answering that one. "Uh...yeah, that works for me."

Huzzah...and just like that, Clan Cumhaill comes through again.

---

I leave the brainstorming of the Great Room and go to check on the others. I knock on the door for the vampires, but there's no answer, so I go to Garnet and Myra's room.

"Hey, you're still here." I hug my bestie and step into her suite.

"I told Garnet I wouldn't leave until I got to see that you've been put back together and wish you well on your honeymoon."

"I appreciate it. Is he around?"

"No. He took Xavier and Benjamin home. Something must've happened with them because Xavier was acting even more dark and broody than usual."

"Yeah, he didn't do well with being confined here. I'm sure he'll feel better once he gets back to Toronto and can check on Karuna. Laurel mentioned she's had a bad flu the past week."

"I'm sure that didn't help his mood any."

"No. I'm sure it didn't."

Myra walks over to the oversized sofa by the fireplace and pats the seat cushion. "Come. Sit with me. Tell me how you're really doing."

I accept the invitation, but I'm not sure where I am with things. "Everything seems to be in a big muddle, you know?"

"I know a lot has happened in the past three days. Maybe the events haven't all settled over you yet."

"Maybe."

I sit with her, quietly thinking about everything that's gone on over the past few days. "We had so much fun during our family fun day. Brendan and Emmet arranged these crazy games for us, Gran and Shannon made more food than ten armies could eat, and we were all together, you know? It was like old times."

"That sounds lovely."

"It was. And the dragons..." I wipe the tears stinging my eyes and laugh at myself. "I don't know why I'm crying."

"You don't have to have a reason. Just keep talking. Odds are, you'll figure it out."

I swipe my fingers under my eyes and continue. "The dragons are so happy here. They can fly and mingle with their kind. Dart has never complained, but I feel how much happier he is here than in our backyard in Toronto."

"Uh-huh. And?"

"I miss Emmet. I know we're both adults and I'm married now, but I hate being so far away from him. It's like a dull ache in my heart I can't get rid of."

"I think it's lovely how close the two of you are."

"Were. See, that's what breaks my heart. We were so close, but now his destiny has him confined to living here."

"Where does that leave you?"

"In Toronto without him...and Da...and Gran and Granda...and Brenny."

Myra presses her hand over mine. "Duck, what is it? Put it into words. I know it's there on the tip of your tongue. Just say it, and I bet we can figure it out from there."

I look into Myra's warm eyes, and I stop fighting. It's just her and me, and I trust that she won't ever hold my ramblings against me...even if what I think is selfish and silly.

"What if I'm not happy in Toronto anymore? What if it was only where I belonged because that's where my family thrived? Here I am at the beginning of my life with Sloan. He moved across the world for me, bought me a house, and has completely sacrificed his history and passions for me, and now...I'm not sure that's what I want."

The warmth of tears on my cheeks grows. Then Myra gets up and brings a box of tissues over for me. "Duck, why do you think Garnet created a portal door to the compound? We tried living in that house in Mount Pleasant. It's a lovely house, but he missed the sun and his pride, and I missed Leniya. So, we made it work. We live in the compound in the savannah, and I spend my days with my home tree."

I blow my nose and blink up at her. "What do you think I should do?"

She chuckles. "I think you're discovering that on your own without me putting ideas into your head. The questions I want you to ask yourself are, what makes you truly happy? Then, how can I make that happen?"

I think about that, and my chest feels tight. "But Sloan's built his Shrine and Nikon bought us a building, and Max, Garnet, and Andy have carved out this place for me leading the way for the fae."

"Every one of those people loves you. Be honest with them. Explain where your mind and heart are, and I guarantee you, the way will become clear."

"You think so?"

Myra winks. "I know so. Trust me, duck. You don't live two centuries as a gatherer of knowledge without picking up a few things."

I lean in and hug her. Over the past two years, Myra has been my confidante, friend, mentor, and the closest thing I've had to a mother since Mam died.

Shannon has always been good to us and taken care of us, but she was Auntie Shannon. She had her life and Liam and the pub to worry about.

Myra's just mine.

"You know...I told Da on Friday night how sad I was that

Mam couldn't be here this weekend. I wanted her to help me get dressed, see me get married, and give me the life talk that would set me on the right path to a life of happiness. You've ticked every one of those boxes for me. Thank you. I hope you know how much I love you."

Myra leans forward and pulls me into a breath-squishing hug. "Oh, duck. I'm honored. I love you right back."

# CHAPTER TWENTY-TWO

I leave Myra to finish packing and strike off to find my newlywed hubby. Maybe Myra's right. Maybe I've known all along things were heading in this direction. Maybe that's why my Team Trouble cases have been hurting my soul so much lately.

Not being able to bring HaiLe's mate home to her.

The trouble in New Orleans.

The conflict with the other guild in San Francisco.

Hell, I even burst out in tears when Dillan suggested he and Eva move out on their own.

Maybe it's all been because my foundation was crumbling. My family unit was getting away from me.

As those thoughts coalesce in my mind, they solidify and take hold.

*Yeah.* That's the tension in my chest...the feeling I've been fighting that something inside me isn't right.

I'm lost in my thoughts as I climb the stairs and almost bump into Sloan on his way down. "Och, there ye are." He grips my forearms to keep me from tipping back on the stairs. "I was comin'—"

His words cut off and his brows crease. A wash of his magical signature tingles over my skin, and the two of us are standing in our room.

"Ye've been cryin' again. Fiona, ye need to tell me what has yer emotions so twisted up. Ye've cried more in the past few weeks than ye did in the two years before that."

I take his hand and draw him over to the sofa. "I haven't been able to figure out what's wrong with me until Myra and I sat for a heart-to-heart."

"Ye came up with yer answer?"

"I think so...and maybe I knew somewhere in the back of my mind, but I didn't want to go there."

Sloan takes my hand in his. "Why, luv? What is it?"

I see the worry in his gaze and read his fears. "It's not you or anything about us. We're solid. You're the best and most right thing in my life. Please don't look like I'm about to tear your heart out."

He lets out a long breath. "I'm glad to hear it because fer a minute there, I thought ye were about to tear my heart out."

"No, but I'm not sure you'll be all that happy with me either...so, I'll just say it and see if Myra's as smart as I think she is."

"All right. Speak yer truth. I'm listenin'."

I do. I tell Sloan about the ache I feel being so far from Emmet and how I miss Brenny, Da, and my grandparents.

I confess how selfish I feel for not being content with my life given how much he and others have sacrificed to make me happy.

And I tell him how much this weekend has taught me that I need to be closer to my family and have Dart and Saxa happy and that maybe Myra's right, and I might want to commute to Toronto but maybe live here.

"I'm so sorry, hotness. Nikon bought us the Acropolis, and you've worked so hard at building your shrine of enchanted objects. It's stupid for me to be pining for my family when they're never more than a portal away, but I feel disconnected from them, and I—"

Sloan presses a finger over my lips. "Ye don't need to apologize to me, luv, and I expect Nikon, Garnet, and all the others will feel the same. I love the home we've built in Toronto, but if it's not the place fer forever, that's fine. Today is the first day of our future, however that looks, and as long as the two of us take it on together, I'm happy."

"What about your shrine?"

"Dionysus can help me create a new secure location here, and I'll move the objects. There's no reason I can't still work downstairs when we go to Toronto in the morning to get the case files for the week. And there's no reason we can't use our Toronto home as a home base when we're not here. Honestly, luv. Nothin' about this is as bad as ye fear."

I draw a deep breath. "It's not what I planned."

"There ye have it. The best-laid plans of mice and men."

I'm still not quite wrapping my head around all this. Could it really be that easy? "Do you *want* to live here? Be honest. I want the bold truth."

He sits back and considers that. "I like the idea of livin' closer to home, sure. From here, I can visit my Da as much and as often as I like, and I don't have to recharge and miss out on what's happenin' at home."

"Yeah, that would be nice for you. But what about life here? I want our home to work for both of us."

"As much as I love yer brothers, I don't think I want a room across the hall, no. I'd like more privacy than that. But as far as I can tell, no one has been using floors four through ten, and there are a great many houses outside the palace walls. Would close be close enough?"

Now it's my turn to consider things. "Sure. Maybe we can find a beautiful old crumbly building in the city and claim it. Would you like that?"

He chuckles. "We could take a tour and see what appeals."

"Scouting the neighborhood. I like that. I know from Kinu and Aiden it's important to be in the right school district." Thinking about Kinu and the kids is like a dagger lodged in my ribs.

"She'll come around, luv," Sloan says, reading me.

I want to believe that, but maybe it's good to get some distance. If Kinu truly believes I put the kids in danger, maybe I should relocate.

I imagine what that might look like...us here. Will that fill up my well? "If we lived outside the palace, could we share meals with them? I think I miss that most of all."

Sloan nods. "How about we share all meals except maybe a dinner or two a week which are reserved for us alone."

"Like a date night?"

"Aye, like that."

"I can get behind that." I rub the center of my chest. "It feels like such an upheaval."

"In what sense?"

"A move like this affects more than the two of us. Bruin has his lady friends in the Don, and Dionysus has his loft and is just getting settled. And what about our grove family? Pip and Nilm just had the baby." Thinking about uprooting everyone like that makes me nauseous. "It's too much."

I can't let my wants alter the course of everyone else's lives.

"May I weigh in?"

We turn to where Dionysus is standing over by the door. "Sorry...I didn't mean to intrude, but Fi pressed her pendant, and I thought I was needed."

I drop the silver pendant and sigh. "Sorry, Tarzan. I didn't realize I was playing with it. Not your fault."

He steps closer. "I didn't mean to eavesdrop, but can I make a suggestion?"

"Of course. What are you thinking?"

"Couldn't we have Nikky make a portal door between a room in your house in Toronto and a room here in the palace? It could be like the portal for Garnet's compound. We could spell it so only family could access it. Then you wouldn't have to decide right this minute about moving."

I check to see what Sloan thinks about that. "It's not a bad idea."

He agrees. "We could try it out and see if it eases some of yer anxiety about bein' so far from yer family. It certainly would give us time to think through the pros and cons of such a move."

"It would also allow us to have meals with the family and for you to *poof* off to see your dad without using up all your wayfarer mojo for the next two or three days."

Sloan nods. "Aye, it's a sound idea. Thanks, sham."

Dionysus nods. "And just so you know? I don't care about my loft. I care about you. If you move and don't mind me following, I'll be there. I lurve you, Jane."

"Thanks. I lurve you too."

"And I can move your grove and build you a crumbly castle and do whatever you need to make you feel at home."

I get up and hug him. "You're the best. I'd be lost without you."

"Same."

When I ease back, I draw a deep breath. "Let's shelve this discussion until after the honeymoon, then revisit. Now that the idea has bubbled up to the surface, maybe things will become clearer for me."

"As ye wish, luv. Fer now, it's late. How about we turn in fer the night, get a good night's sleep, and when we wake up, we'll tackle the last of the island adventures, then portal off to start our honeymoon?"

"That's the best idea I've heard in ages, hotness. Yeah, let's do that."

The next morning, Sloan and I meet up with the others in the Great Room and check in. "Hey, D. How are you feeling?"

I go over to where my brother is sitting in his chair at the breakfast table and hug him from behind.

"Not the first schoolyard shit-kicking I've received, and I doubt it'll be the last. I'm fine, though. Rory's a little blue, but now that she's merged and resting, I'm sure she'll feel better soon."

"Glad to hear it. I don't want our little dragon girl taking this too personally. She was brave and fought hard, I'm sure."

"She was and did. I told her so. Sometimes, no matter how prepared you are, you'll come up against someone who's stronger and more prepared to win that fight."

"It's true. Da used to tell me that all the time."

The boys all nod. I'm sure they remember.

Sloan and I go over to where the food is laid out on the buffet hutch and make our plates.

"Dionysus has his powers back, all right." Sloan chuckles. "He's the only one I know who can rival Lara for preparing a meal."

I chuckle and heap my plate full of golden crepes drizzled in icing sugar, baked apple, and caramel sauce. "If we move here, we can't eat like this every morning, or there won't be any amount of battling that will work off the poundage."

"True enough."

"What, what?" Emmet hustles over. He tilts his head with a sly smile. "Do my ears deceive me or did you say, 'if we move here?' Explain please."

Sloan and I take our plates to the table, and I meet the curious gazes of my brothers, Eva, and the Greeks. "I realized yesterday that amazing as my life is—and it definitely is—part of me has felt adrift and disjointed since our family kind of crumbled and everyone started building separate lives."

Emmet's smile fades, and he nods. "You're not the only one. I decided to stay here because everything in me sings to be on this island, but I hate not being part of the family on the daily."

"Same," Brendan says. "I know I sometimes spent months at a time undercover, but I would drive by the house or the pub or the art studio and catch glimpses of you guys to ground me. It's tough being apart."

Sloan brings over two flavored coffees and sets one down for me. "It's hard fer Fi to face the violence and chaos of the world and not have the solidity of that family unit to stand as her foundation. She's struggled the past few months. I think the toll of her duties overwhelmed her when she hasn't had the contentment of the family to reset her compass on a regular basis."

"You're my stress cleanse." I finish my crepes. "Yes, we were talking about different options that might allow us to spend more time here."

"Do I get a vote?" Emmet asks. "Because, if I do, I vote the two of you definitely move in."

As much as I love that idea, I'm not ready to rush into a move that will disrupt so many others. "We'll keep you posted on how that idea progresses. For now, we're thinking about a direct portal from our house to yours, sharing meals, and spending weekends."

"Even that would be awesome," Brendan agrees.

I let that conversation drop and move on to more immediate concerns. "Eva, after breakfast, would you be able to come with us to the Light Weavers' temple to keep working on unraveling the mystery of what Kyna was saying in her holographic message?"

"Of course, but by tonight, I have to go. I've been called to report to the Choir."

Sloan finishes his coffee and sets his mug down. "Then, let's not keep ye."

A group of us *poof* to the Light Weavers' tower after breakfast to take another crack at unraveling Kyna's message. Dillan hasn't seen his angel in the prism light show yet, so he's gung-ho, and Sloan's been thinking about what the lack of soundtrack could be about for a couple of days now.

Unlike me, he can focus on something in the present and still be mulling over a problem in the back of his mind.

The Force is strong in that one.

"What about asking Mr. Epema?" Emmet suggests.

Calum nods. "It's not a bad idea. Isilon's tagline is that he knows everything past and present."

"Good call. It can't hurt to try. Isilon, will you join us, please?"

He appears in an instant, and I smile. I lost touch with my professor after high school. I'm finding it nice to see him again…even if it's not really him.

He takes in me, then Dillan and Nikon. "It's good to see you three are healed and well."

Nikon nods. "Thank you for releasing us so we could get the care we needed. We intend to make a few updates and changes around here, so people won't have to be portaled out for medical care in the future."

"So, you do intend to return and spend time here?"

"You sound surprised?" I meet his curious gaze.

"I had concerns. Your father was very angry and quite blunt about taking you away from me."

"If you didn't allow us the freedom to choose," I add. "We all love the island, but we won't be prisoners. If we're here, we're here by choice."

He nods. "As you wish."

"That's not why we called you," Emmet says. "We wanted to know if you will help us with Kyna's message. We know she was trying to tell us something, but we can't hear her."

Isilon glides over to where Sloan is fiddling with the prasiolite crystal to get the golden light Eva's giving off to hit the pages of the book and project the image of Kyna in front of us. "You only have one of the three crystals."

Sloan steps back and shakes his head. "This is the only one we found."

"That is your problem. Each of the Light Weaver sisters had a crystal. This is Kyna's, but you're missing the ones belonging to Syma and Lyri."

"All righty then." Dillan slaps his hands together. "Looks like we're on a treasure hunt. May the best team win."

I look at who is here, and yeah. There's me and Sloan, him and Eva, Emmet and Brendan, Calum and Kevin, and Nikon and Dionysus. "Fun. What are the stakes?"

Brenny grins. "How about we make it interesting and offer up bragging rights and an Oh, Henry! trophy?"

Dillan laughs. "Go big or go home, brother. I'm in."

I nod. "We're in."

Everyone pairs off, and there's a roomful of smiles and nodding heads.

"May the best men win," Brenny says.

"Rude. I object to that statement."

It's too late. Brenny and Emmet are tearing out of the inner sanctum, the Greeks are gone, Kevin and Calum are searching the bookshelves and moving around the room, and Eva and Dillan have their heads together making a plan.

"Yer family takes bein' competitive to an entirely new level." Sloan chuckles.

"True story. Now, how do you want to handle this?"

He grins. "What's Occam's Razor?"

"The simplest answer is usually the right one."

His grin broadens. "Exactly. Isilon, where are the other two crystals?"

"Syma's is in the floorboards of her sleeping chamber and Lyri's is in the hollow of the tree of fortitude in the city center."

I laugh and glance around at my brothers to see if they heard.

I don't think Calum, Kevin, or Dillan heard, but Eva definitely did.

She takes Dillan's hand and they portal out.

"Dammit. Where do you think they went first?"

"One way to find out." Sloan takes my hand and *poofs* us to the center square. Eva is standing at the base of the tree and Dillan's feet are already disappearing up into the foliage.

"Okay, they've got this one. We'll go for Syma's floorboards. Do we have any idea where they lived?"

Sloan waggles his brow. "Actually, I do."

Another rush of Sloan's power signature washes over me and we're standing in the upper levels of the golden dildo. "The three sisters lived in the crown of the palace—"

I make a face and groan. "Let's not use the word crown in reference to the top of this structure."

Sloan blinks at me. "That's not what I meant, and ye know it."

"True, but that's where my mind went."

"Of course it is."

He releases my hand and frowns at the massive space. Where each of the floors below are broken into ten-bedroom suites and libraries and gathering rooms, this floor is solely the private space of the three Light Weaver sisters.

It's massive, and my excitement about a slam dunk of finding the crystal falls flat.

"There are a lot of floorboards in this flat."

"Aye, but Isilon said the crystal was in Syma's floorboards, so all this open space and the balconies and the kitchen and living rooms and libraries are irrelevant. We need to focus on the bedrooms."

I turn a circle finding three ornately runed doors, evenly spaced, along the round walls. "Which one?"

Sloan jogs over to the round table in the center of the space and lifts a pendulum into the air. Holding it delicately between two fingers, he tilts his head to the side. "Do you mind if I have the honors?"

"It's your party. You can scry if you want to."

Doubling over, I snort and bust a gut. That was damned good, and the two of us lose time laughing over it.

I regain control and straighten up. "Okay, game faces. Find Syma's floorboards."

Sloan utters his finding spell, and the pendulum goes from swiveling in a gentle circle to pulling in one direction and lifting in the air until its point indicates one of the three doors.

"Bingo. We have a winner." I push off across the space and stop when I get to the door, the importance of the moment catching up with me. "Syma, if you can somehow hear me, we're going to do you and your sisters proud."

I try the door. I'm not sure what I expected, but it opens.

Huh, sometimes a door is only a door.

I step into the private space of a woman I only met and spoke to once or twice a thousand years ago and try my best to be as respectful as I can about who she was and what she and her sisters meant to this island.

Sloan steps in behind me still holding the pendulum. It points the way, guiding him to where it senses the crystal, then it points straight down at the floor.

"So mote it be." Sloan sets the pendulum on the dressing table and joins me on the floor. "Anything?"

"Nope." I've got my nose practically to the smooth wooden floor, searching for any indication of an uneven spacing between boards or a spot where it looks like a section might lift up...but I've got nothing.

Sloan gets down and does the same thing.

I meet his gaze and chuckle. "Look at us. It's a glamorous life, isn't it?"

He grins. "Indiana Jones and Lara Croft at heart."

It strikes me then. "Syma was a Light Weaver. Maybe she

phased the floorboards out of the way when she hid it here. In that case, there's no way we're finding it. We'd need someone with that particular ability."

Sloan sits up and rests on his calves. "Who do you want me to get, Emmet or the Greeks?"

I think about that for a moment, but the decision is easy. "Em. He needs more wins. He still doubts himself too much."

"Text him and see where he is."

I pull out my phone and send him a text.

**Found it. Need you to phase it free. Where are you?**

**In the security office with Astrid.**

I hold the phone out so Sloan can read the reply. He's gone in a *poof* and back in a flash. Emmet looks around and comes to sit with me on the floor.

"Welcome to the private space of Syma. I believe what we're looking for is below these floorboards." I tap my finger on the beautiful old planks of wood.

"I'm surprised you didn't just start pulling up boards," Brendan says.

I shake my head. "I don't think it would be that easy. Syma was a Light Weaver. They hid the city. Don't you think they'd hide the crystals to a secret message in a similar fashion?"

Emmet presses his hands on the floor and stretches his neck from side to side. "Sure, they would. The three of them were so incredibly smart and talented. They were also devoted to keeping the city safe. They knew we'd come here eventually to resurrect the city and they knew I would teach people I trust to help me."

I'm happy Emmet got the chance to be the star of that adventure. He's always felt like he's living in the shadow of our four older brothers. Maybe that's why he turned out to be such a goof or maybe he would've been exactly the same person if he didn't have to follow in their wake.

Still, the moment he took the dip in the prana river, the trajectory of his life changed forever.

He found his niche—his greatness.

Now he simply needs to grasp it and believe in himself.

As the three of us watch, Emmet phases the floorboards out of existence and reaches into the void he's created.

I blink and turn my head from the brightness his magic gives off. He's so powerful, yet I get the feeling he hasn't even begun to understand what he's truly capable of.

He lifts his hand and passes me a triangular crystal of amethyst.

I stand, and Sloan and I examine it while Emmet replaces the floorboards into this plane of existence.

"Well done, Em." I hug him. "Now, how much do you want to bet Dillan's still climbing that tree, searching for the hollow where Lyri hid her crystal?"

"No bet." Emmet laughs. "He's definitely still searching. I bet by now he's cursing up a storm."

"Then let's go help him out."

## CHAPTER TWENTY-THREE

By the time we finish with the tree in the city center and get back to the Light Weavers' inner sanctum, the others have returned and are waiting to witness the hologram in its entirety.

Sloan takes Kyna's triangular prism of prasiolite, Syma's prism of amethyst, and Lyri's prism of chrysocolla and pieces them together. The moment they come into contact, there's a *snap* in the air, and they fuse as one.

Dillan waggles his brow and kisses Eva's cheek. "All right, beautiful. Looks like you're up."

Eva launches into the air, and her dove soars high above our heads. When she positions herself above the strings of crystals and stretches her wings out, the golden rays of heaven's light beam from her.

It takes some adjusting to get the beam to focus on the sisters' prisms and not the crystals strung above, but when that happens, and Sloan gets the focused energy of the crystal to fall on the open pages of the text, Kyna, Syma, and Lyri appear in front of us.

Kyna's gaze lifts to where we stand but doesn't focus on us as it would if she were real. "Well done, Emmet. We knew we could count on you. In these, the darkest hours of our fair city, the one thing that gives us hope is knowing that one day you will return and awaken our incredible Isilon. Thank you."

Syma steps forward. "But you must do more than awaken it, sweet boy. You must protect it. What happened to us must not be allowed to happen again. It is our sincere hope, given your strength and the resourcefulness of those in your company, that you will succeed where we have failed."

Lyri takes the stage next. "We left you everything we know about the enemy and the missteps and underestimations that led to our defeat. Please study the errors of our past to secure success in your future."

Kyna gestures a sweeping hand around the room and glows with the hot pink aura Emmet gave off the few times that power overloaded him. "All is not as it may seem, Emmet. Remember all we taught you and see beyond that which appears before your eyes."

The message ends then, and the images of the three Light Weaver sisters dim and fade away.

We're all quiet for a moment while the impact of that settles in. I step over to my brother and hug his arm. "They believed in you, Em. They knew you'd get the city up and running and that you'd find the crystals and piece together their message."

Calum pats his shoulder. "They chose their champion well. You're going to do them proud, and we're going to help you."

"Damn straight." Dillan holds his fist up for a bump. "That whole part about the resourcefulness of the company you keep is us in a nutshell. We got you."

Emmet gives us a nervous smile. "I hope you're right. Yeah, for whatever is coming down the pipe, I need you guys to back me up."

"You can count on me to be here, by your side, the whole time." Brenny offers us a straight face for as long as he can, then laughs. "Because—who are we kidding—where else can I be?"

The tension of the message begins to settle, and instead of being overwhelmed, Emmet begins to relax into the idea that he's meant for something more than he expected of himself.

He might not have the confidence to hit that head-on yet, but we'll get him there.

"Do you think their message about preparing for what is to come has anything to do with the kids being Crescent Called?" Calum asks.

Sloan's sly smile tells me he'd already considered that possibility. "I'm more intrigued by Kyna's statement at the end. *All is not as it may seem...See beyond that which appears before your eyes.*"

Yeah, cryptic.

It's enough of a cranial puzzle to intrigue a man like Sloan. "I assume she meant they've hidden clues or tools for him in spatial pockets where no one else would be able to find them."

Sloan taps his index finger on the tip of his nose. "That's where my mind went too."

Dionysus' phone rings and Lady A's *Bartender* chimes as his ringtone. He answers the call and smiles. "Hey, Liam... Yes, sir, I'm on my way."

When he hangs up, I chuckle. "Bartender?"

"It was either that or *Wild Again* from *Cocktail*, but I thought Bartender was more current and more on the nose."

I laugh. "No argument. So, where are you off to?"

"Shenanigans. Liam put together what he needs to get the bar stocked up for tonight's 'Welcome to the Island' party at the tavern."

He leans closer. "Jane? You didn't forget you put me in charge of the welcome party, did you?"

"No way. I just didn't know it was tonight."

He nods. "It is, and since you are going to be one of the two event bartenders, you're on the hook for helping us get the place ready for customers."

What's that? No battles. No blood.

Just taking down chairs and dusting off glasses…

"I honestly look forward to it. You go get Liam and the supplies, and we'll meet you there."

---

When Dionysus portals off to get Liam and the supplies, Sloan *poofs* me, Kevin, Calum, and Brendan to the cute yellow tavern on the main thoroughfare from the palace down to the meadow. Nikon is dropping Emmet up at the palace and meeting Sarah to take her to Blarney to pick up some girlfriends who've longed to spend time with her.

I feel bad that she's been stuck here alone with my brothers since Mother Nature put her on assignment. Brenny and Em are amazing, but Sarah is a girl's girl and is used to not only belonging to a full coven but also leading it since the death of her High Priestess a couple of years ago.

"So, here it is," I say as we enter. "I know it's not Shenanigans, but I think it's got potential."

Calum and Kevin step deeper into the space and take in the interior.

"I take it you've been here before?" I ask Brendan.

"Yeah, a couple of times. Em and I talked about what it would be like to start our own bar, but Sarah would've been our only customer at the time."

"Not the case any longer."

"Nope."

"Have ye given any thought to the kinds of spirits and ales the different species might need ye to provide?" Sloan asks.

"Nope."

I laugh at Brendan's blank expression. He isn't as used to Sloan as my other brothers. My hubs is always thinking three or four moves ahead. It can be tiring until you get used to it and resign yourself to the fact that it's his way.

I get us started on that conversation. "I know the Quasti drink nectar but have no idea if they are more animals in the woods or creatures in a bar."

"More animals in the woods," Isilon says, appearing next to us.

"Hello, again. What can we do for you?" I ask.

"Nothing. I felt the energy of the demi-god a moment ago and was curious about his level of excitement."

I chuckle. "Dionysus is always excited at the prospect of a party. He's planning a 'Welcome to the Island' event tonight and we're here to get the tavern in working order."

"You should join us," Emmet says, snapping in with Nikon and Sarah. "It's going to be a good time."

Isilon looks like he's not sure what to do with an offer like that. "Perhaps I will."

I pull up my phone and open a picture of one of my favorite GQ looks on Sloan. "If you do come, wear something like this. Mr. Epema is great and all, but beige pants, white collared shirts, and plaid jackets only get you so far. This is a great outfit for a fun night at the tavern. I think you've got hot for teacher potential."

Calum snorts. "Are you really pimping the sentient city's ride?"

"Sure. Why not? Even Data had Tasha Yar. If we're all going to be neighbors and working together, why wouldn't I help him acclimate into the twenty-first century?"

He doesn't have an answer for that, so I take it as a win.

"Okay, we're off." Nikon smiles. "Shopping and picking up a few friends to join us for the evening."

Sarah flashes me a wide grin and rushes over to hug me. "I'm so excited to see my girls. They're going to love having the tavern to catch up at. Thanks for making this happen, Fi."

I wave that away. "I just brought up the idea. Nikon's the hero of the girls' night out."

Nikon waggles his brows at me. "If I'm going to be a hero, that's not a bad one to be."

The two of them snap out, and we're left looking at the old tavern. "Okay, everyone. Let's take ten minutes to explore and let our minds turn over ideas of what this place might become. Then we'll meet back here and brainstorm."

Brendan claps once. "And break."

---

Exploring the tavern and the inn on the second floor, I'm surer than ever that this place could be great. It's out of date. There's not enough flair to anything, but the bones are good.

"How many rooms are there?" Sloan climbs the stairs with me as we access the second level.

"Not sure. We'll have to count."

"I'm thinking Brenny and I can make this our home base," Emmet says. "Then, if anyone needs anything or new arrivals come, they can grab a drink and take a room up here for a day or two while we determine the best accommodations for their needs."

"That's good thinking," I agree.

We crest the top step, and I take in the view. Glancing at the streets below, I think about the last time I was standing in this exact spot. "I can still see you standing there, scowling up at me." I point at the spot on the corner where Sloan begrudgingly waited for me to speak to Betrys in private.

"Ye were too free with facts about the future, and I worried yer interference would set a course," he explains.

"It did set a course," Patty says, sitting on a chair behind where we came in.

Emmet yipes and spins.

I press a hand to my chest, my heart pounding at the base of my throat. "Geez, dude. You scared the crap out of me."

"Sorry, Red. I was sittin' here, mindin' my own when yer lot arrived."

"No. I'm sorry. Did we intrude?"

"Och, no. Nothin' like that. I was feelin' melancholy and missin' my sister. She never was one fer taverns, but I suppose she came here to collect me enough times that it made her a regular."

The sadness and self-recrimination in Patty's voice are hard to take. Emmet takes that as his cue and excuses himself to check on the rooms available for us to fix up.

I meet Patty's sorrowful gaze. "That was a lifetime ago. You're a different man now."

"Aye, that's true. When ye met me then, we hadn't been here long since my break with our kind. I didn't approve of their ways and was foolish enough to think if I stood my ground and made it known, they'd listen and maybe amend a few things."

"No such luck, eh?"

He winks at me and pushes the bridge of his spectacles up his nose. "No. They stripped me of all titles, took my family possessions, and raided my gold. I told ye once it was a source of great shame fer my kind to be relieved of our gold."

"I remember."

"Well, they did it again and again and again. When they finished with me, there was nothin' left of the man I once was. Bets saw the truth of it and packed our bags."

"You're not the first to have to rebuild," I say. "And if I say so myself, I think you've done all right."

He nods. "In the end, perhaps. Betrys' husband, Anghus, wasn't keen to leave. It caused trouble between the two and created a rift between him and me as well. Still, I made enough of a mess of things in our realm that Bets thought it best to seek shelter with me."

"That must've been hard fer all involved, sham. I know first-hand how the land that made ye can root itself deep inside yer soul. To give it up and to know ye were never to go back...weel, I couldn't imagine."

Patty smiles at Sloan. "I was a drunken mess fer a lotta years after. Then, one day, my sister said it was time to pull up my bootstraps and become the man she knew I was supposed to be. She said she had it on good authority I was supposed to come to an agreement with the Queen of Wyrms and that companionship between us would lead me to a long and happy life."

Sloan casts a look at me and arches a brow. "Did she now?"

*Sure, throw me under the bus. Nice.*

I shrug. "Don't look at me like that. I needed to do something. The Patty I found back in time was in trouble, and I couldn't let that stand."

He shakes his head. "No, I suppose ye wouldn't be yerself if ye could. Still, ye take risks too easily."

*I can't argue that.*

Patty squeezes my hand. "Weel, I'm glad she took that one, lad. I never knew who told Betrys such a thing. I figured it was a seer or a card reader or someone—Bets was always goin' to seek guidance from those sorts—but I was ever so grateful fer the new life path it led me to."

"I'm glad it worked," I say.

He tugs on my hand, and I slide into a seat at his table. "I didn't know it was yer guidance until ye returned from yer visit back in time and gave me the family crest. I think knowin' the full story meant even more to me than holdin' that marble shamrock in my hand."

I meet the glassy gaze of my friend and blink fast to keep from glassing up myself. "You're happy and whole. That's all I care about."

"Aye, I am, and I'll be forever grateful, *a stór*."

Having Patty call me his treasure does it. I'm blinking back more than watery eyes now. I'm wiping tears and laughing at myself. "Does being back here make you happy or sad?"

"A mixture of both, but I think that's to be expected. It all goes to make us who we are, right?"

"Right. I happen to love who you are."

Patty winks. "Right back at ye, Red."

There's a shout of alarm downstairs, and I jump to my feet. Sloan *poofs* out, and Patty and I are left running down the steps. When I get down there, I see the problem immediately.

Liam's standing behind the bar with a massive splat of pink paint on his left shoulder.

"Who got you?"

"Dillan. The asshole waited until my hands were full, holding trays of glasses, and pegged me off."

"Hearsay." Dillan grins. He holds up his empty hands to show us he isn't holding a weapon. "No witnesses. No proof. I deny that allegation."

I laugh and perform the same cleaning spell over Liam's shoulder as I did for Sloan. When Fionn taught me that one, it was meant for us to get blood and dirt out of our clothes before a formal dinner.

Who knew it would also work for paintball?

"With the chaos of the realm battle, then the battle at the gate and recovering at Stonecrest Castle, I've lost track of who's still in the game."

Brenny grins. "Right? Let's just say not everyone is broadcasting their status. The players are dwindling, but I think it adds an element of intrigue not knowing who's left. Are we down to two? Still at four? See…intrigue."

Dillan snorts. "You need to get out more, dude."

Brendan flashes him his middle finger. "He says to the man destined to live the rest of his existence sentenced to this island."

"Sentenced?" I repeat, not liking the sound of that word. "Is that how you feel?"

Brendan turns to me and shrugs. "Not usually, no, but there are times. I love being here with Em, don't get me wrong, and

Sarah's great, in a cardigan and knee socks, girl next door kinda way, but let's just say there are a few areas in my life that are lacking."

"Why didn't you say so?" Dionysus holds up his hands. "Brother mine, does my reputation not precede me? Hello? You have access to the god of feast and wine. If you have carnal needs that need to be met, I'm your man."

I roll my eyes and run a hand over my face. "Did one of my besties just become my brother's pimp?"

Calum laughs. "No, a pimp is for the girls. Dionysus would be his hook-up handler."

Brendan laughs. "I don't know that we have to go that far, and maybe the influx of people over the past few days will help, but there is a definite demographic missing on this island."

"Sexually aggressive biker chick, you mean?" Dillan suggests.

"Hey, no kink-shaming." Brendan points.

"No. Never," Dionysus agrees. "This is good. I can work with this. Is it only women you're looking for? Are you flexible? Curious?"

Brenny chuckles. "Nope. No curiosity. Just women."

"And how aggressive do you like?"

Brendan's cheeks flush pink, and he waves in consternation. "This conversation jumped rails somewhere along the line. I'm not asking for a mail-order hook-up, just that maybe we could invite some new blood occasionally. Maybe, someone we're not related to or who is married or waiting for Mr. Right."

I chuckle. "I'll bring Suede the next time I come. She had a thing with her father this weekend, but she's always up for a good time. And she seems to like the Cumhaill boys."

Dionysus nods. "A great choice. I'll ask her. Wait, is that weird?"

"For you to bring your ex-girlfriend to have a penis party with other guys?" Calum laughs. "For other people maybe. For you...not so much."

"Andromeda's girlfriends rock." Dillan winks at Eva.

"Oh, and I have reaper friends I could invite too," Eva says. "Reapers can get very aggressive. How do you feel about weapon play?"

Brendan's got a deer-in-the-headlights thing going on, and it's way too funny.

I raise my hands and slow the roll of this conversation. "Lots of ideas. Lots of possibilities. How about we get back to the point of our story? Tonight, we're having the first social event in a tavern that has been closed and dormant for over a thousand years. How about we get busy getting ready for that?"

"Are we still going to brainstorm ideas?" Kevin asks. "Because Calum and I were thinking a mechanical bull with a matted corral over there by the stairs would be cool."

"Done deal!" Emmet grins. "Excellent idea. What else have we got?"

"Coyote Ugly bar dancing," Dionysus says.

Emmet laughs. "Also, a great option. Anyone else?"

# CHAPTER TWENTY-FOUR

"Just like old times, isn't it?"

I'm scrubbing down the brand-new black granite bar top Dionysus installed a few minutes ago and grin at Liam. "Yeah, except when did we ever have taps this nice or a bar this clean?"

Liam laughs. "With Kevin's designer taste and Dionysus' god powers, there's no stopping us."

"Right?"

We're not even kidding. The place is tricked out.

Other than the mechanical bull and the padded corral around it, the layout is very similar to Shenanigans. The front door faces the bar on the far back wall, a bank of booths on the left and right walls, some four-tops inside that, a dance floor in the middle, washrooms down the back hall to the left, kitchen behind the bar to the right.

"Yo, Brenny, how's the sound system coming, bro?" Kevin shouts.

"It's coming."

Calum pushes through the saloon doors with a tray of washed glasses. His apron is soaked. "You're set for glasses and plates."

The sound system cuts in, and Ed Sheeran's *Bad Habits* starts playing.

"There we go." I get into the beat.

"Now we're talking." Emmet finishes setting up the chairs.

Our family has all, at one time or another, served, bussed, tended bar, and worked the cook line at Shenanigans. Even years after my brothers moved on and were working on the force, they donned their pub persona and pitched in if the need arose.

This tavern is no different.

"Hey, what are we going to call this place?" I finish with the bar to hang the stemmed glasses and get the tumblers in place.

"Too Cumhaill." Emmet grins.

I laugh. "Yeah, that would be great if everyone could read Irish and know to pronounce it 'Cool,' then Too Cool would work. Odds are, anyone without the Irish in them will pronounce our name phonetically and miss the joke."

"Yeah, you're probably right." Emmet sighs. "What about Shenanigans 2?"

"Electric Boogaloo," Calum and I both say at the same time. "Jinx!"

The two of us get laughing, and Emmet rolls his eyes. "Guys, get serious. We need a name."

"What about The Craic House?" Brendan suggests.

We all get a laugh out of that.

"Points for hilarity, but I think not. We'd get the joke, but maybe people coming here from other realms might get the wrong idea."

Emmet nods. "And if my pick got tossed because of people not knowing Irish, yours does too."

It goes on like that, everyone working hard to get the tavern up to code while laughing and having a good time. Honestly, I don't care if anyone shows up tonight. We'll have a good time.

"Did somebody say party? Well, let the fun begin."

I straighten and turn toward the group coming through the tavern doors.

I laugh. "What happened to island protocols? Are we letting in any old riffraff now?"

Tad laughs. "Hey, we pledged our oath to the island when the shit was hittin'. We're legit."

I wave that away. "Yeah, I suppose. Welcome."

Clan Cumhaill abandons our posts to greet the Heirs of the Order. "Hey, guys. What brings you by?"

Tad swings around and points at Dionysus. "Someone said there was a party tonight and I should round up the usual suspects to kick off the tavern opening and send you two off on your honeymoon in a true Order fashion."

"Oh, hell." I don't like the sound of that. "We don't want to spend the first two days of our honeymoon hungover and puking."

Ciara holds out a little box with a red bow. "Fer the happy couple on the eve of their honeymoon."

I wait until Sloan steps in beside me and open the top of the box. It's a little baggie of pills. I laugh, knowing exactly what they are. "These are your magical sobriety tablets."

Ciara grins. "Yer welcome. Ye see, I knew ye'd try to play the card of responsible drinkin', and we'll not hear of it. Ye may be Irish by blood and now by marriage, but yer still not Irish enough to hold yer own against us on a night out."

"Challenge accepted." I hand Sloan the little box. "Put this in our room on my bedside table with a glass of water, will you?"

"As ye wish, luv."

Brendan is the only one not in the loop. "Brenny, you know Ciara and Tad, but this is Eric, Jarrod, Darcy, and Davin. Also known as the Heirs of the Order."

"Or at least the ones old enough to be out after nine and drink," Jarrod says.

"True. There are others who are still young and innocent."

"Hey, good lookin'." Ciara grins at Emmet. "Aren't you going to give your ex a hello kiss?"

Emmet grins, waggling his ebony brows, and meets her chest-to-chest. When his arms go around her, and his fingers grip the back of her long hair, I'm surprised.

When he bends her backward and sticks his tongue down her throat, I'm stunned.

"That's what I'm talking about," Dillan says. "Hellooooo, nurse."

Liam lets out a shrill whistle and bangs a hand on the bar. "Yeah, baby."

I blink and look at Sloan. "That sailor has been out to sea too long."

"That's what I'm saying!" Brenny adds.

I laugh and look away. There's no sense weighing in on my brothers' love life. I learned long ago it doesn't do any good and what makes me happy isn't what makes them happy.

"Wow, come up for air, Cumhaill," Quon Shen says as he, Samuel, and Ahren come through the front doors.

"Dayam, son," Ahren says in his thick Southern drawl. "You got to let a beautiful bouquet like that breathe, Hoss."

Emmet straightens and eases back from the kiss. "Hey, beautiful. I've missed you."

"If that's the welcome I get from you missing me, it's worth it."

Brendan is looking on with a sad pout, and I have to laugh. "Don't worry, dude. Your time is coming. Seriously though, you should've mentioned something to Dionysus sooner. He lives for fun, frolicking, and fornication."

"And a few other f-words too," Dionysus adds. "That's the after-party plan. First, we have the island welcome so go put on one of your tamer playlists and let's get this evening started."

Brenny nods. "Consider it done."

By the time Nikon returns with Sarah and her friends, the welcome party has begun, and half a dozen white witches join the festive air. I recognize a few of them from the time we spent in Blarney and am happy to catch up with the two who used to be Sarah's roommates, Yasmine and Erika.

"We appreciate being invited to stay," Erika says. "We've missed Sarah so much."

I gather the empty glasses and set them on my tray. "I know that goes both ways. Have a wonderful night."

Sarah nods, her gaze flickering over to where Emmet is glued to Ciara.

I knew he wasn't over her and the feelings they share, but he's *really* still not over her.

Carrying my tray back to the bar, I set the glasses onto the rolling mat of the washer and lean toward the bar. "Maybe we're not the only ones who need a portal gate to give easy access to the ones we love."

Sloan twists on his bar stool to follow my gaze. "Maybe not. They never split because they didn't love one another."

"No. I know. I just kinda hoped he'd move on to Sarah. She's thoughtful and lovely and—"

"And yer not the one makin' the choice."

I roll my eyes. "I know. And I get it. You're right."

He grins and finishes his beer. "I hear the words comin' out of yer mouth, but I don't think they're registerin' with yer head."

"Har-har. No. I really do get it. Sarah's just so lovely."

"You can say that again." Nikon joins Sloan on the barstools. "We had the best time. That's why we were late. We totally lost track of time. She's amazing."

I pour Nikon a glass of Gran's blackberry pear wine and slide it across to him. When he pivots in the chair and lifts his glass to salute Sarah across the room, I try to catch up.

Was I rooting for the wrong teams?

Sloan meets my gaze and shakes his head. "Everything

happens as it's meant to, *a ghra*. Without yer nudgin'."

I grin. "Who me? I wouldn't dream of interfering."

He laughs. "Go ahead and try to sell that to someone else. I ain't buyin'."

Nikon turns back around and takes an appreciative swallow. "Not buying what? What did I miss?"

"Nothin', sham," Sloan says. "We're glad ye enjoyed yerself. By the sounds of it, Sarah's lookin' forward to doin' a lot more shoppin' and settin' up house."

Nikon nods. "Yeah, we've already made plans for Wednesday night when we take her friends back."

Sloan pegs me with a knowing look.

I make the international gesture of locking my mouth and throwing away the key. That appeases him because he lets the subject drop.

"Shame. Shame. Shame." Dillan walks through the crowd, his black jeans highlighted by a bright pink splotch. "We have a winner, folks. The grand Assassin is none other than our retired reaper and my angel wife. Let's give it up for Eva."

Eva joins us, grinning and waving at the crowds.

We all give her a round of applause, and she comes to stand at the end of the bar. She's dressed in white leather and has her wings out, ready to kick ass as a guardian angel.

She's badass beautiful and turns every head in the bar. "The pleasure was all mine. I loved that game. We should play it more often."

I chuckle and start setting up to make a round of cosmos. "Should we be intimidated that the ex-reaper finds an instinctual joy in killing us?"

"Only for fun." Her dimples show. "I'd never let anything really happen to you."

I rim a few glasses with sugar and pour. "Good to know. Congratulations, sister mine. You make us proud."

I hand her a drink and lift one for myself to make the toast.

The boys around me all do the same.

"To Evangeline," I say.

"To Evangeline," the room echoes.

Eva drinks, tipping her head back as her throat works to down the entire contents of her glass. When she's done, she drags her tongue along the sugar and makes eyes at Dillan.

He moves in for a kiss, and it's no surprise when yet again, one of my brothers makes a public display that has heads turning. When he eases back from the kiss, he touches noses with her and smiles. "Safe home, my love."

We all raise our glasses. "Safe home."

With that, Eva smiles at us and waves. When she bursts into a golden mist and disappears, we're left looking at a love-struck Dillan sighing in contentment.

Liam laughs and passes him a tumbler of whiskey. "Dude, you're so whipped it's incredible."

He accepts the drink and lifts it in thanks. "You don't even know the half of it, my man."

I see where that comment is headed. "We don't *need* to know, thanks. We're happy for you, D. You met a one-of-a-kind woman, you treated her right, and you earned her love. Good on you."

He accepts the accolades and takes the barstool on the end to sit and nurse his drink, content to occupy his time with his thoughts.

I know it's tough on him when Eva goes away on assignment, but he respects her calling and trusts her skills to bring her home to him when things wrap up.

I couldn't be prouder of him.

Setting another round of beer, cosmos, and whiskey on my tray, I ensure I'm ready to make a run into the crowd.

I'm pleased to see so many of the newcomers out to say hello. There aren't many humanoids yet, and like the Quasti and the Petal People, many of the others are more wild creatures than tavern drinkers, but still, we've got a good crowd.

"The heirs are gettin' on well with yer Hunter-god friends," Sloan says as he follows my assessing gaze over the sea of bodies.

"Yeah, I'm glad. I'm not great at compartmentalizing friends. If everyone can get along, that works for me."

They should get along. They've fought together a few times, first when Samuel and I came to blows, and the dragons invaded to take my side, then during the battles of the Culling.

It's funny. So many of my deepest friendships have been made over battles and fighting for our lives.

"This is a wonderful party," HaiLe says, stepping into my path to claim a couple of drinks.

Kidok and Pi are sitting with her, and I make sure to hand the boy a drink. If he's old enough to defend his brother in battle, watch his father die, and spend time in a leprechaun prison, then he's old enough to drink a pint at the tavern. "Welcome to the island, all. I wish you all a safe and happy life to come."

"Thank you, Fiona," HaiLe says.

Kidok nods and raises his hand to accept another tumbler of whiskey.

"If you have liquor requests, Dionysus is making a list of ales and spirits from other realms that we might not know about. Feel free to ask him to import something for you. It's his divine designation, and he's keen to make sure everyone has their libation of choice."

Kidok smiles. "I'll be sure to do that. Thanks, Fi."

"Not a problem." I glance around, searching the faces in the crowd. "I'm not sure where he went, but he's not far, I'm sure."

HaiLe laughs. "No. He's not far. He blocked the street with the large, billowing castle from the meadow and he's in there jumping around, playing with my cubs."

I laugh. "That makes sense. He loves the bouncy castle, and he loves kids. So, yeah, I'm sure he'll be back when he tires out."

"Does he ever tire out?" HaiLe asks.

"No. Not really." The two of us share a laugh, and I get back to making my rounds.

I'm almost back around to the bar when Nikon snaps in with his sisters, Andromeda and Politimi, and four other women dressed to impress and ready to party.

I feel Nikon's magical signature ramp up and meet his gaze, expecting him to speak to me on an internal channel. He doesn't.

Brendan's head lifts from where he's chatting with Calum and Kev, and Nikon points at Politimi behind her back.

*Seriously? Are you offering your sister up for a one-night stand with my brother?*

Nikon's head swivels over to meet my gaze, and he laughs. *Not without her previous approval. We're immortals, Fi. Our views on casual sex aren't the same as yours. Maybe when you've lived four or five centuries, you'll understand. Don't worry. If Brendan has a thing for aggressive biker chicks, Politimi has him covered.*

I roll my eyes. *My concern isn't that she does or doesn't fit the bill...* Politimi closes the distance, and Brendan's all swagger and coy smirk. Why do I even try? *Never mind. I'm out.*

I return to the bar, Nikon's amusement leaking into my mind.

I smack my tray down on the bar and look at Liam, Dillan, and Sloan. "Am I a prude? Sexually repressed? Old fashioned? What?"

Liam chokes on the whiskey he's drinking and holds up his hands. "I'm out."

I turn my gaze on Sloan and Dillan. "Well?"

"Yer none of those things, luv. What makes ye ask?"

Before I can answer, there is a thundering crash in the sky outside, and Dart's breaking in on our mental connection. *Angry cockatrice mate is making his move on Cadmus.*

"Shit." *Okay, buddy, we're coming. We'll meet you at the meadow. Get Saxa and Kaida ready too.* I break the connection. "Emmet, you and Sloan are with me. We've got a cuckold cockatrice problem. Nikon, get the kids in off the street."

I run around the bar and reach for Sloan and Emmet. The

scraping of legs across the wooden floor brings Davin and Darcy rushing over.

"We've got more experience with airborne dragon fights than you guys—no offense," Davin says.

"None taken. It's a fact. Sure. Sloan, we're meeting at the meadow. Hands in."

Sloan waits until the five of us have made contact and *poofs* us to the meadow. I don't wait to sort the others out. Saxa is here for Sloan and Kaida enjoys Emmet. The Perry twins can sort their mounts out on the fly.

*"Feline Finesse."* I call the spell as I throw myself into the air, catch Dart's elbow, and swing up to land on his back. Running to the frill at his shoulders, I grab the handle of my saddle on his first spike. "Take us up, buddy."

The power of Dart's thrust into the air never fails to amaze me. I brace my knees, clamp my jaw, and wait for the pull to end and the butterflies in the pit of my stomach when the pull ends.

Dart tilts his wings and catches a gust of wind, pulling us up and back. The shift in position changes my center of gravity and I focus on planting my feet solidly beneath me.

The yellow dragon on my right is Saxa with Sloan. The blue girl on my left is Kaida with Emmet. Davin and Darcy join us a moment later riding Torrim and Chezzo.

"What the fuck is that?" Darcy shouts, pointing at the rooster-dragon love child trying to take Cadmus' eyes out with its talons.

"A cockatrice," Dionysus says, joining us on Contessa McSparkles.

Okay, yeah, six of us up here might be overkill.

I'm about to instruct Emmet and Dionysus to fall back when the satanic cluck of a demon chicken shrieks behind us, and Mrs. Cockatrice joins the fight.

At first, I think she's coming to help split up the fight and squawk some sense into her mate.

No such luck.

The moment she gets within range, she extends her talons and grabs hold of Cadmus too.

"Oh, hells no. You don't get to turn this around on him." I may not be overtly motherly with the dragons, but don't you dare attack them unjustly. "Dart, get us closer. Bruin, we've got airborne demon roosters attacking one of our own. Do you feel like some aerial assault?"

*Can I hurt them?*

"Since they're trying to blind Cadmus and kill him, sure. Go ahead."

*Yer the best, Red.* Bruin releases from me in a rush.

"Tough as Bark." My armor engages, and I reach out to Dionysus. *Tarzan, can you open a link so I can talk to everyone up here?*

*Anything you need, Jane.*

*Thanks.* The moment I feel the mental channel link our minds I relay the play. *Boys, these cockatrices aren't Isilon compatible. Their visas have been rescinded. Emmet, you get to the security office, talk to Astrid about an alternative realm to send them that won't put them in danger, and program the Boundary Gate.*

Kaida peels off the group. *On it.*

*The rest of us will contain the fight, push them to the other end of the city, and force them through the gate.*

Bruin roars off to my right as he materializes on the back of the cockatrice male. The look on the female's face is priceless.

What? You didn't expect a bear to attack your mate mid-air? Too bad. So sad.

Bruin rushes forward on all fours and has the male shrieking and flipping to see what's on him.

The five of us are all jockeying, the Perry twins rushing in and retreating, trying to get Cadmus free of the male's hold.

A gust of blue fire roars past us and Dart grunts as he adjusts to keep me from getting fried.

*Friendly fire. Sorry, Fi. Cadmus can't see for blood, and a blind dragon under attack will not be good.*

*No. I guess not.* I glance across the night sky and curse how far we are from the Boundary Gate. There's no way we'll get there in time to get them out of this city before Cadmus is blind and lame.

*Dionysus, can you portal all of us as a group to the Boundary Gate?*

*I'm saddened that you still have to ask.*

I chuckle. *Sorry, sweetie. Let me try again. Dionysus, I need you to use your awesome godly perfection to move our entire group in one aerial portal above the Boundary Gate.*

*On it. Hang on.*

The five of us on our mounts, plus the cockatrice couple, plus Bruin portal out and reappear in the far end of the city over the Boundary Gate.

*You're amazing. Now, let's bounce them out of our city.*

The five of us spend the next few minutes positioning ourselves to free Cadmus, but no matter what we do, the male cockatrice won't release his hold.

*Maybe comin' at the male is the wrong tack,* Sloan says. *If it were me, I wouldn't care if I was attacked half as much as if my wife was.*

*Good point, hotness. Okay, Bruin. Let's try attacking the female and see if we can get him to let go of Cadmus in defense of his mate.*

Bruin roars, pushes off his position, and spirits from the male over to his mate. The moment the female feels him dig his claws in, she lets out a horrific squawk.

I honestly don't know why she gets a say in any of this. She's the Cheater McCheater face.

*Tarzan. Tell Nikon and Sarah we need to open the gate to kick these two out. Emmet? Does Astrid have a place to send them yet?*

*Programming the destination now. Get ready to bounce them.*

*Bruin, she's not freaking out enough. We need her mate to lose his mind and come after you.*

*Och, is that all? Thanks fer usin' me as a replacement victim to the demon chicken.*

I laugh at how crusty he is. *You know I love you. Now, make her squeal.*

*I love it when you talk dirty,* Dionysus interjects.

The Perry brothers are laughing on the connection.

*Ignore him, boys. He can't help himself.*

Nikon snaps in with Sarah, and the two of them get positioned in front of the massive doors of the gate and start working their magic to release the security wards. Once they're finished doing that, a massive influx of portal energy builds and the link to the other realm begins to glow.

*Now, boys. Let's push them through.*

On my command, the four dragons and Contessa McSparkles take another run at getting the male to release Cadmus. The poor guy is exhausted and either he's suffered a wound I can't detect, or he's about to pass out.

I hope it's the latter.

*We need the female to really need his help.*

*I've got an idea.* Dionysus steers Contessa away. Then she comes in head down with her spiraled unicorn horn poised as a lance.

The approach is hard and fast, and the horn pierces straight through the meaty part of Mrs. Cockatrice's left wing.

She makes an incredible show, screeching and kicking as her flight falters and she begins to fall out of the air.

That gets the male's attention, and he throws Cadmus' limp body to the side as he dives to help his mate.

"Gusting Gale." I hold up my palms and force them closer to the doors. *Bruin, don't get caught in their wake. You're done, buddy. All we need to do now is show them the door.*

Nikon has snapped Sarah to a rooftop off some distance to keep her out of the way. Now that the massive bronze doors are open and glowing with power, we press as one, forcing the cockatrice pair bit by bit until the dragons are surrounding them in a half circle at the front of the gate and they've got no choice but to leave or face us all.

The male lets out one helluva squawk, but by this point, it's all talk. They're beaten, and they know it. The welcome mat has been revoked.

The two land on the ground in front of the gates and the male postures while the female makes her way through first. Her left wing hangs almost limp at her side, but it's not the type of wound that won't heal in time.

"Buh-bye." Dionysus waves as the magic dissipates and the doors close.

*Okay, Em. They're gone. Lock it down.*

*Yep. Got you on the screen.*

Nikon and Sarah return to reinstate the wards, and when they give us the thumbs-up, we lead the dragons back to the meadow.

"Well done, Contessa." I stroke the unicorn's feathered wings. "Thanks for your help, everyone."

The Perry twins dismount from their dragons and come over to high-five us. "No need to thank us. That was savage craic."

Nikon snaps in with Sarah and Emmet. He brushes his hands together and grins. "All in a night's work. Everyone back to the tavern. There is still plenty of night left for drinking and carrying on."

Before he snaps us all back and we get sucked into the next adventure, I touch his wrist. "I think we'll pass, Greek. We're several days late on starting our honeymoon, and I, for one, think we should go while the going's good."

Nikon nods and hugs me, then Emmet does the same, and then Dionysus takes over.

"Enjoy yourself, Jane. I heart you."

"I heart you right back." I kiss his cheek and take a step back, sliding my palm against Sloan's. "Okay, so, give our goodbyes to everyone, no contacting us unless the world is literally about to crumble, and we'll see you in a week to ten days."

I squeeze Sloan's hand. "Back to our room to grab our stuff, Mr. Cumhaill."

He chuckles. "As ye wish, Mrs. Mackenzie."

# ENDNOTE

Thank you for reading *Hazards in the Hidden City*, book 4 in the Case Files of an Urban Druid series. While the story is fresh in your mind, and as a favor to Michael and me, please click HERE and tell other readers what you thought.

A quick star rating and/or even one sentence can mean so much to readers deciding whether to try a book, series, or a new-to-them author.

Thank you.

If you want more of the Clan Cumhaill adventures, you can find book 5 in the series, *Hexes in Texas, on Amazon*.

# AUTHOR NOTES - AUBURN TEMPEST

## WRITTEN OCTOBER 11, 2022

I'm smiling as I write this because I love me a happily ever after. Fi and Sloan's courting has taken us through nineteen books. Can you believe it?

Michael told me from the beginning, "No romance," and I tried...but I couldn't help myself. Then he said, "This isn't going to be a triangle, is it? I hate that." I assured him it wasn't. I knew from the beginning Fi's heart belonged to Sloan Mackenzie. Then, about the eighth or ninth book, he said, "Isn't it about time for some nuptials?"

That made me laugh out loud.

There, I got the marriage book out of my system, and hopefully, you had some adventure and some fun at the same time.

In the end, Fi got her way and took two years to ease into her powers, figure out who she is, and make space in her life and her future for Sloan.

He was never worried. He knew his destiny was to be the man at her side and he never wavered.

FYI: Mr. Epema really was my grade 11 English teacher, one of my favorite teachers of all my school days, and one of the smartest men I knew growing up.

Each morning, there would be a really hard word written on the chalkboard when we came in. He called it "Dr. Epema's game of Epemology." (Instead of etymology – see what he did there?) We were tasked to derive the meaning of the word by breaking down the roots and origins.

It was before the days of Google or cell phones and was a test of intelligence.

I was never any good at it, but it was the entire class against him. Then we got to try to stump him. It rarely happened, but we might have gotten him once or twice.

Mr. Epema was also the first to encourage me to write stories, telling me I had a unique gift for verbiage. My sixteen-year-old self took that as a compliment. I'm not sure that's how it was meant…lol.

Either way, he meant a lot to me. Teachers are amazing. They have the unique position to build and guide and inspire their students to be more than they realize and might never realize the impact they had.

I doubt Mr. Epema would remember me, but I certainly remember him.

Off to start editing the next Elementals book.

Blessed be,

Auburn Tempest

Facebook page: https://www.facebook.com/groups/167165864237006

Or feel free to drop us a line: UrbanDruid@lmbpn.com

## AUTHOR NOTES - MICHAEL ANDERLE

### WRITTEN OCTOBER 12, 2022

Thank you for not only reading this book but these author notes as well!

How in the hell? I JUST got through writing author notes for Mantle & Key book 08 where I talk about romance. Then I open Auburn's author notes…

To see she is giving me shit about romance!

Now, I probably did say something about romance when we first started the series. But it's a cool ingredient in a story (and frankly a great one if you want to hook readers), but I HATE love triangles.

I realize that might not be how you see romance (many women treat love triangle stories as a man does a football game. It's SPORT and you have to know who wins in the end), but I feel pain for the losing guy in the romance story.

Why would I want to read a book that does that to me?

Probably why I'm not a huge reader of romance. I'm pretty empathetic, so all of the emotions going up and down, back and forth would leave me emotionally drained. No catharsis for me.

But I silently give a toast in appreciation to the reader who explained why love triangles are a huge draw for romance readers. You have helped me understand, and perhaps if I had spent more time talking to you, a few more of my confusions would have been laid to rest.

Now, back to Auburn, Fi, and Sloan.

By the time we got to book eight or nine I was run through the wringer with their relationship. As I mentioned above, I feel the characters when reading and even I was getting the impatient "get a move on, already" feel each time I read a story. I realize in the timeline of the books it wasn't THAT long, but damn, it felt like forever to me.

I promise I will never ask Auburn just how many books she can make a SLOW romance burn.

If I do, I'm not reading the books until the characters get hooked up! *(Editor's note: <snicker>)*

Talk to you in the next book!

Ad Aeternitatem,

Michael Anderle

MORE STORIES with Michael newsletter HERE:
https://michael.beehiiv.com/

# BOOKS BY AUBURN TEMPEST

Join us on the Facebook page: https://www.facebook.com/groups/167165864237006

Or feel free to drop us a line: UrbanDruid@lmbpn.com

**Find Me**

Amazon, Facebook, Newsletter,

Web page – www.auburntempest.com

Email – AuburnTempestWrites@gmail.com

**Auburn Tempest - Urban Fantasy Action/Adventure**

**Chronicles of an Urban Druid**

Book 1 – A Gilded Cage

Book 2 – A Sacred Grove

Book 3 – A Family Oath

Book 4 – A Witch's Revenge

Book 5 – A Broken Vow

Book 6 – A Druid Hexed

Book 7 – An Immortal's Pain

Book 8 – A Shaman's Power

Book 9 – A Fated Bond

Book 10 – A Dragon's Dare

Book 11 – A God's Mistake
Book 12 – A Destiny Unlocked
Book 13 – A United Front
Book 14 – A Culling Tide
Book 15 – A Danger Destroyed

**Case Files of an Urban Druid**
Book 1 – Mayhem in Montreal
Book 2 – Sorcery in San Francisco
Book 3 – Necromancy in New Orleans
Book 4 – Hazards in the Hidden City
Book 5 - Hexes in Texas

**Chronicles of an Urban Elemental**
Book 1 – Incendio: Fire Born
Book 2 – Magicae: Powers Dawning

If you enjoy my writing and read sexy/steamy romance, my pen name for the books I write in Paranormal and Fantasy Romance is JL Madore.

You can find me on Amazon.

# BOOKS BY MICHAEL ANDERLE

**Sign up for the LMBPN** email list to be notified of new releases and special deals!

**https://lmbpn.com/email/**

For a complete list of books by Michael Anderle, please visit:

**www.lmbpn.com/ma-books/**

# CONNECT WITH THE AUTHORS

**Connect with Auburn**

Amazon, Facebook, Newsletter

Web page – www.jlmadore.com

Email – AuburnTempestWrites@gmail.com

**Connect with Michael Anderle and sign up for his email list here:**

Website: http://lmbpn.com

Email List: http://lmbpn.com/email/

https://www.facebook.com/LMBPNPublishing

https://twitter.com/lmbpn

https://www.instagram.com/lmbpn_publishing/

https://www.bookbub.com/authors/michael-anderle